Also by Ana Huang

KINGS OF SIN SERIES
A SERIES OF INTERCONNECTED STANDALONES
King of Wrath
King of Pride
King of Greed
King of Sloth

TWISTED SERIES
A SERIES OF INTERCONNECTED STANDALONES
Twisted Love
Twisted Games
Twisted Hate
Twisted Lies

IF LOVE SERIES
If We Ever Meet Again (DUET BOOK 1)
If the Sun Never Sets (DUET BOOK 2)
If Love Had a Price (STANDALONE)
If We Were Perfect (STANDALONE)

if the sun never sets

ANA HUANG

Bloom *books*

Sourcebooks, Bloom Books, and the colophon are registered trademarks of Sourcebooks.

Published by Bloom Books, an imprint of Sourcebooks
P.O. Box 4410, Naperville, Illinois 60567-4410
(630) 961-3900
sourcebooks.com

Originally self-published in 2020 by Ana Huang.

Cataloging-in-Publication data is on file with the Library of Congress.

Printed and bound in the United States of America.
LSC 10 9 8 7 6 5 4 3 2 1

Playlist

"Hello" Adele
"Just a Dream"—Nelly
"All I Have to Do is Dream"—Lauren O'Connell
"Show Me the Meaning of Being Lonely"
—Backstreet Boys
"Ain't It Funny"—Jennifer Lopez
"Just Give Me a Reason"—Pink featuring Nate Ruess
"Back to Your Heart"—Backstreet Boys
"Fallin'"—Alicia Keys
"All of Me"—John Legend
"Little Do You Know"—Alex and Sierra
"I Try"—Macy Gray

CHAPTER 1

THIS WAS IT. THE MOMENT SHE'D WAITED THREE years for.

Twenty-five-year-old Farrah Lin smoothed a hand over her skirt as she walked toward her manager's office. Sweat dampened her underarms—thank god she'd worn black today. Sweat stains were the last thing she needed during a promotion meeting.

"Nice top." Matt fell into step with Farrah, *GQ*-ready in a black Helmut Lang blazer and Diesel jeans with a smirk pasted on his handsome face.

Farrah flashed a tight smile. "Thanks."

Like Farrah, Matt worked as a design associate at Kelly Burke Interiors. Unlike Farrah, he'd bypassed the junior grunt years and sailed straight into a midlevel role. All thanks to his godmother, Kelly Burke herself.

Farrah wouldn't mind so much if Matt worked hard. He had talent, but he treated his job like it was a hobby he could pick up whenever boredom hit. Given the size of his trust fund, it was possible his job *was* a hobby.

Case in point: KBI had a *one-hour lunch break* rule, which

Matt obliterated by skipping out for two or more hours in the afternoon on a regular basis. No one said anything, because he was Kelly's best friend's son and the apple of their boss's eye, but his blatant disregard for the rules infuriated Farrah.

Then again, part of growing up was knowing when to keep your mouth shut. So she did.

They reached their supervisor's office. Farrah knocked and held her breath, both out of nerves and in an attempt not to inhale Matt's overwhelming cologne. The man smelled like an ` store on steroids.

"Come in." The thick oak door muffled Jane Sanchez's summons.

Farrah opened the door, and Jane gestured to the two brass-framed, ivory leather chairs across the desk from her. "Take a seat."

As Kelly's right-hand woman, Jane ran a tight ship. She oversaw the nuts and bolts of all projects, managed client relationships and the firm's twelve employees, and brought donuts to the office every Friday to celebrate that week's wins. As far as managers went, she was great.

Nevertheless, Farrah's sweat intensified. Nothing wracked her nerves like a Friday afternoon meeting with a higher-up.

"First, I want to thank both of you for how hard you worked on the Zinterhofer project. It was a tough one, and we all had to pull long hours to complete it on time. But I'm pleased to say Z Hotels is *thrilled* with the outcome." Jane beamed.

Farrah and Matt smiled back. For the past ten months, they'd worked nonstop on the Z Hotels flagship property overlooking Central Park. Landon Zinterhofer, heir to the Z luxury hotel empire, had taken over the brand's mid-Atlantic portfolio last year. His first order of business: modernizing the NYC outpost and broadening its appeal to wealthy young travelers instead of just the Old Guard of high society.

KBI rarely assigned two associates to a project—not when Kelly was the principal designer—but Z Hotels was their biggest client.

"That's great!" Farrah's skin tingled with pride. She may not have led the project, but she'd put a ton of time, sweat, and creative energy into it. Redesigning an entire hotel—including 253 rooms and dozens of public spaces—in ten months was no cakewalk.

Good thing Farrah thrived on challenges. Besides, Z Hotels looked fantastic on her résumé, and the project was a straight shot to a senior associate position at KBI, five years ahead of schedule.

Well, almost a straight shot.

"However, we all know why we're here." Jane's eyes turned serious behind her red-framed glasses. "Last year, I mentioned one of you will be promoted to senior associate pending exemplary performance on the Z Hotels project. Even though senior associates usually have at least eight years of experience, Kelly and I agreed you're both talented enough to take on the increased responsibilities, and we'd much rather promote internally than hire externally. Z Hotels was your test."

Farrah resisted the urge to grip her necklace. Instead, she clamped down on her chair's armrests until her knuckles turned white. Beside her, Matt slouched in his chair, dripping confidence.

"You both did an excellent job and impressed us with your diligence, creativity, and commitment. I wish we could promote both of you, but we're a small firm and we don't have the capability right now."

Get on with it already. Farrah appreciated the praise, but she was going to pass out if Jane didn't get to the point soon.

"That being said, I want to congratulate—"

Oh my god, this is it. Farrah was finally going to get what she'd been working so hard for these past few years. She was going to be—

"Matt. You're the newest senior design associate at Kelly Burke Interiors. Congratulations." Jane adjusted her glasses, sounding unenthused.

A senior associate at the tender young age of—what?

Ice water replaced the blood in Farrah's veins. She must've heard wrong.

There was no way Matt—who couldn't keep the names of their vendors straight and who complained that reading blueprints gave him a "headache"—got promoted over Farrah.

No freaking way.

"Wow, thanks so much." Matt grinned, not appearing at all surprised by the news. "This is such an honor."

Jane smiled tersely. "It was Kelly's decision. Matt, can you give Farrah and me some privacy? I need to speak to her alone."

"Of course." Matt patted Farrah's shoulder on the way out. "Better luck next time." He oozed condescension.

Farrah flip-flopped between the urge to throw up and the desire to clock Matt in the face.

No. You are not a violent person. Take a deep breath. In one, two, three. Out one—aaaargh!

Jane examined Farrah with a worried frown. "How are you feeling?"

How do you think I'm feeling? Farrah bit back her caustic reply and forced a smile instead. "I'm fine. I'm happy for Matt."

Her manager sighed. "Farrah, you and I both know you're supremely talented. That's why we promoted you to a midlevel role so quickly after you joined the firm. You did exceptional work on the Z Hotels project. *Exceptional.*" She shook her head. "Please do not take this as a negative reflection of your work or your role here at KBI. You're a valued member of the team."

"But not valued enough to receive the promotion."

Jane hesitated. "The final decision wasn't mine to make."

"I know. It was Kelly's." Farrah met the other woman's gaze. "Tell me the truth. Did the fact that Matt is Kelly's godson play a role in her decision?"

Jane didn't answer, but the look on her face said it all.

Disappointment snaked through Farrah. She'd idolized Kelly since she was a teenager and had been over the moon about interning at KBI after she won the National Interior Design Association's student competition in college. Sure, Kelly as a person was more aloof, competitive, and demanding than she'd expected—not exactly mentor material—but Kelly was also one of the top interior designers in America. She *had* to be demanding.

But Farrah thought Kelly valued talent. Hard work. Meritocracy. It was one thing for her to push up Matt's promotion to a midlevel role. There were no limits on those. It was another for Kelly to promote Matt over someone who'd given the company everything she had these past three years.

Matt hadn't given a shit about the Z Hotels project. He'd seen it as an opportunity to schmooze with a hotel heir and add a line to his résumé without doing any of the hard work. Farrah was the one who'd burned the midnight oil every night, scrambling to pull things together. She was the one who'd spent hours on the phone with contractors, smoothing over issues and misunderstandings. She was the one who'd ensured they delivered great results on time, even if Kelly received all the glory.

Farrah didn't think she was entitled to a promotion, but dammit, she'd *earned* it.

"There'll be another promotion opportunity in two years," Jane said. "Be patient. Your time will come. I promise."

Maybe that was true, but Farrah knew she'd never win in a game where nepotism ruled. Still, she wasn't a risk-taker by nature, which was why the next words out of her mouth surprised her as much as they did the woman sitting across from her.

"I quit."

CHAPTER 2

"THIS PLACE IS SICK." BLAKE RYAN TOOK IN THE MATTE hardwood floors, high ceilings, and wall of windows offering spectacular views of the Hudson River and city skyline. "Thanks for hooking me up."

"Anytime. Glad to have you in the city for good." His oldest and best friend, Landon Zinterhofer, clapped him on the back. "Besides, I'm not the one who paid for it."

Blake laughed. His new two-bedroom waterfront West Village condo cost an arm and a leg, but it was worth it. He'd been flitting around the world for too long, never staying in a city for more than a few months at a time. It'd been fun at first, but now he craved stability, and there was no place he'd rather settle down than in one of his favorite cities in the world: New York.

"How'd the hotel turn out?" he asked.

Landon had fought his mother tooth and nail on the revamping of her precious New York flagship hotel, but he'd worn her down and spent the past year running around like a crazy person. Between his project and Blake's constant travels, this was the first time they'd seen each other face-to-face in half a year.

"Great." Landon raked a hand through his black hair. "We got fantastic press and the new interiors are amazing. Even better than I'd imagined. I could refer you. The design firm did a top-notch job."

"The bar design is set," Blake reminded his friend. Besides buying his apartment and ending his nomadic lifestyle, he had another reason for coming to New York: Manhattan was getting its very own Legends.

Since Blake's original Legends sports bar took off in Austin four years ago, he'd expanded the brand into a renowned international chain at a breakneck pace. From London to LA, Legends was the place to go on game days. Even on nongame days, it buzzed with activity, thanks to its bar Olympics, theme and trivia nights, and celebrity guest bartenders. It was a rite of passage for NFL, NBA, and MLB players to do at least one stint behind the bar of their local Legends. Blake had even bought back Landon's share of the company last year.

They'd been equal partners, and the Zinterhofer name and connections in the hospitality industry had played a role in Legends's rapid ascent to the top, but Landon had given Blake the startup capital as a friend helping a friend. The more Landon became enmeshed in his mother's business, the less time he had for Legends, so splitting as business partners had been a mutually beneficial decision.

Yes, the Legends empire was alive and well, but Blake's vision for the New York branch wasn't just a regular ol' sports bar. It was going to be different. Elevated. And he couldn't wait to unveil it to the world this October.

T-minus six months.

Blake was successful enough now to have a team that dealt with the details and grunt work he'd shouldered in the early years, but he liked to be present and oversee things before any grand opening.

New York was going to the biggest opening in Legends history, and he sure as hell was going to be here every step of the way.

"I'm not talking about the bar." Landon opened the fridge and handed Blake a beer like he was in his own apartment. He'd connected Blake with the seller—a famous fashion designer who'd moved to the South of France after tiring of city life—so Blake couldn't complain too much. "I'm talking about this apartment."

"What's wrong with the apartment?"

"Nothing. The apartment is great. The decor sucks."

Blake cracked open his beer with a frown. "Give me a break. I bought this place a week ago."

Landon raised a skeptical brow. "So you're planning to decorate it all by yourself?"

Blake grimaced. While he appreciated a nice home, he had no desire, patience, or time to tackle a design project. Besides, you don't *need* anything other than a couch, coffee table, and TV in your living room. Right?

"Bro, let me set you up with the interior designers I used for the hotel. They do residential work too. There was one who was particularly good, and she's much nicer than the other two."

An ache spread through Blake's chest at the words *interior designers*. It was sad, how the slightest thing could still remind him of her after half a decade.

Blake wondered how she was doing. They weren't friends on social media, and her accounts were private, but he managed to squeeze an update out of Sammy every now and then. Last he heard, she was living in New York.

His stomach did a dumb little flip when he realized they were within fifteen miles of each other. He hadn't reached out to Farrah after he ended things with Cleo—partly because he'd been in such a dark place the first few years and partly because he didn't think he deserved her forgiveness or sympathy.

But now that they were in the same city...

Blake's mouth dried. He shouldn't. He didn't want to barge in and upend her life after five years, but he missed her so damn much. It was selfish, but he wanted to see her again. Maybe, after all the time that had passed, she didn't hate him as much.

"Blake?" Landon prompted. "What do you think about hiring a designer?"

"Fine." Blake was too flustered by memories of warm chocolate eyes and golden skin to argue with Landon. "I'll hire a damn designer."

Note to self: Text Sammy and get Farrah's number.

"Excellent." Landon grinned. "I'll set up a meeting. They'll have this place feeling like home in no time."

Home.

It'd been so long since Blake had a home, he'd forgotten what it felt like. He didn't visit Austin enough for it to count.

After they finished their beers, he and Landon moseyed over to the balcony to watch the sunset with fresh drinks in hand. The proud lines and towering heights of New York City beckoned in the distance—the grays and browns of hundreds of buildings softened by the soft glow of sunset, the lights in the windows twinkling like tiny beacons of hope, and the sharp, iconic spire of the Empire State Building piercing the sky with an arrogance that was unapologetically New York.

Blake soaked in the sight while another pang wrung his heart. Manhattan's forest of skyscrapers, pulsing energy, and glittering lights reminded him of another city he loved long ago and far away.

He'd been a boy back then, unsure and terrified of what the future held.

Now, he was the owner of a multimillion-dollar business empire. His dreams had become reality, and most of the time, that was enough. When Blake was at an opening, or on the floor greeting customers, or coming up with ideas to make Legends bigger and better than it already was, adrenaline rushed through him, and he felt like he was on top of the world.

But sometimes, when he returned to his soulless hotel room at night or woke up next to a woman he'd never see again in the morning, a hole opened up in his stomach and sucked all his emotions out until he was nothing but an empty shell.

Still, anything was better than being back in Austin.

Screeching tires. Twisted metal. Blood. So much blood.

A familiar wave of darkness crested within Blake's chest, threatening to drown him. He gritted his teeth and forced the darkness back into the box where he kept all his demons, safe from prying eyes—including his own.

There, the demons lurked—plotting, scheming, scratching at the inside of the box with their gnarled, poison-tipped nails. Sooner or later, they'd break free, and Blake could only hope he'd be alone when it happened. He didn't need to drag anyone else into the abyss with him.

"We've come a long way." Landon raised his beer. "From Texas to New York. What a ride."

"True." Blake pushed his turbulent thoughts aside and slapped a smile on his face. "But it ain't over yet."

"Not even close."

They clinked bottles.

Blake kicked the box of demons deeper into the recesses of his mind. One day, they'd break free. But not today.

Today, he was going to stop dwelling on the past. That chapter of his life was over.

It was time for a new one to begin.

CHAPTER 3

FARRAH SENT OUT EIGHTY RÉSUMÉS IN ONE WEEK.

The number of responses she received? Zero.

Of course, it was early. The job market in New York was brutal; it could be weeks or months before she heard back.

That was the ugly truth and not one she was keen on sharing with her mom, which was why Farrah ended their weekly call with guilt twisting her gut.

It's for the best.

Cheryl Lau was all about stability, and she would freak out if she found out her daughter had quit a safe job with nothing lined up.

"Here." Her roommate and best friend, Olivia Tang, pushed a large milk tea across the counter. "This'll make you feel better."

"Thanks," Farrah muttered. She sucked on the sugar-laden drink and tried not to think about what a huge, horrible mistake she'd made. She'd felt so empowered, quitting on the spot, and had been gratified to see how hard Jane tried to get her to stay. Jane had even called Kelly, who'd decamped to the Hamptons until Labor Day. Kelly, true to form, had been furious and made it clear she thought Farrah was a selfish, ungrateful brat who'd be photocopying construction documents at a low-rent studio had it not been for KBI.

Needless to say, she hadn't incentivized Farrah to stay.

But now, Farrah was having serious doubts about the wisdom of her move. Yes, she had a few months' worth of rent saved up, but New York was one of the most expensive cities in the world. Even if she cut out all nonessential spending, the living expenses would eat into her rent savings until she only had a one- or two-month safety net.

"It's only been a week, and you're so talented. You'll find a job in no time." Olivia radiated confidence. "Don't stress, babe."

"You're right." Farrah's résumé blinked at her from her open laptop: 3.9 GPA from California Coast University. NIDA competition winner. Three top-tier internships. Three years of increasing job responsibilities at Kelly Burke Interiors, where she'd worked on several high-profile hospitality projects, including Z Hotels.

She was a catch. If only she could get someone to take the bait...

"You're right," she repeated. "I'm being silly. I just need to be patient."

"Exactly. Now, since you have plenty of free time, how about going on a date with Ken?" Olivia wiggled her eyebrows.

Farrah groaned. Olivia had been pestering her to go out with her coworker for months.

"You know I hate blind dates."

"I do, but I also know you haven't had sex in...hmm, how long has it been again?" Olivia tapped her chin.

Farrah glared at her. She hadn't had sex in a year, and they both knew it. It wasn't that she didn't *want* to. She'd just been so busy with work, and dating in New York was freakin' hard. It had been a long time since she'd found a guy attractive and non-douchey enough to want to sleep with him.

If she were being honest, the last guy she'd *really* been attracted to had been—

No. Don't go there.

Farrah swallowed the lump in her throat and twisted her necklace around her finger, shoving aside thoughts of blond hair and devilish blue eyes. The pain in her chest wasn't as great as it used to be, but it was still there, a lingering reminder of the boy she'd never been able to forget.

Perhaps that was why Farrah had such high standards. She'd experienced what explosive chemistry felt like, and everything else paled in comparison.

"Oh, that's right. *A year.*" Olivia snapped her fingers. "Twelve months of no action, and no, your battery-operated friend doesn't count. If you don't break your dry spell soon, you'll explode into a million pieces of lost orgasms, which is not ok. I just deep cleaned the apartment."

"You deep clean the apartment every week."

They had a clear breakdown of house duties—Olivia cleaned and handled the bills (two of her greatest joys in life were the scent of Lysol and a zero-dollar payment balance), while Farrah handled home supplies and grocery shopping.

"Exactly."

A sigh escaped Farrah's lips. "Fine. Set me up."

She was going to regret this, but once Olivia got an idea in her head, she was like a pit bull with a bone.

Besides, maybe it was time for her to be more proactive. She couldn't experience explosive chemistry if she didn't look for it, right?

"Yay!" Olivia tossed her empty container of boba in the trash and clapped in excitement. "I can't wait. It's about time your vagina got some love."

Farrah's drink went down the wrong pipe, and she coughed for a full minute before gasping, "Leave my vagina alone."

"Honey, everyone has left your vagina alone for the past year. Your fault, by the way."

"You're fired as my best friend."

"Not accepted," Olivia said cheerfully. "I've never been fired in my life, and today is not the day to break that trend."

This is what I get for living with my best friend.

She and Olivia had shared the same tiny apartment in Chelsea since they'd moved to New York after college. It was ridiculously expensive considering how small it was, but you couldn't beat the location. Plus, it had one feature any New Yorker would kill for: an in-unit washer and dryer.

Olivia, who was a year older than Farrah, had lived here for ten months with a rocker chick she'd detested before said chick fled to Brooklyn and Farrah moved in. They'd been close in Shanghai, but they'd developed an unbreakable friendship over the past few years. Most of Farrah's college friends had stayed in California, and though she'd kept in touch with them, they weren't as close anymore. Olivia was her ride or die, and she wouldn't have it any other way.

Except in certain situations when she was tempted to speed up the *die* part, like now.

Farrah's phone rang, interrupting her daydreams of strangling her roommate, even though everything Olivia said was true (hence why it was so annoying).

She didn't recognize the number. It was probably a telemarketer, but even a cold call was better than discussing her lonely vagina. "Hello?"

"Hi, is this Farrah?"

Her brows knit in confusion. "Yes. Who's this?" The deep baritone sounded somewhat familiar.

"This is Landon Zinterhofer."

The answer almost sent Farrah into another coughing fit.

Who is it? Olivia mouthed.

Farrah shook her head, her mind racing with a thousand possibilities. What the hell was *Landon Zinterhofer* doing calling her personal cell? Was there a problem with the hotel? But they'd already finished the project, and Jane said he'd been thrilled with the results.

"Hello?"

Farrah realized she hadn't answered him yet. "Yes. I mean, no. I mean, hi." She swatted at Olivia, whose expression had morphed from curious to amused at Farrah's fumbling response. "How did you get my number?"

She winced. The question came out ruder than she'd intended.

"I called KBI, and they told me you no longer work there. I had them give me your personal cell." Landon sounded apologetic. "I realize I may be overstepping my boundaries, and I'm sorry for calling so late on a Friday night."

"It's ok. I...decided to pursue other opportunities outside KBI." Nonexistent ones. But he didn't need to know that. "Is something wrong with the hotel?"

"No, the hotel's great. In fact, you did such a good job, I wanted to see if you'd be willing to help a buddy of mine. He just moved to New York and his apartment's looking a little sad. The guy can't decorate to save his life." Landon laughed. "Anyway, he needs an interior designer, and I think you'd be a great fit. If you have time, of course."

Farrah clutched her phone so hard, she heard it crack. Every word out of Landon's mouth sent her spiraling down another tunnel of shock, disbelief, and excitement.

"You want me? Not KBI?"

What are you doing? her mind screamed. *Don't sabotage yourself!*

But she didn't understand why the heir to one of the country's largest hotel chains was seeking her out for a project. KBI had plenty of amazing designers, and she didn't even specialize in residences.

"It's unorthodox," Landon acknowledged. "But like I said, you stood out on the hotel project, and your personality is, er, better suited for this than your colleagues."

Now that, she believed. Neither Kelly nor Matt would win Miss or Mr. Congeniality anytime soon.

"I realize this is short notice, but my friend will pay twenty percent above your full rate and—"

"I'll do it!"

Farrah's shout caused Olivia's head to pop up from the couch, where she'd retreated with her latest erotica book.

Farrah cleared her throat. "I mean, I think I can find the time."

"Great. Are you free for a lunch meeting on Monday? One p.m. at the Aviary. I'll introduce you to my friend and get the ball rolling. Meal's on the house."

The Aviary was the signature restaurant at Z Central Park— the same hotel Farrah helped redesign. An average meal there cost several hundred dollars a pop.

"Yes. Sounds good."

Farrah hung up and pinched herself. *Ow.*

Holy shit. This wasn't a dream. Landon Zinterhofer just called her and offered her an interior design gig—at twenty percent above her full rate.

She didn't know what her full rate was, but she'd figure it out.

Farrah had no plans to freelance full-time, but this was the perfect project for her to sink her teeth into while she waited for callbacks from design firms.

I'm not going to be broke and forced to move back home!

Farrah couldn't hold it in any longer. She squealed and did a little happy dance that had Olivia staring at her like she'd sprouted a second head and antennae.

"Who was that? Is everything ok?"

"Yes." Farrah grinned from ear to ear, breathless with exhilaration. "Everything is perfect."

Farrah spent the weekend researching the nitty-gritty of how to be a freelance design consultant, from standard hourly rates to drawing up a client contract. She also threw together a portfolio and brought it with her to the lunch meeting. Even though Landon had all but guaranteed her the job, she wanted to make a good impression on his friend. He was, after all, the one who would be paying her.

Farrah strode into the Aviary. Natural light flooded through the domed glass ceiling and the walls of windows overlooking the park. It was one of her favorite rooms in the hotel and the one she'd worked most on.

Confidence coursed through her as she took in the sleek gray chairs, sculptured tables, and strategically placed plants. An indoor waterfall cascaded over a sheet of black slate, providing a soothing white-noise soundtrack for the business negotiations and high-society gossip sessions taking place throughout the restaurant. She could see Central Park through the windows—a vast, rolling green carpet speckled with patches of lakes and encircled by a forest of sun-drenched skyscrapers.

She could do this. So what if she'd never tackled a project from start to finish by herself? She'd figure it out. She had the design chops, and that was what mattered the most.

Farrah zeroed in on where Landon sat by himself at the prime table in the corner.

A broad grin stretched across his face when he caught sight of her. "Farrah. Thanks for coming."

"It's my pleasure, Mr. Zinterhofer." She shook his hand. With his wavy black hair, deep brown eyes, and bronzed skin—not to mention that tall muscular body—Landon could pass for a male model. Farrah recognized this, but she didn't feel one flicker of attraction. Maybe she needed to take her libido to the repair shop. "Thanks for thinking of me."

"Please. Call me Landon. And of course. You're one of the best interior designers I've had the pleasure of working with." Landon winked at her. "Don't tell Kelly that. She doesn't like being second."

He thought she was better than Kelly Burke?

Farrah tightened her grip on her portfolio to prevent herself from screaming like an idiot.

Thank god Landon was a hands-on management type of guy. He hadn't micromanaged their project, but he'd made it a point to learn everyone's names and listen to their ideas, no matter how junior they were.

Landon Zinterhofer, you are a thousand blessings in one.

"Are we waiting for your friend?" Farrah smoothed her napkin over her lap. She hoped the friend was as friendly and easygoing as Landon. She'd dealt with nightmare clients before at KBI; sometimes, she still woke up in the middle of the night, drenched in cold sweat as faded screams of *I said eggshell white, not ecru!* echoed in her head.

"He's already here. He went to the rest—ah. There he is." Landon nodded at someone behind her.

Farrah put on her most professional smile and turned, ready to knock her new client's socks off.

But her greeting died a quick death when she saw the tall gorgeous blond striding toward them.

No.

Cold tendrils of shock slithered down Farrah's spine as the temperature plunged to subzero levels. She was imagining things. There was no way that was him. The universe wouldn't be so cruel.

But there was no denying those ice-blue eyes. The cut-glass cheekbones. The deep dimples that faded as disbelief replaced his smile. He looked as stunned as she felt.

The twist in Farrah's heart confirmed what her brain refused to acknowledge.

That was him.

The first—and only—man she'd ever loved.

The one who broke her heart.

The one she thought she'd never see again.

Blake Ryan.

CHAPTER 4

THE CHATTER IN THE DINING ROOM FADED AS BLOOD roared in his ears. His stomach plunged into free fall...and all Blake could do was stare, stupefied, at the brunette seated across the table from his best friend.

I'm hallucinating.

His brain must have associated *interior designer* with the only interior designer he knew and conjured up the illusion to torture him. The deep-chocolate eyes, soft red lips, and faint scent of orange blossoms mixed with vanilla...she seemed so real, it was cruel.

How many times had Blake dreamt of her, only to wake up to an empty bed, plagued with regrets over what could've been?

A deadly python of emotion constricted his chest and dripped poison into his veins, gluing his feet to the floor. The deafening *thump-thump-thump* of his heart drowned out every other sound in the restaurant.

I'm going crazy.

"Blake, this is Farrah. Farrah, this is my friend, Blake." Landon's introduction sailed through Blake's haze of consciousness. His friend's voice sounded far off, like the people you heard in dreams. The ones that try to shake you awake when all you want to do is sink deeper into your delusion.

Landon gave Blake a frown that said, *Why the fuck are you acting so weird?*

Meanwhile, Farrah sat, eyes wide, fingers strangling the black leather portfolio in her lap. Her face matched the color of the white linen tablecloth.

Blake's breath hissed out in shock. *This is real.*

He'd fantasized about their reunion a million times, but now that it was happening, he had no clue what to do.

He just stood there, gawking at her like an idiot.

Say something. Anything.

"You haven't aged a day."

Anything but that.

Landon choked on his water while pink rose on Blake's cheekbones. He couldn't remember the last time he'd been this flustered. He felt like a damn schoolboy with a crush, one who'd waited five years to see the girl of his dreams again, only for his first words to her be... *You haven't aged a day.*

He wanted to die.

Landon's shoulders shook with suppressed laughter, but Farrah's expression remained smooth and hard as stone.

"Thanks," she said. Zero emotion, not even sarcasm.

The Farrah who Blake knew would've called him out on his lame-ass greeting faster than a teenager could text in class, but the Farrah he knew also used to look at him like he hung the stars in the sky—until he fucked it all up.

"Do you know each other?" Landon asked, controlling his mirth long enough to ask the world's most obvious question.

Blake forced his legs to move. He sank into the chair next to Landon and tried not to shake too much as he lifted a glass of water to his lips. "We studied abroad together in Shanghai."

He felt Landon's sharp inhale beside him. He'd told Landon about Farrah one drunk night after he and Cleo split for good. Blake had been spiraling, drowning in guilt and regret and booze, and his usual filter had been down for the count. In its absence, confessions about Farrah and what happened in Shanghai tumbled out. Blake hadn't divulged Farrah's name, but Landon was a smart guy. Blake could tell by the look in his friend's eyes that Landon had already pieced the puzzle together.

The waiter showed up and took their orders. Blake didn't remember what he ordered. He didn't care; he was too busy staring at Farrah.

It'd been five years, and god, she was even more beautiful than he remembered. More sophisticated and self-assured. Time had sculpted her features into a masterpiece, and her slim figure had blossomed with curves. She was no longer a girl but a woman—one who sent desire curling through his gut even as his heart ached.

Farrah, on the other hand, hadn't so much as looked at him since he sat down.

"So." Landon filled the silence. "Farrah, as I mentioned on our call, Blake is looking for a designer for his new condo. Two bedrooms, two baths, in the West Village. It'll be his primary residence from now on, so he needs someone to spruce it up. Make it feel like home." He nudged Blake. "Right?"

"What? Oh, uh, yeah."

Get your shit together, man.

"Right." Landon's gaze ping ponged between Blake and Farrah. "About the compensation. Since this is so last minute, Blake will pay twenty percent above—"

"I can't do it." Farrah's quiet refusal brought the conversation screeching to a halt. She kept her focus on Landon as she explained, "I'm sorry for wasting your time. I appreciate you thinking of me, and I'll pay you back for this meal. But I just remembered I have, um, another project I need to work on, and I won't have time for this. In fact, I should probably—"

"Double."

Farrah stiffened at Blake's offer. "What?"

"I'll pay you double your rate if you agree to work with me."

"That's not going to—"

"Triple."

Farrah's gaze slammed into his. Her eyes smoldered with disbelief, and Blake couldn't fight the small grin of victory on his lips. *Finally. A reaction.*

"You don't know how much my rate is."

"How much is it?"

After a beat of hesitation, she said, "Three hundred dollars an hour."

"I'll pay you nine hundred dollars an hour. But it has to be exclusive. You'll work only on my apartment for the duration of our contract period."

"Jesus, Blake," Landon breathed.

Across the table, Farrah's lips parted with shock.

Nine hundred dollars an hour was a shit ton of money, but Blake could afford it. He wasn't as rich as Landon, but thanks to both Legends' success and a slew of smart investments over the years, he had enough of a financial cushion to absorb the cost. Besides, he didn't care about the money. He cared about Farrah.

He'd bitten the bullet and asked Sammy for her number over the weekend. Sammy had been wary of Blake's sudden desire to reconnect with her, but being the good friend he was—as well as the only one in their old Shanghai group who knew the truth about Blake's feelings for Farrah and what happened with Cleo— he'd relented.

Blake had stared at the ten digits all weekend, trying to work up the courage to call her. He'd chickened out every time, but now here she was, right in front of him.

It was like the universe had tired of his waffling and given him the kick in the ass he needed.

This was a sign.

Of all the designers in all the world, she was the one Landon invited here.

Two people in a city of eight million, reunited against all odds. Coincidence? Hell no.

Farrah was the one who'd taught Blake to believe in fate, and like everything else about their relationship, he'd carried it close to his heart all these years.

"Do we have a deal?" Blake kept his tone even, but inside he was a chaotic storm of need and emotions.

Say yes. god, if she says yes, I will never ask you for anything else ever again. Except maybe for a team other than the Patriots to win the Super Bowl, but I'm willing to negotiate on that front.

Farrah fiddled with her necklace while indecision flickered across her face. After an eternity, she bit out, "Yes."

Blake released his breath and sent a quick thank-you up to the heavens.

"It's a deal." He grinned, revealing his trusty dimples in all their glory, and held out his hand.

After a brief pause, she took it.

A current of electricity sizzled through his body the second they touched, and judging by the way Farrah's nostrils flared, he wasn't the only one who'd felt it.

Blake's grin widened.

The universe had handed him his second chance on a platter, and this time, there was no way in hell he was going to fuck it up.

CHAPTER 5

FARRAH MADE IT TWO BLOCKS BEFORE SHE FELL APART.

She'd sat stone-faced through lunch, hauled ass to a department store near Z Hotel, and bulldozed her way into a restroom stall before she collapsed into a heaping mess.

Blake freakin' Ryan.

Of all the times he could've walked back into her life, he had to do it now, when she was (1) unemployed and therefore unable to brush off his generous offer and (2) so sexually frustrated she'd gotten turned on by a handshake.

Farrah shivered when she remembered the strong, warm grip of Blake's hand around hers and the resulting shock of electricity that had traveled up her arm and into her chest, making her heart beat in a way she didn't think it capable of doing anymore.

She'd dated other guys since Shanghai. Some of them she'd liked; some of them she hadn't. None could turn her into a live wire of emotions like Blake could.

Smoky memories of long nights, passionate kisses, and whispered secrets crawled into Farrah's brain, drowning her in the past.

I think you're a smart-ass who's too stubborn for your own good. I think you drive me crazier than any person ought to. And I think I might die if I can't be with you.

You said once every second counts, and I don't want another second to go by without you knowing that I am totally, completely, one hundred percent in love with you.

A sob escaped her throat. Farrah pressed a fist to her mouth, struggling to remain calm before she turned into a girl-crying-over-a-boy-in-a-public-restroom cliché. Even though her eyes were already glazed with tears. Even though her chest ached so much she wanted to curl up in fetal position on the floor, germs and potential cholera be damned.

She wasn't in love with Blake anymore. She needed trust for love, and he'd lost hers long ago. But dammit if he couldn't make her heart pound with one smile and her body clench with one touch. Their physical chemistry had always been off the charts, and apparently, the flames still burned hot after all these years.

A call from Olivia lit up her phone and yanked her thoughts off the dangerous path they'd taken.

Farrah swallowed and composed herself before answering.

"Hello?" A slight waver. Pretty good, considering snot and dried tears streaked her face. Farrah yanked a few so-thin-they-were-transparent squares of toilet paper from the roll and wiped her face. It was like exfoliating her skin with sandpaper.

"Hey! How'd the lunch meeting go?" Olivia asked.

"Fine. What are you doing calling me from work?" Farrah stalled, debating whether to clue Olivia in on today's developments now or wait until they were face-to-face.

Now, she decided. Olivia was going to shit bricks. She'd hated Blake since he broke up with Farrah, and Farrah was already bracing herself for the hurricane once she told Olivia she'd accepted Blake's job offer.

"I'm on a coffee break," Olivia said, which surprised Farrah almost as much as seeing Blake at the Aviary. Olivia worked long hard hours as an analyst at Wall Street's most prestigious private equity firm, and she rarely took a break on the clock. "I have six minutes and twenty-seven seconds before my break is over, so give me the deets quick."

"Ok." Farrah took a deep breath. "Long story short: I got the job, and they're paying me nine hundred dollars an hour."

Always lead with the good news first.

"Oh my god!" Olivia whisper-yelled. "That's amazing! *Nine hundred dollars an hour?* We have to celebrate! I won't make it out in time for happy hour today—this deal we're working on is the bane of my existence, I swear—but I'll pick up ice cream and wine on my way home. We can have a proper celebratory dinner this weekend."

"Sounds great."

There was a pause. "Why do you sound so *not* excited about this? Is it the client? He's a jerk, isn't he? Or is he a creepy old perv? Remember, if he tries anything, you can take one of your stiletto heels and jam it up his—"

"It's Blake."

"Blake who?"

"Blake Ryan."

Another pause, and then, "*Your new client is Blake Ryan?*"

Her yell pierced Farrah's eardrums. Farrah winced and held the phone away from her ear as Olivia uttered a stream of curses so colorful and fantasy-murder scenarios so graphic, she could've moonlighted as a horror author.

Once she stopped for breath, Farrah interjected. "Look, I get it. The situation is not ideal." That was putting it mildly, but Farrah didn't want to fan the flames of Olivia's anger. "But I don't know when I'll get a new job, and I need the money. He's paying me a *lot*, Liv. Like…enough to cover half a year of expenses if I'm smart about saving."

She could hear her friend ruminating in the silence that followed. "Have you asked yourself why, exactly, he's paying you so much?"

Farrah frowned. She'd been so surprised by Blake's sudden reappearance in her life, she hadn't stopped to think about the reasons behind his offer. "No…"

Suspicion seeped into her veins. Why *had* Blake been so insistent on hiring her? He'd kicked her to the curb for his ex-girlfriend, and they hadn't spoken in half a decade. Plus, he could hire any designer in the city for the price he was paying.

They weren't friends on social media, but she'd stumbled on articles about him over the years. His sports bars were doing well. Really well. Despite herself, a flicker of pride flared in Farrah's stomach at his success.

Farrah had walked into the meeting intending to quote $150 an hour, given that this was her first freelance gig. Once she'd realized the client was Blake, she'd jacked the price up to $300, desperate for an excuse not to have to see him again. When he not only agreed but *tripled* her rate, Farrah nearly had a heart attack. Not even Kelly Burke commanded $900 an hour.

"He's up to something. Be careful," Olivia warned. "The boy is your kryptonite. Don't do anything stupid."

Not so much a boy anymore.

Farrah's mouth watered when she remembered how good Blake looked. College Blake had been hot, but he'd possessed a boyishness common among twenty-two-year-olds. Grown-up Blake, with his stubble and lean muscles and confident, panther-like stride? He was fiercer, grittier, and he exuded a raw, hard masculinity that turned her knees to Jell-O.

"Like what? I'm designing his apartment. It'll take a few months. That's it." The words rang false to Farrah's own ears.

"Uh-huh." Skepticism coated Olivia's voice. "I mean it, Farrah. Stay as far away from Blake as possible. I've seen his picture in magazines from time to time. He's still fine as hell, which makes him dangerous. Don't sleep with him, and for god's sake, *don't* fall in love with him again."

Now that made Farrah laugh. "I won't fall in love with him again." She was horny, not an idiot. Her body might crave Blake, but she'd built enough defenses around her heart to keep an invading army at bay.

"Good." Olivia sounded satisfied. "So he's Landon's friend, huh? What are the freakin' odds?"

"Well, Landon is from Austin." Now that Farrah thought about it, she remembered Blake mentioning back in Shanghai that his best friend was a hotel heir. Landon was the one who'd floated him the capital to start his bar. Blake might even have mentioned him by name. Farrah couldn't believe she hadn't put two and two together until now.

"So are millions of other people. god, this world is too small." Olivia sighed. "Shit. My break is up. We'll discuss later, ok? In the meantime, buy yourself something nice, like a big bottle of vodka. You need it."

Farrah snorted. "Thanks."

She hung up, took a deep breath, and unlocked the stall. Thankfully, the bathroom had emptied, and no one was there to witness what a mess she was.

Farrah splashed water on her face, letting the cool liquid fortify her.

Blake's project would take a few months, max. She could go that long without giving in to her base desires. Right?

Another image of Blake's dimpled smile and broad shoulders flashed through her mind, and heat sluiced through her.

Dammit.

Maybe it was a good thing she'd agreed to go on that blind date with Olivia's coworker. Hopefully, it'd take the edge off.

Farrah stared at herself in the mirror. Her reflection blinked back, uncertain and uneasy.

"Farrah Lin, what have you gotten yourself into?"

CHAPTER 6

"I RECEIVED YOUR QUESTIONNAIRE." FARRAH FROWNED at the paper in her hands. "Half the answers are blank."

"I didn't know how to answer them." It was the truth. Blake couldn't name a single design style if his life depended on it, much less which ones he liked and didn't like. "Besides, I figured it'd be easier to discuss in person."

His mouth tugged up into a smile when Farrah side-eyed him.

Sure, he could've tried harder to answer the questions, but the less he answered, the more time they'd have to spend discussing them in person.

Time. They'd never had enough of it. Not in Shanghai, and not at that all-too-short lunch meeting the other day. But now that Blake and Farrah were client and consultant, he was determined to milk every second they had together.

And no, Blake was not above petty ploys like leaving half his new-client intake questionnaire blank.

Farrah walked through his apartment, examining the layout and current decor. "Landon wasn't kidding when he said you didn't have a lot of furnishings."

"I moved here not too long ago. Didn't make sense to buy a bunch of stuff myself when I was going to hire a professional."

He hadn't planned on hiring a designer until Landon pushed him, but Blake kept that part to himself.

"Have you worked with a designer before?"

"For the bars, yeah, but those were pretty high-level. My team took care of the details. Since this is my home, I intend to be *very* hands-on." Blake's dimples winked into view. "Expect to see a lot of me over the next few months."

Farrah looked as thrilled as a mouse in a snake's cage. "In that case, I'll go over the different phases of the project, so you know what to expect. First, we'll start with the planning phase, which is what we're doing now. This is where I get to know you and your tastes, budget, and lifestyle needs."

I need you.

Blake swallowed his reply. First, because it was cheesy as hell, and second, because he didn't want to scare her off. They'd just gotten reacquainted, and Farrah wasn't the type to let her guard down that easily. It'd taken months before she'd opened up to him in Shanghai, and given how they'd ended things...well, he was pretty sure an apology card and box of chocolates wouldn't cut it for a reconciliation.

Farrah continued, oblivious to his internal strategizing. "After planning is the design phase. I'll put together a few sketches and design boards for you to choose from. Once we finalize the design, I'll hire the contractors, order the furnishings, and source the materials. That takes the longest time, given contractor schedules, shipping delays, and unforeseen circumstances. I'll minimize those as best I can, but they pop up in any project. Finally, we execute. The contractors do their thing, we hang the art, arrange the furniture, and so on until your dream home is complete. Any questions?"

What Blake heard was, this was going to take a while. Excellent. "Nope. Sounds good to me."

They entered his bedroom, and he tried. He really did. But Blake couldn't stop his mind's autoplay of X-rated fantasies at the sight of Farrah next to his bed.

Him shoving her tight gray skirt up and feasting until she screamed his name, her riding him while he sucked her nipples, them sixty-nining and coming all over each other's faces.

His blood rushed south, turning him to steel, and Blake realized there was a major flaw in his brilliant win-Farrah-back plan: until he actually won her back, he was going to suffer from a serious case of blue balls.

"What is that?" Farrah's tight voice interrupted his arousal-slash-horror.

"Hmm?" Blake hoped she wasn't talking about the erection straining against the confines of his jeans because that would be super awkward.

"That." She tilted her chin toward his nightstand.

Blake followed her gaze to where a little elephant figurine sat next to his alarm clock. It'd been his loyal companion all these years, traveling with him to London, Peru, Australia, and everywhere in between. It was the first thing he packed when he had a trip.

"Blake Jr." His mouth tilted up when he remembered the night Farrah gifted him the souvenir from Thailand. That was the night of their first dinner together off campus, just the two of them. He'd fallen a little in love with her then, even if he hadn't known it at the time. "Handsome and ageless, just like his owner."

Farrah rolled her eyes. "Poor thing, still stuck with a vanity name." A strange expression crossed her face. "Why'd you keep it for so long? It's a cheap souvenir, and it doesn't exactly fit with your new life." She gestured at their sparsely decorated but well-appointed surroundings.

Because it reminds me of you.

"Because it's important to me."

His response soaked into the air and charged it with electricity. He could feel the shift on his skin and in the pulsing of his veins.

Farrah's cheeks tinted pink. She opened her mouth, closed it, then shook her head and replied in a professional tone that didn't match the sparks crackling between them. "I think I have everything I need." She tucked her notebook into her bag, and Blake detected a slight tremble in her hands. "I'll work on the sketches and call if I have any further questions. In the meantime—"

"Farrah—"

"Send me photos of any interiors you like," she rushed. "You can email them, or I can create a shared Pinterest board. The Pinterest board is easiest."

"It's great seeing you again."

You could have heard a pin drop in the silence.

Farrah hoisted her bag on her shoulder, her face hard. "This is a professional relationship."

"Never said it wasn't."

"Then don't look at me like that."

"Like what?"

"Like you—" She stopped. "Just don't. Don't pretend you don't know what I'm talking about. If you try to cross the line between client and consultant, I will walk off this project no matter how much you're paying me. 'Either party may terminate this agreement for any reason with ten business days' notice.' That's in the termination clause of our contract. Am I clear?"

Blake raised his hands in defeat. "Crystal. But—no, hear me out first—we'll be working together for a while, and we have history. We don't have a typical freelance relationship. I promise I won't do anything that makes you uncomfortable, like try to kiss you"—*even though I want to*—"or braid your hair while we gossip over Chinese takeout"—he grinned when Farrah's mouth edged up into a smile—"but we can talk about stuff other than, I dunno, leather patterns."

She raised her eyebrows. "Leather patterns?"

"Are they a thing? Doesn't matter. All I'm saying is, there's a big gap between professional and overly personal." Blake's voice softened. "I know we didn't end things on a great note in Shanghai, but that was a long time ago. I'm not the jerk I used to be. We can have a fresh start."

Farrah pressed her lips together. "Fine, as long as you're aware of what the boundaries are."

"I got the map drawn up and tattooed on my brain."

"Good."

Farrah's phone buzzed right as they exited the bedroom. When she read the incoming message, her eyes lit up and a delighted smile stretched across her face.

Jealousy smashed into Blake—sudden, fierce, and potent. She used to smile like that for him. *Who's the fucker texting her?*

Was it her boyfriend? She wasn't married—he'd checked for a ring at the Aviary. But maybe she was dating someone. She was beautiful, smart, witty, kind. She must have men beating down her door.

Green smoke clogged his throat and made it hard to breathe. Blake couldn't expect Farrah to have remained single and celibate all these years—it wasn't like he had—but he still wanted to tear the head off any asshole who'd touched her or so much as breathed in her direction.

Irrational? Yes.

Did he care? Fuck no.

But asking her about her love life definitely crossed the

boundaries they'd just discussed, so Blake fumed in silence while Farrah responded to Fuckface's text.

"I have to go." Farrah looked up, that smile still lingering on her lips, and the fire in him stoked hotter.

Don't ask, you idiot. Do. Not. Ask.

"Date with your boyfriend?"

His question landed with the subtlety of a pile of bricks.

Farrah flashed him a warning glance but didn't dignify his obvious fishing with an answer. "I'll call you when the sketches are ready."

It wasn't a no.

The front door shut behind her, leaving silence and a seething, jealousy-riddled Blake in her wake.

CHAPTER 7

THE SMELL OF BOOZE AND FRIES HIT FARRAH THE second she entered Tavern 14, a happy-hour favorite in the heart of the East Village. Per usual, it was packed with people eager to take advantage of half-off drink specials and $2 sliders.

Farrah pushed her way through the crowd and searched for her date. She was about to text and ask if he'd arrived yet when the group of beanie-wearing artist types in front of her parted, and she saw him at a high-top in the corner, sipping a beer and scrolling through his phone.

A grin took over her face. It had been too long.

"Sammy!" Farrah raised her voice so he could hear her above the noise.

Happiness flooded Sammy Yu's sculpted features when he saw her. "Farrah!" He stood up and walked around the table to hug her. He smelled like soap and fresh laundry, and the scent was so familiar, she choked up. Nostalgia was getting the best of her these days. "It's so good to see you."

"Likewise. It's been, gosh, two years since we last saw each other?" Farrah and Sammy kept in touch via text and social media, but he lived in San Francisco and in-person meetups were rare. The last time they'd caught up in person was when she flew to California to work on a boutique hotel project for KBI. Sammy had visited New York a few times since then, but they'd both been so busy, they couldn't align their schedules.

"Two years too long. How've you been?"

"Good. You? Still taking SF by storm?" Farrah teased.

Sammy's cheeks colored. With his deep brown eyes, chiseled face, and tall, muscular body, he was as gorgeous as ever, but now he had an additional draw: his bakery, Crumble and Bake, had become a major attraction in San Francisco and had garnered him praise from foodies and celebrities alike. It was so popular, he'd recently opened a branch in LA, where the line on opening day wrapped around the block. Farrah saw photos of the spectacle online.

Sammy himself had become a quasi-celebrity among the food crowd, with more than a million Instagram followers and a booming YouTube channel where he posted baking tutorials.

Farrah knew he'd encountered major resistance from his family when he ditched his math degree and a NASA career for baking, but Sammy was crushing it.

"Hardly. I'm just a baker, not Mark Zuckerberg."

"Mark Z can kiss my ass. You're much better."

Sammy cracked a smile. "Thanks. Hey, you want a drink? On me."

"I got it. Don't argue," Farrah warned. "You're the guest."

He laughed. "Fine. But I got the next round."

"Deal."

Once they got their drinks, Farrah and Sammy snagged one of the few booths in the bar right after it opened up and caught each other up on their lives. She told Sammy about quitting KBI, her birthday trip to Jamaica, and the time she accidentally crashed a Met Gala afterparty. Sammy told her about his San Francisco exploits and the ups and downs of running a famous bakery—including hundreds of propositions and NSFW (not safe for work) images from rabid, sugar-crazed fans.

"Must be tough." Farrah laughed when Sammy punched her in the arm.

"It's all fun and games until you accidentally open one of the pictures in front of your three-year-old niece," Sammy grumbled. "My sister nearly impaled me with her nail file. Besides, I don't like the attention. I just want to bake my croissants in peace. I don't know how Kris deals with this shit."

"Too late now. You're a star, baby," Farrah sang. "Kris deals with it because she's Kris. She'll clock any paparazzi that come too close."

"True."

Kris Carrera, another friend from study abroad, was engaged to Nate Reynolds, one of Hollywood's hottest stars and a paparazzi favorite.

"Have you kept in touch with anyone else from FEA?" Farrah stirred her drink, now watered down from the ice.

"Pretty much everyone in the group except for—" Sammy stopped short.

Olivia.

The name hung in the air, unspoken, like a guillotine waiting to drop.

Farrah felt a pang in her heart. There'd been a time when Sammy and Olivia were *the* couple. Their relationship made it out of FEA intact—the only one in their group to do so—only to implode a few months later. Farrah had been in New York with them, but even now, she wasn't sure what happened. Sammy and Olivia refused to talk about it.

How could two people go from being so in love to hating each other's guts so quickly?

Then again, Farrah of all people knew how much things could change in the space of minutes.

"Have you kept in touch with Blake?" The question fell out unbidden.

Sammy's eyes flickered with surprise. "Yeah, a little. Why?"

"Well…" Farrah debated whether to tell him about her new project. She didn't want discussion of Blake to hijack the night, but she needed a sounding board beyond Olivia, and there weren't many people who knew what had happened between her and Blake in Shanghai. "I'm kind of, um, working for him."

"What?"

Farrah filled Sammy in on the details.

"Wow." He rubbed a hand over his face. "What are the odds?"

"Yeah. I mean, I'm over him," Farrah said quickly. "It's been five years. It's just weird."

"Mm-hmm." Sammy surveyed her with a shrewd eye. "You're sure you're over him?"

Pretty sure.

She chalked the way her heart pounded when she caught sight of the elephant figurine up to surprise. As for the heat that licked at her skin when she'd imagined all the things she wanted to do to Blake in that big bed of his…well, that was nothing a night with her battery-operated boyfriend couldn't sort out.

"Totally sure."

Sammy appeared unconvinced. "Maybe this is a sign," he mused. "For you to bury the hatchet and move on. You can be friends again."

Farrah snorted. "Right."

They could be civil, but friends? She didn't think so. It was hard to be friends with someone who broke your heart.

"Hey, I'm not making excuses for Blake. He did a shitty

thing in Shanghai. But we all make mistakes—some bigger than others—and deep down, he's a good guy. Like you said, it's been five years. You don't have to marry him; just give him a chance to prove he's changed. It'll make your life easier, considering you'll be working together."

Farrah pondered Sammy's advice. It sounded similar to what Blake had said earlier.

She wasn't angry about what happened in Shanghai anymore. She used to be. god, she'd been pissed. But the anger had iced over as the years passed, leaving behind a thick wariness no man had been able to penetrate. Her relationship with Blake had proved fairy-tale love existed in real life, but it also proved that every fairy tale had a dark side, that happily-ever-afters sometimes came with less-than-happy epilogues, and that the One Big Love could crush your heart as easily as they stole it.

Anyway, it wasn't like Farrah was in danger of falling in love again. In lust, maybe. But that was a whole other matter.

"You're way too nice. You know that?"

Sammy ruffled her hair, causing her to scowl. "Just dispensing my daily dose of wisdom. Forgiveness makes the world go 'round and all that."

"Does that apply to Olivia?" she asked hopefully, smoothing a hand over her tousled locks. She was opening a can of worms by mentioning her roommate's name, but she was sick of this cold war between her friends. Sammy thought she and Blake needed to make up? He and Olivia needed to make up. Stat.

Sammy's smile fell. Tension crowded his shoulders, and a steel edge crept into his voice. "It's not the same."

Most of the time, he was the same good-natured, easygoing Sammy from their younger years. But like everyone else in the group, he'd hardened over time. More secrets, more bitterness, more cynicism—especially when it came to past heartbreaks.

"Why not?"

Sammy set his jaw. "It just isn't."

Farrah knew when she was fighting a losing battle. She changed the subject, not wanting to ruin their reunion. "How long are you in town for?"

She'd been pleasantly surprised when she received Sammy's text while she'd been at Blake's apartment. She hadn't known he was in New York, but it was a nice distraction from the unsettling chemistry that burned between her and Blake.

Chemistry, like coincidence, was a bitch who couldn't read the room.

Sammy relaxed. "I leave tomorrow morning. Sorry for the late notice today, by the way—I'm in town for business and didn't think I'd have time to meet up, but my meeting tonight got canceled."

"Don't worry about it. It's always nice to see you."

They stayed at the bar and chatted until the happy-hour crowd thinned and gave way to the night-owl set, but Farrah could tell neither of their hearts was in it. Their conversation had dredged up memories best left forgotten, and every once in a while, their sentences would taper off as they stared at their drinks, both lost in memories of what used to be.

CHAPTER 8

"WE'RE NOT INSTALLING A SHARK TANK."

"Why not? Ice-T has one," Blake protested. "I saw it on an *MTV Cribs* rerun. Besides, I'm the client. If I want a shark tank, I should get a shark tank."

Farrah huffed in exasperation. "First, you should not be taking life inspiration from Ice-T. Second, you're right. You're the client, and if you want a shark tank, I'll get you a shark tank. But it kind of goes against the understated theme you want, don't you think?"

Blake shrugged. "It'll be a statement piece?" He hid a grin at the annoyed look on Farrah's face.

Annoyance was good. It was a step up from indifference.

"I'm kidding," he said, taking mercy on her. "We can scrap the shark tank."

Blake and Farrah sat on a bench by Central Park's Bethesda Fountain, poring over the sketches she'd put together for his condo. He was the one who'd suggested they meet in the park instead of at a café or his apartment. It was a beautiful day, and he hoped the casual atmosphere would encourage her to lower her guard.

It was working, sort of. Farrah seemed more relaxed than she had during their walkthrough, but he hadn't succeeded in getting her to talk about anything except work—yet. The day was still young.

"Thank god." Farrah scratched something out on her notepad. "So, design two, no shark tank?"

"Yep." Honestly, Blake liked all the sketches and had chosen one at random. He trusted she knew what she was doing. "Okay. That's it for work today. What do you say we take a walk?"

Farrah slanted him a sharp glance. "I have to get started on the next phase of the project."

"Right now? At this very moment? Come on, it's Friday afternoon," he cajoled. "Look at this weather! The sun is shining, the birds are chirping, the—"

"Joshua, Peter, if you don't stop that this instant, you're grounded for the next two weeks!" a woman screamed as a young dark-haired boy head-butted his twin. His brother pushed him in response, and the two fell to the ground, wrestling.

Their mother stormed over with fire in her eyes. "Have kids, they said. It'll be so rewarding, they said," she muttered loud enough for Blake and Farrah to hear.

"The kids are out in full force." Farrah completed Blake's sentence. Her eyes twinkled with amusement.

"Yep." Darkness swirled in his chest as he watched the kids wrestle. The pain wasn't as sharp as it used to be whenever he saw children, but now and then, he wondered what his life would be like had things with Cleo worked out. Would they have been happy? Would he have enjoyed fatherhood, or would it have felt like a noose, constricting around his neck until he couldn't breathe?

Questions he'd never have the answers to.

Blake shoved the insidious whispers of guilt aside and flashed a charming smile. "So how about that walk? According to my trusty mental map, it's well within the boundaries."

"I guess I could go for a walk," Farrah said reluctantly. "It is a beautiful day."

Success.

Farrah was ice, but he was fire, melting her down inch by inch. Blake had a lot of things to atone for. She thought he'd played her in Shanghai, and he was tempted to let her continue thinking that. It was, in his mind, more palatable than the truth, which was that he was a fucked-up human being. A part of him wondered if he should even pursue Farrah again.

She was too pure, and he was too broken. The world saw a businessman with a perfect smile and perfect life, but the image Blake presented concealed the jagged shards and haunting thoughts inside. It was a side of him he'd never let Farrah see, not only because he didn't want to drag her into his spiral of shame and regret, but because he was afraid she'd take one look at the chaos and run the hell away.

If Blake were a good person, he would leave Farrah alone so she could move on with someone more deserving. But he was a selfish bastard, and now that she was in his life again, he couldn't let her go. She was the light to his darkness, the angel to his demons, and his only excuse for trying to crawl back into her heart was that he loved her.

Even after all these years.

Even after all that had happened.

Their elbows brushed as they left Bethesda Terrace. Tingles shot through Blake's arm, chasing away his doubts, at least for the time being.

"Have you been to the Ravine and Loch?" he asked.

Central Park was one of Blake's favorite places in the city. It covered over eight hundred acres, but most people flocked to the popular spots: Bethesda, Sheep's Meadow, Bow Bridge. He preferred the hidden gems, the quiet spots that surprised you with their beauty if you were lucky enough to stumble upon them.

"Nope." Farrah munched on her lower lip. "I don't come here often. I usually stick to downtown."

"Hmm. One of those."

She side-eyed him. "What do you mean, *one of those*?"

"People who think downtown is the only part of Manhattan worth visiting."

"Uh, yeah, it's the best part of the city. Midtown is the worst and uptown is boring."

"Downtown snob."

"You live in the West Village!"

"True, but I regularly venture past Twenty-Third Street. Downtown is great, but there's cool stuff up here too."

"What do you know? You've only been living here for a few weeks," Farrah grumbled. "I've been living here for years."

"Yet I've been to the Ravine and Loch, and you haven't," Blake teased. He made it a point to visit at least one new place every time he visited New York. That was one of the city's biggest draws: one never ran out of new things to see or do.

"You are *seriously* making me regret this walk."

Blake's dimples made a timely appearance. "Trust me. You won't regret it once you see this place."

It took them another half hour to reach their destination. During that time, Blake coaxed personal details out of Farrah, like what she did for her recent birthday (in mid-March, a month ago) and whether she was still friends with Olivia, Kris, and Courtney. The four of them had been glued at the hip in Shanghai.

Farrah had gone to Jamaica for her birthday, and yes, she was still friends with them. In fact, Olivia was her roommate.

It wasn't much, but it was a start. At least she was talking to him about nonwork-related topics.

Meanwhile, Blake regaled her with tales of his travels, including the time he'd visited Luke Peterson, one of his closest friends during study abroad, in Wisconsin and bought a crap ton of cheese as souvenirs. Some of it hadn't been wrapped properly, and when he opened his suitcase to unpack, it'd stunk so bad he had to toss the entire bag and its contents into the trash.

Blake hadn't been able to eat cheese since.

Farrah laughed, causing his chest to glow with warmth. He'd missed that sound so damn much.

There wasn't a lot of foot traffic in the North Woods, and Blake could hear the soothing sound of the waterfalls in the distance before they saw it.

"I can't believe this is in the city." Farrah followed him through the woods toward the stream. "I feel like I'm in Upstate New York."

"For good reason. It was designed to look like the Catskills or Adirondacks." The roar of waterfalls intensified. Blake stepped out of the woods and spread his arms. "Welcome to the Loch."

"Wow," Farrah breathed. The stream meandered through the ravine's verdant canopy, creating a scene so idyllic, it felt like they'd stepped into a painting, and the white noise from the waterfalls drowned out the city commotion in the distance, transporting them to a secret paradise where only the two of them existed. The fresh, earthy scent of the streamside vegetation tickled her nose, and she sucked it in with an eager inhale.

Blake settled on one of the big rocks by the stream and patted the seat next to him.

After a brief hesitation, Farrah sank beside him. "I feel like a tourist in my own city." She tilted her face up, her hair shining with various hues of black and brown beneath the sunlight. It was an unusually warm day for mid-April in New York, not that Blake was complaining. "This place is so relaxing."

"It's better than therapy." Blake ran his hand over the sun-baked rock, taking solace in its rough, warm solidness. "I try to visit every time I'm in New York. Although I live here now, so I guess I can come all the time."

"Why did you move here?" She sounded genuinely curious.

"I love the city. I'm opening a new bar here and figured it was time to settle down in one place." He shrugged. "Everything aligned."

Farrah wrinkled her brow. "Settle down? Haven't you been living in Texas?"

"No." Blake curled his hand around the edge of the rock until it dug into his skin. "My family's there, and I visit from time to time, but I've been traveling, going where business takes me. A few months here, a few months there. It's fun, but it gets exhausting." He noticed the smile on Farrah's face. "What's so funny?"

"I remember a time when Shanghai was the only city you'd visited outside the U.S. Now you're basically a professional globetrotter."

He chuckled. "I wish. Most of my travels are for business, but I sneak in some fun here and there." Study abroad had opened his eyes to the possibilities that lay beyond the white picket fences and Sunday football games of Texas suburbia, and he'd never been able to go back. Not for more than a few days at a time.

The bad memories and his strained relationship with his father also played a role, but he kept that to himself.

"What's your favorite place you've visited so far?"

Blake thought about it. "Depends. If we're talking food, Tokyo. Nature? Norway. Wonders of the world? Machu Picchu."

"You went to Machu Picchu for business?" Skepticism drenched Farrah's voice.

"Llamas love beer and fútbol. My business doesn't discriminate based on species," he said, eliciting another laugh. Blake grinned. Two in one day. Now they were getting somewhere. "On a serious note, I want to expand Legends into a bigger international brand, so I travel a lot, researching markets, meeting with licensing partners, that sort of thing. Machu Picchu was just for fun, though. Have you been?"

"Not yet." Farrah traced a star with her finger on the rock. "I've been so busy with work, I haven't been able to travel as much as I want, except for my birthday weekend. Though I have more flexibility now since I don't have an office job. Not that I'm planning to take a vacation in the middle of your project," she added quickly.

Blake wouldn't mind—as long as he could go with her.

"Landon told me you left your design firm right before you took on my project." *Talk about fortuitous timing.* "Are you looking to start your own company?"

"Maybe one day. Not now. I'm working with you as a freelancer, not a one-person studio." Farrah traced another star. "Anyway, that's not why I left."

When she didn't elaborate, Blake asked, "So why'd you leave?"

"It's a long story."

"We have time."

"Not really. It's getting dark."

She was right. The bright afternoon sun had softened to the warm yellow of golden hour. Sunset approached, turning the sky into a palette of soft pastels.

"We could continue this over dinner. Not a date," Blake added when Farrah frowned. "Just a meal between old friends." He was stretching the definition of *friends,* but at least she didn't correct him. "There are a couple of great restaurants around here."

"Maybe, but I can't." Farrah unfolded herself from the rock. "I have a date."

The green-eyed monster reared its ugly head again. "Oh. Boyfriend or just a date?" he asked. Light, casual, but hard tension ran beneath his words.

She hesitated. "Just a date."

Relief fizzled through him—at least she didn't have a boyfriend—but the tension remained. Was this the same douche who'd texted her the other day? Where the fuck was he planning to take Farrah? Probably to some cheesy Italian restaurant where he'd try to get her drunk on red wine in the hopes of hitting a home run on the first date.

Farrah doesn't like red wine, you asshole.

Some might call him crazy for holding a mental conversation with a guy he'd never met, but those people could fuck right off.

Blake shoved his hands into his jacket pockets as they exited the park. The city's energy crackled in the air and danced along his skin, burning off some of his steam.

It wouldn't do him any good to act like a jealous prick, so he recalibrated.

"If you change your mind about dinner or your date turns out to be a flop, I'll be at the Egret on the Upper West Side. Best damn burgers in the city—at least, until my place opens." Blake grinned until his cheeks ached. "Their drink specials run till eleven, so I'll be there till late."

Farrah ignored the bait. "Good night."

"Good night. Enjoy your date."

Total lie.

It was wrong and petty of him, but as Blake watched Farrah walk away, he couldn't help but hope she had a really, really bad date.

CHAPTER 9

FARRAH WANTED TO POKE HER EYES OUT, AND THEY hadn't even made it to the main course.

Olivia's coworker was cute, she'd give him that. Ken had dark hair, green eyes, and a nice smile. No complaints on that front. Too bad he also had the personality and self-absorption of a wet sponge, not to mention the maturity of an eighteen-year-old rushing a fraternity.

"Anyway, I was on the phone with this guy, and he was all like, 'Dude, you should totally come to the Hamptons this summer, the parties are *sick*.' And I was like, 'Dude, we go to the Hamptons every summer. Let's go somewhere *different*, ya know? Let's go to Martha's Vineyard!' So, he…"

Farrah's eyes glazed over. While Ken droned on, she sipped her red wine and tried not to stare too hard at the cutlery, lest she pick up a knife and stab herself or Ken to put them out of their misery. She hated red wine—it gave her migraines, and one sip made her skin flush redder than an angry lobster—but Ken had ordered the bottle without asking, and she was desperate.

Not even the restaurant could make up for the disastrous

evening. They were at a cute little Italian place in NoMad that Farrah had always wanted to try. No doubt Olivia gave Ken a nudge when it came to choosing the date spot, but that wouldn't save Olivia from the imminent pain coming her way.

I am going to kill her. How could she possibly think I'd like this guy?

"So." Farrah tried to steer the subject away from Ken's summer exploits. "You like to travel."

"Yeah. My family has a NetJet membership," he bragged, naming a private jet company that offered leases for the country-club crowd.

"What's the most interesting place you've visited?"

"Easy. Ibiza."

Farrah's brow furrowed. "Ibiza?"

"In Spain. Españaaaaa." Ken dragged out the last *a*.

"I know where Ibiza is." She fought the urge to "accidentally" spill her wine all over his precious Rolex, which glinted obnoxiously beneath the lights.

Farrah had gone home to shower and change after meeting Blake at Central Park and, thanks to subway delays, arrived late for her date. Ken had greeted her by telling her she was exactly seven minutes late, according to his "Seventy-five-hundred-dollar state-of-the-art Rolex, which is never wrong" but that he forgave her because she had "nice legs."

She should've walked away right then and there, but she gave him the benefit of the doubt for Olivia's sake.

Liv, you're a dead woman.

"Well, the nightlife there is wild." Ken chuckled like he was thinking about things too naughty to say in public. "I had my first orgy there."

Guess they weren't too naughty to say in public.

"Great." Farrah forced a smile. How the hell was she supposed to respond to that? "Have you been to, um, other places? Ones without orgies?"

"Eh." Ken shrugged. "London, Paris, Rome. The usual."

"Anywhere outside Europe?"

"Nah. Where else would I go?"

Jesus. How did this guy get into private equity? Farrah thought the industry was for smart people. "I don't know, maybe one of the other continents," she said, unable to hide her sarcasm. "Asia, Africa..."

"Yeah right. I don't want malaria, and Asia has weird food. If I wanted to eat crickets—ow!"

"I am so sorry." Farrah wasn't sorry at all. "Did I step on your foot?"

If only she'd worn her four-inch stilettos instead of her three-inch ones. That would've made her stomp more painful.

"Yes," Ken groaned.

"My bad."

Farrah gulped another mouthful of wine. This was what she got for caving to a blind date in an attempt to battle her attraction to Blake. It'd backfired. Immensely. Because Ken made Blake look like the Boy Scout love child of Mother Teresa and the Dalai Lama.

The waiter arrived with their entrees: veal medallions sautéed in lemon and capers for Ken, pappardelle al ragu for Farrah. Her mouth watered at the smell, even as her stomach churned at the thought of sitting through another course with King Douche over there.

Ken poked at his veal. "Is this medium rare?" he demanded. "I only eat veal that's medium rare."

"Yes, sir, it's medium rare, as you requested." The waiter wore a professional smile, but the flicker of annoyance in his eyes showed he was dying to spit in Ken's food.

Farrah hoped he already had.

"Good. If it isn't, I'll be very upset. You can leave now." Ken shooed him away. Actually *shooed him away.*

That was the last straw.

Farrah's face burned with secondhand mortification. She'd never seen such atrocious behavior in real life. The way people treated service workers said a lot about them as a human being, and she'd seen all she needed to see tonight.

"You're an asshole."

The forkful of veal froze halfway to his mouth. "Excuse me?"

"You heard me. You're an asshole. Not only that, but you're also boring, insufferable, and kind of racist, and I should've done this twenty minutes ago."

Farrah didn't like making scenes. As her mom always said, keep the dirty laundry indoors because it was none of your neighbors' business. But she'd be lying if she said she didn't revel in the way Ken sputtered when she threw her wine in his face. The deep red liquid dripped down his chin and soaked into his white Brooks Brothers shirt, ruining it beyond repair.

The entire restaurant gasped.

"You bitch!" Ken spluttered. Then he noticed the droplets on the face of his watch and forgot all about Farrah. "My Rolex!"

Farrah didn't stick around to see what he'd do next. She did, however, slip their waiter a twenty-dollar bill on her way out. Lord knows Ken was the type who'd brag about dropping $7,500 on a watch while stiffing waiters on their tips.

"Sorry about the mess I made," she whispered while Ken wailed about his watch in the background.

"No problem." The waiter grinned from ear to ear. "It was worth it."

Farrah stepped into the cool evening air, glad to be away from

Ken's histrionics. She hadn't taken a single bite of her pasta, which was a damn shame, because it'd smelled amazing. But there was no way she could look at Ken's face for another second without throwing up.

Her head swam from the red wine, and her stomach growled in anger as she trudged toward the subway, debating where to go next. She could pick up food on her way home. There were plenty of decent restaurants in Chelsea. Farrah usually enjoyed her alone time, but Olivia also had a date tonight, and the thought of eating takeout alone in their empty apartment after a failed date seemed so sad.

She did have another option...one she hadn't entertained until now.

If you change your mind about dinner or your date turns out to be a flop, I'll be at the Egret on the Upper West Side. Best damn burgers in the city.

It was a bad idea, and Farrah didn't need any more bad ideas tonight.

But a burger sounded amazing, and Blake had said the Egret's drink specials ran until eleven. She needed a stiff drink—one stronger than wine—almost as much as she needed food and normal company after her date from hell.

Would it really hurt to meet up with Blake for one little burger? It wasn't like she was planning to make out with the guy.

On the other hand, Farrah didn't want to give him the wrong impression. She didn't know what Blake was up to, but she doubted he invited all his freelancers out for drinks on a Friday night.

But he hadn't made any unwanted advances toward her. He'd been friendly and professional this entire time—perhaps friendlier than he might have been with other people, but like he said, they had history.

Her brain ping-ponged between decisions. Meanwhile, her stomach growled again, sounding even more pissed off this time.

Farrah reached the subway station. She had two options—uptown or downtown. She took a step to her left, then changed her mind with a groan and walked to the right, toward the line that'd take her uptown.

CHAPTER 10

THE CLOCK TICKED TOWARD 7:30 P.M.—CLOSE TO POST-dinner territory.

Blake finished his last fry without taking his eye off the entrance to the Egret. His hope of seeing Farrah walk through the door dwindled by the second.

"Who're you waiting for? Margot Robbie?" Justin, the bartender, joked. Blake visited the Egret every time he was in town, and he'd struck up a friendship with Justin. "You've been staring at the door all night."

"None of your business." Blake pushed his empty plate across the counter. "Can I get a Stella?"

He should've known better than to expect Farrah to show up. She wasn't the type to walk out on someone in the middle of dinner, and even if she *did* walk out, why would she come here? As much as he'd like to think otherwise, they weren't friends again.

Blake wondered what Farrah and her date were up to. They must've finished dinner by now. Were they getting after-dinner drinks? Taking a romantic stroll by the riverside? Going back to Mystery Douche's place for a night of wild sex?

Blake gritted his teeth so hard his jaw ached.

"Jeez, here's your beer." Justin slapped the bottle in front of him with a wary look. "No need to glare at me like you're planning my murder just because I took longer than usual. It's packed."

"It's not—never mind. Thanks," Blake muttered. He took a swig of his beer. The cold brew did nothing to ease his mind.

"I spy someone that'll wipe that grumpy look off your face." Justin lowered his voice. "Blond. Three o'clock. Staring right at you."

Blake turned his head. His gaze collided with the petite blond at the other end of the bar. Wavy golden hair, bright blue eyes, full pink lips. She was gorgeous, but he couldn't summon even a flicker of interest.

Unfortunately, she took their eye contact to mean he *was* interested.

"Don't fuck it up," Justin warned with a grin. He made himself scarce just as the blond sidled up to Blake with a flirtatious smile.

"Hey. Do you mind if I join you?"

Bold. Then again, she didn't look like the type of woman who got rejected often.

Blake did mind and would much rather wallow in peace, but he didn't know how to tell her that without sounding like an asshole, so he responded with a noncommittal shrug.

The blond plopped herself on the barstool next to him, undeterred by his lack of enthusiasm. "I'm Cathy."

"Blake."

"Nice to meet you, Blake." Cathy leaned forward, giving him an eyeful of her generous cleavage. "What's a handsome guy like you doing here all alone on a Friday night?"

Blake *really* didn't feel like flirting tonight. He could leave, but a small part of him held on to the hope Farrah would show up. The best course of action was to extricate himself from the conversation—by telling her a story that'd have her running for the hills.

Hmm. I could tell her I have herpes. That should do the trick. Then again, with my luck—

"He's not alone. He's with me."

Blake thought he'd imagined Farrah's voice until the faint scent of orange blossoms and vanilla wafted into his nostrils. He spun around, his face splitting into a grin when he saw her standing behind him.

She came.

Just like that, his mood did a one-eighty.

"Sorry I'm late." Farrah touched his arm, and an electric shock worked its way up to his shoulder, causing it to tingle in a way that couldn't be healthy. She turned to Cathy. "Thanks for keeping him company until I got here." Her tone made it clear it was time for Cathy to leave. Pronto.

Cathy sighed. "All the good ones are taken." She slid off the stool and strutted away, causing a waiter to stumble over his own feet.

Farrah withdrew her hand, but Blake's shit-eating grin didn't waver. "You came."

"Don't read too much into it," she warned. "I'm hungry and you said this place had good burgers, so here I am."

"I thought you went to dinner. Date didn't go well?" he asked casually.

"I don't want to talk about it." Farrah took Cathy's seat. "I just want a burger, fries, and a stiff drink."

"Coming right up." Blake flagged down Justin. "One Egret Burger special and a vodka soda. Make it strong."

"You got it." Justin slid an appreciative glance in Farrah's direction and chuckled at the resulting scowl on Blake's face before disappearing into the kitchen.

"My go-to drink." Farrah sounded surprised. "You remember."

"Of course I remember." Blake examined the flush on her cheeks. She'd always hated how she turned red after drinking, but he thought it was adorable. "Red wine?"

Her hands flew to her face. "Is it that obvious? I must look like a tomato."

"You look beautiful." It was an understatement. Farrah always looked beautiful, but tonight, she fucking glowed. Her hair fell in glossy waves down her back, and her red lipstick made her lips look even fuller and lusher than usual. She wore a black dress that clung to every curve and a pair of killer heels that showed off her long, shapely legs.

A hot coil of arousal tightened in Blake's gut.

Right. Time to change the conversation before his mind wandered in a direction that'd land him in trouble.

Boundaries. Stick to 'em (for now).

"Also, thank you for saving me from that woman. I was about to tell her I had herpes. I don't!" Blake added quickly when Farrah choked on her spit. *Fuck.* "It was an excuse. To get her to stop talking to me."

"So you thought you'd tell her you have *herpes?*" Her eyes gleamed with amusement and disbelief. "You could've just said you didn't feel like talking."

Blake frowned. *Huh. She has a point.*

Justin brought out Farrah's food and drink. "Let me know if you need anything else," he drawled. He winked at her and earned himself another glare from Blake.

"She's fine," Blake snapped.

"Why don't you let the lady speak for herself?" A spark of

mischief lit up Justin's eyes before he shifted his attention back to Farrah. "If you need another burger, beer, or someone to show you around town...I'm your guy. I'm Justin by the way."

Farrah laughed while Blake's hands clenched into fists.

"I'm Farrah, and I'll keep that in mind," she said, peering up at Justin from beneath her lashes.

Was she *flirting* with him?

A snarl ripped from Blake's throat. "She doesn't like beer, and she's lived in New York for years. She doesn't need you 'showing her around.'"

"I don't know." Farrah sounded thoughtful. "You did say I should explore outside downtown more often." She cocked her head at Justin. "How well do you know Uptown?"

A huge grin overtook Justin's face. "Very well. I can bring you to—"

"Nowhere." Blake's gaze drilled into Justin, who looked like he was trying not to laugh. "Don't you have other customers to tend to?"

"Sure, but none are as beautiful." Justin winked at Farrah again, causing her to blush. "But I should return to work before I get into any more trouble. With my boss, I mean."

The Egret's manager was the chillest dude on the planet and didn't give two fucks about what his staff did as long as no customers complained.

Justin slid a sly glance in an apoplectic Blake's direction before refocusing on Farrah. "Holler if you need anything, beautiful." He sauntered off before Blake could wring his neck.

Farrah smiled at the bartender's departing back. "He's so nice."

"Nice? He's the biggest man whore in the five boroughs," Blake fumed. "Trust me when I say he was not talking about a stroll along the High Line when he offered to 'show you around.'"

Farrah brushed off his concern. "It was harmless flirting. He's charming and quite hot. I can see why he's such a hit with the ladies." Her gaze followed Justin as he made drinks for a group of older women who blatantly ogled him. "I'm not usually a tattoos girl, but he makes them work."

Blake hadn't started the night planning murder, but if that was how it had to end, so be it.

"He only got those tattoos to pick up girls," he growled, even though he wasn't sure if that was true. "And that's not the only thing he picked up."

Sure, insinuating Justin had STIs was petty, but Blake didn't give a shit.

"I'll take your word for it," Farrah said, not looking concerned enough for his liking. She bit into her burger, and her eyes widened. "Oh my god. This is incredible."

"Told you. Best burgers in the city." Some of Blake's ire melted at the blissful look on her face. "Try the fries. They put a special house seasoning on them."

"Mmm. Mm-hmm." Farrah stuffed her mouth full of fries and nodded.

Blake laughed. "In exchange for good food, I think it's only fair you tell me what happened on your date tonight. It must've been bad for you to resort to drinking red wine."

His best course of action was to redirect Farrah's attention toward a topic that had nothing to do with tattoos or bartenders. If that topic happened to be a shitty date, even better.

His next best course of action would be to punch Justin in the face, but that was a backup plan in case the other man was dumb enough to flirt with Farrah again.

Farrah swallowed and wiped her mouth. "Fine. But no laughing. Promise."

"Cross my heart and hope to die."

As Farrah recounted her story, Blake had to call on every shred of willpower not to burst into laughter. Jesus, her date sounded like something out of the movies.

"I can't believe you threw a drink in his face," he chortled.

"Neither can I, but he was such a jerk." Farrah side-eyed him. "Why do you look so happy?"

"I'm not happy," Blake said with a wide grin. His earlier anger toward Justin had simmered down...though he would still punch his so-called friend in the face for trying to get into Farrah's pants.

"I'm glad you're enjoying my misery." She nudged him with her foot, and his stomach did a stupid little flip.

"Hey, it all turned out for the best. You're not miserable now, are you?"

"No," she said with no small amount of reluctance. "I'm not."

Their gazes met. Blake's heartbeat ratcheted up another notch. Her eyes never failed to mesmerize him. They held him willingly captive, sucking him in until he got lost in their endless, dark depths.

In that moment, he could almost imagine they were on a date. The banter, the laughter, the sizzle of awareness between them... it felt like old times.

That adage about time healing all wounds? Bullshit.

There'd been a hole in Blake's heart since the day he and Farrah broke up, and no matter how many years passed, it remained as empty as ever.

Until now.

Farrah tried to hide it, but Blake spotted a flicker of emotion in her eyes. It wasn't love—not the love that used to fill him with so much warmth, he thought he'd never need the sun again. But it was the first crack in her icy mask since they'd reunited, and it was enough to send hope spiraling through his chest and into the space her love used to occupy.

CHAPTER 11

Six (ish) hours later

THIS WAS A BAD IDEA. CAPITAL *B*, CAPITAL *I*.

Farrah wasn't sure how she ended up snuggled into a dark booth at one in the morning with the ex-love of her life, but she was sure it didn't bode well for her heart.

Perhaps her ill-advised suggestion to check out a new lounge in Chelsea had something to do with the fact that she was a *little* drunk. Red wine, multiple vodka sodas, and a tequila shot would do that to you.

Fortunately (or unfortunately), Farrah was too intoxicated to consider the consequences of her actions.

She tapped her finger on her chin, trying to think of something good. "Never have I ever…Googled my own name."

It was their third round of a game they'd played often in Shanghai. Farrah hadn't played it since she'd graduated from college, but it was a nice throwback to her young, wild days.

"Bullshit. *Everyone's* Googled their own name." Blake

narrowed his eyes at the smirk on Farrah's face. "No? What kind of person are you?" He took a pull of his whiskey.

"One who has no interest in what the internet has to say about her. Tell me the truth. How many times do you Google yourself a day? Two? Three?"

He rolled his sleeves up. "What kind of person do you think *I* am? Five. Minimum."

The laugh burst out of Farrah's chest, unexpected and genuine. Blake's chuckle joined hers not long after.

The buzz, the lighting, the music...they were doing things to her. Lowering her inhibitions, making her forget the bad memories. They still lurked in her subconscious, but they didn't hurt as much, which was why Farrah asked the question she'd been dying to ask since she first laid eyes on Blake again.

"Are you still with her?"

She didn't think so. She'd seen no signs of another person living in Blake's condo, and if he and his girlfriend were still together, they wouldn't live in different cities. Not when he had a choice of where to settle down.

But Farrah wanted to know for sure.

"Who?"

"Your girlfriend." She finished the rest of her cranberry vodka. She was way past her drink limit, but between Nightmare Ken and the way her insides heated around Blake, she needed extra fortification. "The one you dumped me for."

The lingering laughter in the air faded. Blake paled. "You don't want to talk about this."

"I do." Maybe it was the alcohol talking or some sort of latent emotional masochism, but Farrah wanted to know everything about this girl—who she was, how she and Blake met, what their relationship was like. "It's been five years. I'm over what happened between us. But I'm curious."

Blake's nostrils flared at the word *over*. He leaned back, away from the light, until shadows wrapped themselves around his face and the upper half of his torso. "We're not together anymore."

"Why'd you break up?"

The silence stretched for so long, Farrah thought he didn't hear her. Then he answered, "We couldn't make it work."

"Congratulations. You just gave the vaguest answer possible."

Blake leaned forward again, his eyes hard, his jaw set. He looked almost angry, and she had no clue why. "Why are we talking about this, Farrah? Right here, right now?"

What remained of their carefree conversation hardened into something tense and dangerous. Farrah swallowed hard, her skin tingling from the change.

"Because it's the elephant in the room, and an elephant isn't part of my design plan." Her lame attempt at a joke landed with a thud. She lifted her chin. "Look, we have a history together, but it's just that: history. What happened between us happened a long time ago, and I don't want it hanging over every meeting and conversation we have. So let's clear the air once and for all."

"You think me telling you what happened with my ex will clear the air." It wasn't a question.

She lifted a shoulder. "Maybe. You did dump me for her. You can't blame me for being curious."

"Stop using that word," Blake snapped.

"What word? Dump?" Farrah's eyebrows rose. "That's what happened, isn't it?"

Except it wasn't. Dump was too colloquial, too common. It didn't adequately describe the pain Farrah felt the night Blake told her he'd gotten back together with his ex-girlfriend and that he just wasn't that into her anymore. Sorry, thank you, goodbye.

No, he hadn't dumped her. He'd reached into her chest and dug out her heart, layer by layer, piece by piece, discarding and stomping all over them until Farrah had been sure she would die. She'd been raw, exposed, and bleeding, and he hadn't even cared.

The memory tore at the scabs on her poor heart, so much so that Farrah had to down the rest of her drink in one gulp to ease the pain.

What the hell was she doing here?

Blake wasn't a client. He wasn't a friend. He was a liar and a cheater, and if she were smart, she'd leave right now and never look back. But her ass remained glued to her seat.

I'm an idiot.

"Technically." Regret swirled in Blake's crystal eyes. "For the record, I know I acted like a jerk in Shanghai, and I am so, so sorry about what I did. But I'm not the same person I was back then."

"Forgive me if I don't take your word for it." Farrah played with her glass. "When'd you guys break up?"

A tense silence. "Five years ago. A few months after we went home."

"Are you freakin' kidding me?" The words exploded out of Farrah. "You broke up with the girl you were supposedly so in love with less than a year after you got back together?"

Blake was even more of a jerk than she'd realized.

A muscle ticked in his jaw. "I didn't say I was in love with her."

"Yes, you did. You said, quote, 'I love her.'"

"*Love* and *in love* aren't the same thing."

"When you put it that way," Farrah said sarcastically. "We've got the King of Semantics here."

Her breath whooshed out of her lungs when Blake gripped her chin with one hand and leaned in, so close all she could see, smell, and feel was him. Her traitorous body went liquid even as her mind screamed at her to knee him in the balls.

Blake's eyes glinted, as dark and fathomless as the sea at

night. "I've only been in love with one person my entire life. She's the one I dream of every damn night, and she's the one who can break me with one tiny glance. I would jump off a fucking tower for that girl, and you know what? Her name sure as hell isn't Cleo."

Cleo. His ex had a name. Farrah filed this information away for future use—what kind, she didn't know, because her brain had turned foggy and she couldn't get oxygen into her lungs fast enough. She was burning, on fire from the weight of Blake's gaze and the heavy implication behind his words, and there wasn't a rescue in sight.

"Aren't you going to ask me who she is?" His question whispered across her lips like a dangerous, silken challenge. Daring her to accept the game. Daring her to say yes.

"No." Farrah mustered every ounce of strength she had to tear herself away from Blake's touch and kicked herself for almost falling prey to his good looks and charisma. Look where that had landed her the first time around. "I don't care."

"You're lying." His voice didn't change, but his eyes smoldered with blue fire.

"I'm not." *Breathe.* "I told you, I'm over you. I couldn't care less about your love life."

"Fine." Blake went silent, tapping his fingers on the table like he was contemplating his next move. A minute passed before he stood abruptly and held out his hand. "Let's dance."

Talk about whiplash. "You've got to be kidding me."

"Do I look like I'm kidding?"

No. His face was as grim and serious as a tombstone.

Farrah narrowed her eyes, took his hand, and followed him to the dance floor. She didn't know what game Blake was playing, but she wouldn't be the one who backed down first.

Of course, the DJ chose that moment to segue from the electro beats he'd been playing all night to a sultry R&B jam whose soft croons evoked images of silk sheets and entwined bodies.

But this wasn't about the music or the dance. This was about... what? Proving to Blake, or herself, that she was over him? That he didn't affect her anymore?

If so, it didn't work, because the minute Farrah's body pressed against Blake's and the scent and feel of him filled her senses—warm, masculine, and so damn familiar—she wanted to run. She was sinking into quicksand, but she was too damn stubborn to pull herself out even if she could, so they stood there, their hearts beating as one, their eyes locked in a silent challenge.

"It's funny how we ran into each other after all these years," Blake murmured. His warm breath skated over her lips. Goose bumps erupted on her skin in its wake, and she shivered.

"We didn't run into each other. Landon introduced us." Farrah tried not to focus on how hard and strong Blake's body felt against hers. It made her painfully aware of how long she'd gone without sex. One year. The last time she'd been with a guy hadn't been all that great either. She'd faked her orgasm with a few half-hearted screams, not that the guy had noticed.

She also tried not to remember the way her heart jumped when she spotted the jealousy in Blake's eyes earlier that night. Yes, Farrah had been riling him up by flirting with Justin—though she hadn't been lying when she said Justin was H-O-T—and she hated that she cared. Hated that she'd wanted to make Blake jealous, even though jealousy didn't mean anything in the grand scheme of things. Some people got jealous when their partners paid too much attention to the cat.

Still, it'd been gratifying to see Blake's face darken when she complimented Justin. What that said about her, she didn't want to know.

"Yeah, but out of all the interior designers in the world, he chose you." Blake's silky voice brushed over her, a satin cobra waiting to strike. "One might even say it's fate."

"It's coincidence. I don't believe in fate," Farrah lied.

Another bedroom-playlist-worthy song came on. Farrah gritted her teeth. What was the DJ trying to do, induce another baby boom?

Blake pulled her closer; his arousal pressed against her thigh, thick and powerful, and Farrah's mouth went dry. Her mind hazed over with both memories and fantasies—his hands tangled in her hair, his mouth pressed against her core, her body bowing beneath waves of pleasure.

Liquid heat flooded between her thighs, and she prayed her knees wouldn't give out from under her.

"If this is making you uncomfortable, we can stop." There it was. The challenge. She heard it in his voice, saw it in his eyes.

"I'm not uncomfortable." They were so close her lips *almost* brushed his when she spoke.

"Good." Blake tightened his grip on her hips, and her pulse jumped. "Because you're shaking."

Farrah pressed her pelvis against him, smiling when she saw his throat bob with a hard swallow. "I'm not the only one."

This wasn't them. Not the Blake and Farrah she knew. But time, heartbreak, and secrets had twisted them into darker versions of themselves, ones that resorted to playing games like this. Their banter at the Egret earlier that night seemed like a lifetime ago. By now, Farrah had lost track of how they got here or what they were doing. They sure as hell weren't dancing.

Blake dipped his head, and she felt the faintest touch of his lips against hers. Not a peck, not even a brush, but a whisper of a promise.

Farrah's chest clenched with fear and anticipation. Her body wanted this. Her brain did not. As for her heart...well, it didn't know what it wanted.

He's a client.

He's an ex-lover.

He broke my heart.

He can make my body melt.

It's too risky.

What's life without a few risks?

It would be so easy to give in. Farrah's apartment was a five-minute walk away, and Olivia had to be asleep by now. She could sneak him in without her roommate ever knowing.

Blake's heart beat in time with hers.

Thud. Thud. Thud.

Their mouths moved another millimeter closer.

Warning sirens screamed in Farrah's head as the inferno in her body raged.

She had two seconds to decide.

Appease her body...or protect her heart?

Blake's lips parted, and she shoved him. Hard.

Farrah ripped herself out of his embrace, her heart skidding at five hundred miles a minute. The fog in her head cleared enough for her to realize they'd smashed past the boundaries she'd insisted they adhere to.

She'd deal with that later. Right now, she needed to get out here.

"I'm leaving." Her voice sounded far away to her own ears. "It's late."

Blake nodded. He'd won—she'd backed down first—but for a victor, he looked awfully defeated.

Farrah grabbed her belongings and hurried out the door. Her feet hit the cracked pavement, and she didn't stop running until her redbrick building came into view.

Stupid. Stupid. Stupid.

By running away, she'd showed her hand. Despite what she

said, she wasn't over Blake. An irrational, primal part of her still wanted him, and now they both knew it.

Farrah could've stayed and played the game through to the end, but that wasn't an option.

She had too much to lose.

CHAPTER 12

"WE HAVE YOU FULLY BOOKED FOR MEDIA IN THE TWO weeks leading up to the grand opening. In fact, *Mode de Vie* wants to do a big lifestyle feature for their October issue. The interview will be in June, and they requested a photo shoot at your apartment. Is it going to be ready by then?"

"Yeah, Angus beef is fine." Blake watched two contractors assemble the stadium-style seats in the special events section of the bar. The heavy thud of hammers hitting nails and the screechy whine of high-powered drills filled the air. Blake loved those sounds. It was the sound of shit getting done, of success and hard work; it was also the one area of his life that hadn't gone to hell.

His chief of staff glanced up from her clipboard with a frown. Patricia Hart was a lot of things—competent, assertive, organized to a fault—but she was *not* tolerant of people slacking off. Not even when that person was her boss.

"We moved on from discussing the food ten minutes ago. We're going over your media schedule now. Get it together, Blake."

He crossed his arms over his chest, half-amused, half-annoyed. "How much do I pay you to talk to me like that again?"

"A lot." Patricia's smile dripped saccharine. "Now, about your apartment. Is it going to be ready in time for the *Mode de Vie* shoot? The interview is the third week of June."

"I think so."

"You *think so* or you *know so*?"

Blake scowled. Patricia was his best hire and an indispensable part of his team. He came up with the vision and strategies; she implemented them, and he paid her a crap ton of money to do so. She also kept his ass in line and didn't take shit from anyone.

But sometimes, he wished he'd hired someone a little more accommodating.

"I know so."

I hope so.

Farrah told him the apartment would be finished in July, taking into account potential contractor issues and shipping delays, but that was *if* there were contractor issues and shipping delays.

"Good." Patricia ticked something off on her clipboard. "That's all for today."

With her auburn waves and endless legs, she could moonlight as a model. Blake recognized her beauty, but even if she weren't an employee, it did nothing for him. He was a black hair, brown eyes, smart-mouth kinda guy.

"Great. Call me when the liquor distributor comes back with a quote. I don't want a repeat of New Orleans."

Both Blake and Patricia grimaced when they remembered the jackass distributor who'd charged them three times the standard price for two dozen cases of shitty well liquor. Their New Orleans manager had signed the contract in a haze of grief after losing out big in Vegas the previous weekend, and by the time Blake and Patricia found out, it'd been too late.

"Of course. It won't happen again." Patricia eyed him cautiously. "You've been distracted lately. Is everything ok?"

Blake's eyebrows shot up. He and Patricia didn't discuss personal matters. Ever. Theirs was a professional relationship—a great one but professional nonetheless. She did her job, he paid her, and that was the way they liked it.

"Yeah. I've just had a lot on my mind."

Correction: he had one person on his mind. All the damn time. Blake replayed his and Farrah's near kiss the way he used to replay tapes of his old football games. He studied them, analyzed them, broke them down frame by frame until he could pinpoint every mistake, every unconscious tic and tendency, and every player's strengths and weaknesses.

After replaying his night with Farrah on a loop for two weeks straight, Blake was sure of three things: (1) her body wanted him; (2) her mind shunned him; and (3) her heart was terrified of him.

He felt it in the heat of her skin against his, saw it in the glint in her eyes, and heard it in the rapid *thud-thud-thud* coming from inside her chest.

In his quest for Farrah's heart, her mind was his enemy and her body was his ally. And what do you do with allies? You butter 'em up, give 'em what they want, and keep them on your side.

That would be a helluva lot easier if Blake were anywhere near her body. Farrah hadn't spoken to him since she ran off into the night. His calls rolled to voicemail, and she returned his messages via curt texts instead of calling him back. She also refused to meet him in person, saying she was still getting quotes from contractors and didn't have any updates for him yet.

Blake kicked himself for pushing things too far, too fast. He hadn't meant to, but he'd been terrified that Farrah was telling the truth. That she was over him. He could handle her hating him, but he couldn't handle her treating him like he was just some guy she used to date. Because the opposite of love wasn't hate; it was indifference.

So he'd pushed her. Forced her to show her hand and admit, if only to herself, that she may not love him anymore, but he still affected her. Short term, it gave Blake satisfaction to see the heat in her eyes. Long term, it was a fucking terrible strategy. The more Farrah was aware of her attraction to him, the more she would avoid him.

Case in point: the past two weeks.

"Understandable. This is a big opening." Patricia snapped back into chief-of-staff mode. "Is there anything else you want to go over?"

"No. That's it. Thank you."

Patricia left to supervise the bar setup, and Blake swept his eyes around what would soon be the crown jewel of the Legends empire. The New York branch wasn't going to be just a sports bar—it was going to be a destination. And it wasn't going to be just a destination—it was going to be the hottest destination on New York's nightlife circuit. A sports mecca spread over three stories, complete with a bowling alley, state-of-the-art recreation room, and upscale cocktail bar/nightclub.

In the cutthroat hospitality world, stagnation meant a slow, painful death. You have to innovate to stay on top of the game and beat back the hungry upstarts frothing at the mouth to take your crown.

Blake had no intention of getting dethroned.

That was why it was time to expand the Legends brand. He was keeping the casual, down-home business model where it made sense, but places like New York, Dubai, Miami, and Vegas? They wanted big; they wanted glitzy; they wanted out of this fucking world. And he was going to give it to them.

Now, if only he were on top of his personal life as much as his professional one.

———

Later that night, Blake made the mistake of asking his friends for advice.

"Dude, you're doing this shit all wrong." Justin cracked open his beer. "You gotta play hard to get. Make *her* come to you."

Blake rolled his eyes. "Sorry, I didn't realize we were back in middle school."

"You make fun, but that shit works. Girls like a challenge."

"Not this girl. Not after what I did."

Blake already regretted bringing Farrah up in front of Justin, who was a good bartender and a cool guy but also a major pain in the ass when it came to the opposite sex. Specifically, when it came to advice pertaining to the opposite sex.

Like Blake, Justin didn't have to work hard, if at all, to get a woman into bed. Must have been the tattoos and devil-may-care attitude. Unlike Blake, he blazed a path through Manhattan's female population with the enthusiasm of a drug addict hopped up on coke. His perception of how the whole dating thing worked was warped because he didn't date. His love life was a flimsy string of one-night stands and casual flings.

"What *did* you do?" Justin's eyes gleamed with curiosity. "Forget her birthday? Bang her best friend? Tell her what you really thought about her outfit?"

"No, dickhead. That would be you, you, and oh, you."

"Wrong. I've never forgotten a birthday because I've never asked."

"Charming." Landon entered the room with a fresh bowl of popcorn and a six-pack of beer. "You're in the running to be Bartender of the Year."

"Hey, you don't need to know someone's birthday to be a good bartender." Justin reached for the popcorn before the bowl even touched the table. "I listen to people cry, dispense invaluable life advice, and supply them with alcohol to numb their pain. I'm a goddamned saint."

"I'll call the church," Landon said wryly. He glanced at Blake. "You still moping about Farrah?"

Blake scowled. "I'm not moping."

He, Landon, and Justin were watching the NBA playoffs in Landon's decked-out den. The Celtics versus the Warriors. It was a nail-biter, and a fun night with the guys was just what he needed after a long day at work.

Of course, it would be a lot more fun if his guy friends weren't acting like jerks.

"Sure you're not." Landon chuckled. "This girl has got you more twisted than an episode of *Game of Thrones*. You should've seen his face when he saw her again for the first time," he told Justin. "He just stood there like an idiot, gawking at her."

Justin guffawed. "I'll one-up you with the way he nearly tore my head off for just *talking* to her at the Egret a few weeks ago."

"Fuck you both." Blake tossed a handful of popcorn at his so-called friends. "And you weren't 'just talking' to her." He glared at Justin, his blood simmering again when he remembered the way Justin had eye-fucked Farrah at the bar. "You were trying to sleep with her."

"True. But I try to sleep with everyone. No biggie." Justin caught a kernel and popped it in his mouth, unfazed. "That was the same night you almost kissed, right? And you haven't seen her since? I'm telling you, man, you gotta hit the brakes. Give her a chance to miss you."

"It's been two weeks."

"I mean, you gotta be around her but not, you know, hit on her."

"As much as I hate to agree with J on any of his often dubious advice, he has a point." Landon kicked his feet up on his custom-made, expensive-as-shit coffee table. "You're scaring her off."

"I don't hit on her that often," Blake muttered. "The other night was a slipup."

"Maybe not with words, but she *feels* it." Justin waved his hands in the air. "Women have a sixth sense about this sort of thing and—oh, shit! The Celtics just scored. Up by two, baby!"

As Landon and Justin redirected their attention to the game and their mutual loathing of the Warriors, Blake pondered his friends' advice.

What the hell. Might as well give it a shot. It couldn't hurt. Right?

CHAPTER 13

IF SOMEONE HAD TOLD FARRAH LAST WEEK THAT SHE'D willingly go on a road trip to Upstate New York with Blake, just the two of them, she would've laughed in their face.

Yet here she was, ensconced in a rented Range Rover with her ex-boyfriend while they drove around Syracuse, looking for a place to eat lunch.

In her defense, she'd been desperate.

Farrah had gone into a tailspin when she received Blake's text telling her the apartment had to be finished by late June because *Mode de Vie* was shooting a lifestyle feature on him there. It'd almost been enough to make her forget their inappropriate encounter at the lounge two and a half weeks ago.

Mode de Vie. The most influential lifestyle magazine in the country. They always asked for the interior designer's name when they shot at a subject's home, which meant Farrah's name would appear in its hallowed pages in a few months. That was the equivalent of an author getting their book featured in Oprah's Book Club. One mention in the esteemed magazine could vault her from being an unknown to being the brightest star in the sky...*if* her design was good. If not, Farrah could forget about her future in the industry.

Blake didn't want any major remodeling done, thank god, which shaved weeks, if not months, off the process. But seven weeks was still a tight turnaround for redesigning an apartment his size.

Farrah had been a whirlwind of activity since she found out about the new deadline: calling contractors and pushing them for quotes and start dates, sourcing materials, and searching through every website and every store in the five boroughs for the perfect pieces that would transform Blake's apartment into his dream home.

She'd succeeded for the most part.

The only hiccup was the vintage trunk sitting in a little shop in Syracuse, four hours from New York City. Farrah had found it on the store's website but when she called, they informed her they didn't ship large items. She'd have to pick it up herself.

That wouldn't have been an issue, except Farrah hadn't driven since she moved to New York. She sure as hell wasn't going to brave the city streets on her own. None of her friends in the city drove either, and she'd seriously considered hiring an Uber for the eight-hour round-trip drive before Blake called her for a progress update.

She'd mentioned her dilemma; he'd offered to rent a car and drive her, and she'd accepted.

Now, here they were, with the trunk from the shop nestled snugly in the back of their car.

"This looks promising." Blake slowed in front of a diner on the edge of downtown Syracuse. Since it was summer, the town swarmed with tourists instead of students from its eponymous university.

Farrah spotted several out-of-town license plates in the parking lot: Vermont. New Hampshire. Pennsylvania. Fortunately, there were a few parking spaces left. All the other restaurants they'd passed had been packed.

"Fine by me. I'll eat anything at this point." Farrah's stomach growled with a ferocity that could scare off a pride of lions. "Hurry, before someone takes those spots."

Blake smirked. He pulled the Range Rover into one of the empty spots, his muscles flexing against his shirtsleeve as he turned the wheel. Even in a simple white T-shirt and jeans, he could melt the panties off a nun. "I forgot how snippy you get when you're hungry."

"I'm not snippy."

So what if she was? Farrah only had a bagel and coffee for breakfast, and that'd been hours ago. When she wasn't fed, she got a little...well, snippy.

That, plus Blake was acting weird. Not in an overt way. He'd been a perfect gentleman all day. He'd picked her up, let her choose the playlist with no complaints—not even when she played five Taylor Swift songs back-to-back—and didn't blink an eye when she spilled water on her shirt.

Water. On her white shirt. And not a single comment, not even a glance. He'd merely handed her a napkin and hummed along to "Blank Space" while she dabbed at her semitransparent top.

Which is a good thing, Farrah reminded herself. It wasn't like she wanted any extra attention from Blake aside from what their professional relationship entailed.

Heat rose on her cheeks when she remembered their near kiss. She'd woken up the next morning hungover and mortified. They technically hadn't done anything, but the whole experience felt so intimate, they might as well have had sex.

At least, Farrah thought so. Judging by Blake's cool attitude, he didn't feel the same way.

They walked in silence toward the diner. The beautiful blue skies from earlier that morning had darkened into an ominous slate gray, and Farrah smelled the earthy promise of rain in the air.

Despite the few empty parking spaces, the inside of the diner overflowed with patrons, and Blake and Farrah waited thirty minutes before the hostess showed them to a table. By the time they received their food—well over an hour after they'd parked—Farrah was ready to snap someone's head off.

"Jesus." Blake's jaw dropped as Farrah tore into her chicken sandwich with a gusto she usually reserved for Anthropologie sales and Henry Cavill. "You'd give some of my college teammates a run for their money. And these are three-hundred-pound linebackers we're talking about."

Farrah washed down her food with a healthy gulp of her chocolate milkshake. "I'm hungry."

"I can tell." One of Blake's dimples peeked out before it disappeared, and her stomach twisted in a way that had nothing to do with hunger.

They lapsed into silence.

Farrah was beginning to think aliens had kidnapped the real Blake and replaced him with a robot version of himself. He was never this quiet. She felt like she was in the backseat of an Uber with a driver who didn't particularly care to converse with his customers.

"I didn't do this for the money by the way." Farrah tried to fill the silence.

Blake arched a questioning eyebrow.

"The road trip," she clarified. "I found the trunk on the store's website and it seemed so perfect for your living room. All the other trunks I found were off—weird color, wrong size, ugly details. I didn't specifically choose an item that couldn't be shipped so I could bill you more hours."

His laugh boomed against the chatter in the diner. "It's ok. I didn't think you were trying to swindle me."

That was it. No teasing. No banter. Just "it's ok."

Frustration coiled in Farrah's gut. Why? She had no idea. This was what she wanted. A relationship in which they were designer and client, nothing more.

So why did she feel so uneasy?

"Well, thank you for driving me. I know you must be busy, so I appreciate you taking the time."

"No problem."

Farrah gritted her teeth. She wanted to shake Blake until more words tumbled out of him because he was freaking her out.

Their waitress, a Rachel Bilson lookalike with a toothy smile, swooped in. "How's the food? Can I get you anything else?" She directed her question at Blake. Farrah might as well have been invisible.

Blake's dimples showed up in their full glory. "The food's great." He glanced at Farrah. "Do you need anything?"

"No."

He appeared unfazed by her curt response. "We're all good, thanks." He upped the wattage of his smile, and Farrah swore the waitress nearly melted into a puddle at his feet.

As the other woman tottered away on shaky legs, Farrah drained her milkshake with one long, hard slurp. The straw rattled angrily at the bottom of her empty glass.

"Do you want another milkshake? I can call her back," Blake offered, still so annoyingly, irritatingly *polite*.

"No, thanks." The way Rachel Bilson 2.0 eyed Blake, like he was a juicy steak and she hadn't eaten in months, rankled Farrah more than it should have.

She took a deep breath. She and Blake had cleared the air about his ex-girlfriend at the lounge, and now it was time to address the other elephant in the room. "Look, about the other night. We were drunk and got carried away. I mean, we didn't *do* anything, but…" Farrah trailed off, trying to arrange her thoughts into a coherent sentence. "What I'm saying is, I left because, uh, I had to wake up early the next morning." *Lame.* "I don't want you to get the wrong impression about my feelings for you. Not that I have feelings for you."

Ugh. Why was she so bad at this?

"It's forgotten. Don't worry about it. Like you said, we were drunk. I don't think you're in love with me or anything." Blake went back to eating his burger, a little more aggressively than before.

Farrah gaped at him in disbelief. She'd spent three weeks agonizing over that night only for him to brush it off like it meant nothing. Like they hadn't almost kissed, and his arousal hadn't pressed against her thigh so hard it could've drilled a hole through his zipper.

Need slashed through her at the memory, even as she resisted the urge to hurl the rest of her food in Blake's face.

"We should head back soon." Farrah gripped her necklace, the anchor to her swirling thoughts. She needed alone time with her vibrating bedside buddy, stat. "It's a long drive back to the city."

"Are you talking about New York City?" Their waitress popped up again.

Jesus. Didn't she have other customers to serve?

"Yes." Farrah tried not to hold the way the other woman ogled Blake against her, but what if Farrah were his girlfriend? Would the waitress still ogle him like that? Didn't seem smart. "Can we get the check, please?"

"Sure thing, but I'd advise against driving back in this weather." The waitress clucked her tongue, not taking her eyes off Blake. "It's crazy out there."

Farrah stared out the window. Between the noise in the diner and her inner turmoil over Blake, she'd missed the near-apocalyptic scene outside. The gray skies had escalated into a harsh downpour worthy of hurricane season. Angry bolts of lightning streaked through the sky, chased by the furious roars of thunder, and the rain fell so fast and heavy she couldn't see their car parked right in front of the diner.

"There's a severe storm warning until tomorrow. You'll have to hunker down in town," their waitress chirped, like they were discussing a picnic instead of a rainstorm. "There's a nice B and B just down the road. Their owner dropped by earlier and mentioned one of their guests canceled last minute, so they should have a room open. I can call them if you'd like." She whisked their plates off the table.

Dread settled in the pit of Farrah's stomach. The last thing she wanted was to spend a night here with Blake—not when he was acting so weird and not when her body was a live wire waiting to explode. He was like the chocolate milkshake she'd ordered: delicious and nice to look at, but oh-so-bad for her.

Unfortunately, the waitress was right. It was too dangerous to drive back to the city.

A loud boom of thunder rocked the diner, underscoring the need to stay put in town for the night.

Farrah forced a smile. "Thank you. That would be great."

Across the table, Blake turned ashen. "I can't drive in this rain."

"It's ok. We'll check into the B and B." This day was *not* turning out the way Farrah had expected. "Hopefully, the storm passes before morning."

"No." Blake gripped the edge of the table so hard his knuckles turned whiter than his face. "I mean I *can't* drive in this rain. We have to wait it out here."

"What?" Farrah laughed. "We can't wait this out here. The storm doesn't look like it's going to pass anytime soon."

"Farrah, I mean it." He bit out each word like they were poison-coated pills. "I'm not driving in this rain."

Farrah had never seen Blake so shaken. The sight of his turbulent eyes and trembling shoulders awakened a part of her that was infinite times more dangerous than her body's craving for him. It was the part that wanted to dig into his darkest secrets, extract the bloodied bullets, and nurse him back to health, even if saving him meant losing herself.

It's not your job to piece him back together.

"I'll drive," Farrah said softly. She could handle the rain. They weren't going far. "Okay?"

Blake's jaw clenched. After a few seconds, he jerked out a nod.

The waitress returned with their check, confirmation there was one room left at the B and B, and a piece of paper that Farrah was sure contained her phone number, which Rachel Bilson 2.0 slipped to Blake.

He didn't notice. His head bowed, all traces of sunny, irreverent Blake gone. In its place was a darker, brooding version of him that had Farrah's heart aching and wondering what, exactly, had happened to him in the time they were apart.

CHAPTER 14

"FOR GOD'S SAKE, JOY, I SAID I'LL TRY. LOOK, I HAVE TO go. I'm with somcone." A pause, then a grudging, "Love you too. Talk to you later."

Farrah tried to focus on her Kindle app and not eavesdrop on Blake's conversation.

She failed. Miserably.

A second later, Blake stepped out of the bathroom, wearing sweatpants and...nothing else. An orange Syracuse T-shirt sat balled in his fist instead of covering his sculpted chest and six-pack abs. His sweatpants rode low on his hips, eliciting wicked fantasies about what would happen if they inched down *just* a bit.

Farrah gulped. She pulled the covers up to her chest, hyper-aware of her hard nipples pressing against the thin fabric of her own T-shirt, which was so large, she wore it as a dress.

She and Blake arrived at the B and B with no incident but had gotten soaked during their run from the car to the inn. Since neither had planned for an overnight trip, they didn't have a change of outfits. Fortunately, the owners were kind enough to lend them clothes for the night. Unfortunately, Farrah's bra was tumbling in a washer somewhere along with the rest of her clothes instead of hiding her obvious and unwanted reaction to the man standing in front of her.

"Is everything ok?" The question came out breathier than she would've liked. Farrah cleared her throat. "You look upset."

"I'm all right. Family stuff." Blake tossed the shirt onto the chair in the corner. "Shirt's too small," he explained. "Hope you don't mind." Apology and a hint of mischief crept into his expression, one that said he knew what the sight of his bare chest did to her and what he'd find if he pulled the covers off her and shoved her panties aside.

Farrah's thighs clenched. Her mind spun in a million directions, all of them counterproductive to her emotional and, soon, physical well-being. Whatever the female version of blue balls was, she had it. Bad.

"Is it your dad?" She silently applauded her attempt at maintaining a normal conversation when all she wanted to do was run into the bathroom and relieve the ache between her legs.

Blake rubbed his jaw. "Sorta. I was talking to my sister. My dad's fiftieth birthday is in August, and she wants me to fly back to Austin for the party."

"That doesn't sound so terrible." Farrah's brows drew together. Blake didn't have the best relationship with his father, but... "He can't still be mad at you for quitting football."

"Who the hell knows?" Blake leaned against the dresser and crossed his arms over his chest. "I told him why I quit, you know. After I returned home from Shanghai. He all but called me a pussy for worrying about CTE. Said the threat of a concussion was better than failing as a businessman. He was so sure my sports bar wouldn't make it."

Farrah's heart twisted at the bitterness coating his voice. She'd had a tumultuous relationship with her own father when he was alive, but for all his faults, he'd never made her feel less than. "But it did. It's one of the most successful sports bar chains in the country. You built an entire empire in just a few years."

Blake flashed a sardonic smile. "Yes, and do you know how many of my bar openings he's been to? Zero. Not even the inaugural one in Austin. My mom was there, and my sister, but not him. Said he wasn't feeling well, but we came home to him drinking beer and watching football."

In that moment, Farrah saw Blake not as a heartbreaker but as someone whose own heart had been broken so many times by those closest to him.

"I'm sorry," she whispered.

She curled her fingers around the comforter, willing herself not to hug him and pour into him some of the light that seeped out every time he brought up his father.

So many reasons I shouldn't.

"You know what the most fucked-up part is?" Blake's eyes brewed with a storm that made the one raging outside look like a gentle summer rain. "All I ever wanted was to make my dad proud. Even in the moments when I resented him, even when I mailed copies of my *Forbes* and *New York Times* features to him out of spite, hoping to get a rise out of him, I wanted him to look at me and say, 'Son, I'm proud of you.' He never did and probably never will, yet I still hope." His humorless laugh scraped against Farrah's chest. "Isn't that pathetic?"

Screw it.

Farrah swung her legs over the side of the bed and walked over to Blake until they stood mere inches apart. She placed a hand on his arm, afraid to embrace him fully but unable to stop herself from giving him this basic act of comfort. "It's not pathetic. It's human. Maybe your dad *is* proud of you and just doesn't know how to express it."

"It's a few words. Should be simple enough."

"Sometimes the simplest words are the hardest to stay."

A small smile touched Blake's lips. A real one this time. "You always saw the best in people. Even the ones that are broken."

The hairs on Farrah's skin prickled. Something hung in the air between them, so thick and heavy she tasted its tangy sweetness on her tongue.

The truth was, everyone was broken. People weren't shells, hard and glossy like the statues you found in museums. They were messy mosaics, compromised of glittering pieces of love and jagged shards of heartbreak. The lucky ones found someone whose broken edges fit perfectly with theirs, like pieces in a jigsaw puzzle. Two imperfects, holding each other up in the storm. And it would feel so safe, so right that they'd get addicted to the illusion of completeness, forgetting that one wrong move could throw them out of sync, and the other's jaggedness would slice them so deep, they'd bleed from the inside out.

"It's better to go through life wearing rose-colored glasses than searching for demons."

A boom of thunder rattled the windows, swallowing Farrah's words, but Blake appeared to have heard them perfectly.

"Classic Farrah." His fingers grazed her cheek, a featherlight touch followed by the blossoming of goose bumps on her skin and pooling of moisture between her legs.

Blake's gaze dropped to where her nipples puckered painfully against her shirt, and the indifferent, robotic Blake from earlier that day disappeared. In its place stood raw, wicked lust, the kind that had zero compunction about ripping your clothes off, bending you over, and fucking you until you shattered into a thousand pieces of ecstasy.

Farrah bit back a whimper.

Blake's sweatpants did as good a job of hiding his arousal as her shirt did hers—which was to say not at all. She could see his erection through the gray fabric, long and thick and hard. Her core throbbed in response, aching to be filled, and Farrah realized, with all the certainty in the world, that she needed to see this through.

All this time, she'd resisted what she wanted, afraid one concession would lead to another and another, until they toppled like dominoes and created a path back to where she didn't want Blake to go. But here was the thing about resistance: the harder you try to pull away, the harder the object you're resisting sucks you in. It was a clash of wills, and the person who was willing to forfeit a battle was often the one who won the war.

Farrah took a tiny step toward Blake, then another, until her nipples brushed his bare chest.

Blake flinched, his jaw tight, his eyes dark. She could see his pulse beating in the hollow of his throat. She wanted to press her mouth to it, to confirm whether it beat in time with hers and if his blood ran as hot as the fire scorching her veins.

He dragged in a shaky breath. His fingertips brushed her hips, and just when she thought he was going to kiss her, he broke away with a growl.

"I'm taking a shower."

The bathroom door slammed behind him and splintered the spell.

Farrah collapsed against the dresser, panting and woozy from unfulfilled desire and confusion. It wasn't true, what she said earlier about wearing rose-colored glasses. She saw, very clearly, in black and white, what was in front of her.

Blake Ryan was her missing puzzle piece, her broken other half. He was her drug, her addiction, her downfall, and if she wanted to survive, she needed to get him out of her system—even if it meant compromising her heart.

CHAPTER 15

BLAKE SPENT AN HOUR IN THE SHOWER. YES, HE JERKED off—twice—and no, it didn't do jack shit for him because the second he stepped out of the bathroom and saw Farrah sitting on the bed in that tiny T-shirt dress thing of hers, his blood rushed south again like it was never-ending spring break in Cancun.

Fortunately, she was so engrossed in her phone, she didn't notice he still sported a boner the size of Texas.

The earlier heat between them had retreated, but it still lingered in the air like a warning, reminding Blake he must be the biggest idiot in the world to turn down sex with the one woman who could unravel him.

He'd seen it in her eyes. She wanted him as much as he wanted her. But she wanted his body, and he wanted all of her—heart, mind, body, and soul.

Forget his earlier strategy about getting close to her body to reach her heart. If Blake gave in now, it would only reinforce the idea that all he wanted was sex. Hell, he'd all but confessed he still loved her at the lounge, and she'd brushed it off like it meant nothing.

To her, his words were lies. To him, they were an unshakeable truth.

Blake clenched his teeth and sat on the other side of the bed—of course there was only one bed, because the universe took pleasure in torturing him—and stared at the tent in his sweatpants. It glared back at him. *Fuck you for blocking me*, his cock hissed.

I'd say fuck you back, but that's exactly what's not *going to happen.*

Not gonna lie, it wasn't his first time talking to his dick, but it was the first time Big Blake and Little Blake didn't get along.

I'm going crazy.

Blake cleared his throat. "Sorry I took so long. Shower's all yours." He thought a normal conversation would take his mind off the ache in his balls, but now he was picturing Farrah in the shower, and *fuck*, that didn't help at all.

"Thanks. I want to finish this chapter first."

Minutes ticked by before Farrah looked up from her phone.

Blake had angled his body so she couldn't see his hard-on, but the tiny smirk playing at the corners of her mouth told him she was aware of the effect she had on him.

He'd taken Justin and Landon's advice and played it cool all day. It took every ounce of willpower he had plus some he borrowed on credit, especially when Farrah spilled her water on her shirt, and he could see the outline of her bra through the wet fabric.

Ever tried driving through Manhattan traffic with a raging hard-on while humming Taylor goddamn Swift to take your mind off your X-rated fantasies?

Yeah, neither had Blake. Until today.

The play-hard-to-get strategy seemed to have worked...a little too well. He'd noticed Farrah's annoyance when the waitress slipped him her number, and he sure as hell noticed the way her body responded to him earlier. It was the chip in her ice wall he'd been waiting for. Too bad it was chipped in the wrong section.

While the rest of her melted, the defenses around her heart remained frozen.

"What are you reading?" Blake eased under the covers, both to hide his erection and to soak up the warmth. Despite the radiator humming away in the corner, a cold draft permeated the room and pebbled his skin with goose bumps.

"Leo's new book. I always suspected he would be a writer someday." Farrah's mouth softened into a smile, and Blake wanted to strangle Leo Agnelli with his bare hands.

He hadn't kept in touch with Leo. Hadn't kept in touch with anyone from Shanghai, really, except Sammy and Luke, who was an assistant rugby coach at the University of Wisconsin Madison. He and Leo had been friends by default. They'd hung out because they ran in the same circle, not because they had anything in common. Not to mention, Farrah had had a crush on Leo before Blake, something for which Blake had never quite forgiven the Italian.

But Blake would have to be living under a rock not to notice that Leo was the literary world's latest darling. He wrote sweeping tales about family and love that covered continents. His work hovered in that space between popular fiction and highbrow literature, and—wouldn't you know it—the public ate that shit up like a pack of starving hyenas.

"Is it good?" Not that Blake cared. He hadn't read any of Leo's books, and honestly? He didn't plan to.

"It's great." Farrah set her phone aside and unfurled herself from the bed. "I'm taking that shower. Be right back."

The door shut behind her.

Blake laced his fingers behind his head and stared at the ceiling. The water running in the bathroom blended with the steady downpour outside. Thunder boomed, rain lashed at the windows, and the demons that stayed inside their box when Farrah was around crawled out, slowly at first, then all at once.

Screeching tires. Twisted metal. Blood.

The memories slammed into him with the force of a Mack truck going at full speed.

Arguing with his dad over some small thing—Blake didn't even remember what—not because it was important but because he was exhausted, and panicked, and trying not to get crushed between the twin weights of starting a business and preparing to be a father. Storming out of his parents' house with Cleo, despite the thundering rain and hazardous driving conditions.

Not seeing the deer in the road until it was too late.

The car skidding out of control and wrapping itself around a tree.

The blood. The doctors. The devastation. The blinding, suffocating, all-consuming guilt.

Blake's chest rose and fell with short, heavy breaths. Sweat beaded his forehead; the food he ate at the diner churned in his stomach, making him want to throw up. He wanted to purge himself of everything that was bad and unholy and terrible inside him, but he couldn't. There was too much of it, and it rooted itself in his gut even as its cancerous reach spread through the rest of his body. Tainting his heart, corrupting his soul.

"Blake?"

He jerked his head up.

Farrah stood in the doorway of the steamy bathroom with alarm splashed across her face.

"I've been calling your name for five minutes. Are you ok?"

"Yeah." The hoarse rasp scraped against his vocal cords. Blake cleared his throat and tried again. "Sorry, I was thinking about something."

She climbed into bed next to him. It was a huge bed, and

there was plenty of space between them, but the weight of her on the other side slowed his breathing and chased some of the demons away.

"Is it the rain?" Farrah's eyes bore into him, warm as melted chocolate but incisive as a scalpel.

"What makes you say that?" Blake tried to bluff; she wasn't having any of it.

"How adamant you were about not driving in the rain when we left the diner and how tense you were the entire drive." Farrah's brow wrinkled. "You didn't have a problem with the rain when we were in Shanghai. What happened?"

"It's not the rain itself. Not really." Blake was fine with the rain. He was even fine with driving, though it took two years after the accident before he got behind the wheel again. It was when you combined the two that he had a problem. That, and when he was alone with his thoughts during a storm. It always triggered flashbacks, and without people around to distract him, he'd spiral into an abyss of self-loathing that took him days to dig out of. "But I had an accident, years ago, during a storm. And I haven't been able to drive in the rain since."

Farrah's face softened with sympathy. "I'm so sorry. Was everyone...?" She hesitated. "Ok?"

No.

"For the most part. I'd rather not talk about it." Blake raked a hand through his hair and changed the subject. "Tell me something that made you happy. Really happy."

He needed a dose of sunshine.

Farrah's bottom lip disappeared behind her teeth as she contemplated her answer. "My mom and I went to Paris together after I graduated college. Her present to me. The entire trip was fun, but there was one moment when we were sitting on a bench watching the sunset in the Jardin du Luxembourg, eating the most *perfect* croissant, that I thought...*Life is beautiful.*" She blushed. "It sounds so corny, and it wasn't a big moment, but it's one I return to whenever I want to cheer myself up."

"It's not corny." Blake wished he had that relationship with his parents. His dad? Forget it. As for his mom, he loved her, but when push came to shove, Helen Ryan bent beneath his father's will instead of siding with her son. He didn't need her to side with him all the time, but once—just once—would've been nice. "I'm glad you and your mom are so close."

"She's the closest family I have left in this world." Farrah picked the bottom of her shirt. "Although she's not too happy with me right now. I finally told her yesterday that I quit KBI."

Blake winced. "Yelling?"

"Almost shattered my eardrums," Farrah confirmed.

Blake did a quick mental calculation. He'd hired Farrah a month ago, soon after she quit her job, so she'd been keeping her employment status a secret from her mom for weeks now. "She can't be that mad. You're still working and making damn good money too."

His accountant was going to throw a shit fit when he saw how much Blake was paying Farrah, but Blake would cross that bridge later.

"I know, but freelancing isn't the same as having a steady paycheck. My mom's all about stability. It was hard enough getting her on board with the whole interior design thing. She's ok with it now, but when I first told her, she almost had a coronary."

"Stability doesn't always equal success or happiness. I know plenty of people in stable jobs who are miserable."

"Yeah, Asian parents don't see it that way." Farrah smiled a crooked smile, and his stomach somersaulted harder than an Olympic gymnast going for gold. "It's an immigrant thing. My mom will get over it eventually. She's pretty liberal, as far as Chinese parents go. It just sucks, feeling like I've let her down."

"You didn't let her down. You're doing great. In fact, I think you should start your own firm." Blake laughed at the shock on Farrah's face. "Seriously. You've been handling everything so well, even when we had to move the deadline up. You shouldn't have to toil away in an office somewhere, waiting for other people to tell you you're good enough."

"I'm not ready." Farrah's jaw set in that stubborn line he knew so well. "One day, I'll go fully independent. But I've only been in the industry for a few years. I have no clue how to start a business."

"Neither did I and look at me now." Blake's lips curved. "I remember someone once told me, no one has experience running a business until they run a business, and if it's what you want to do and you give it your all, you'll succeed."

A direct quote pulled forth from the wells of memory.

Farrah's eyes widened. "You remember."

"How could I forget?"

She'd been the one who'd pushed him to go for his dreams. Without her, Legends wouldn't exist.

What happened next happened in slow motion.

Farrah closed the distance between them until her orange-blossom-and-vanilla scent wrapped around Blake.

His breathing turned shallow. He needed to get out of here. He'd barely been able to stop himself from kissing her earlier; he didn't have enough willpower to do so again.

But he didn't—couldn't—move.

The scene hazed over like they were in a dream world. A part of Blake wondered if he *was* in a dream.

Then Farrah's lips touched his, and he stopped giving a damn whether this was real.

Whatever it was, Blake was going to enjoy the hell out of it while it lasted.

CHAPTER 16

BLAKE'S RESISTANCE: GONE.

Their kiss was an earthquake that split him apart at the seams. Five years of built-up tension and longing exploded at once, cracking his ironclad control and threatening to change the landscape of his life forever.

Five years of hopes and dreams, all leading to this moment.

What started as a tentative embrace morphed into an all-out, down-and-dirty battle of the senses. Their lips collided, and their hands roamed to the cacophony of rain and thunder outside. The force of the storm beat in time with Blake's pulse as he devoured every drop of the chocolate-eyed siren in his arms.

Farrah tasted of sunshine and redemption, and he captured her moans in his mouth, desperate to etch every inch of her into himself.

"god, it's been so long," she breathed. She ground against him; nothing but two thin layers of fabric separated them, and he could feel how wet she was.

Carnal desire shoved aside whatever rational thought Blake had left. He flipped her over and pinned her hands above her head, soaking in the sight of Farrah's flushed cheeks and swollen lips. "Too long," he agreed. "But nice to see you remember my name."

"Still cocky as ever." Farrah's laugh faded into another moan when he nipped at the sensitive spot beneath her ear.

"Right again." Blake pressed his hardness into her soft core, just in case his double entendre wasn't clear, and absorbed the tiny shudders that wracked her body. He cupped one breast through her shirt and swept his thumb over her nipple, watching as it tightened and rose into a peak that begged to be sucked.

He was so turned on, it hurt. The beast inside prodded him to take her, to raise her legs over his shoulders and bury himself so deep nothing could ever tear them apart; the man wanted to savor every fucking second. He'd waited years for this; he wasn't going to throw it all away in a matter of minutes.

Yes, Blake had stamina, but at this rate, he'd be lucky if he didn't come after a handful of thrusts.

"Do something," Farrah demanded, her words thick with lust and impatience.

A smoky promise edged into his chuckle. "As you wish."

Blake caressed her inner thighs, savoring the silkiness of her skin, before he pushed her panties aside and rubbed his thumb over her most sensitive bundle of nerves. Farrah's head fell back when he slipped two fingers inside her, gritting his teeth at how tight and wet she was. He was going to lose it, and they'd just gotten started.

Blake balled his other hand into a fist, straining for self-control, as he worked up a rhythm that had Farrah crying out with pleasure.

"This is exactly what we need," she gasped, her breath ragged against his lips. "More. Please." She spread her legs wider, a not-so-subtle hint of what she was begging for, but a cold sliver of ice sliced through the fog in his mind and forced him to pull away.

Farrah whimpered in protest.

"What do you mean, this is exactly what we need?" A voice in Blake's brain whispered he didn't want to know the answer, but it was too late. The question was already out there.

She blinked up at him. "This. Us. Sex." Her clinical, matter-of-fact response—so at odds with the heat in her eyes—sent another spike of ice through his chest.

Blake felt pathetic, getting so hung up over semantics. If he were smart, the way his cock screamed at him to be, he'd resume what they were doing and deliver so many orgasms, neither of them would be able to walk straight.

Any inclination to do just that died with the next words out of Farrah's mouth. "One night to get each other out of our systems. It's what we need."

The ice melted and simmered, transforming into lava at the pit of his stomach. Blake shoved himself off her and stumbled off the bed.

Get each other out of our systems.

Like they were a disease. A drug. An addiction that needed to be purged.

"No."

Farrah's jaw hung open. She scrambled to sit up, her cheeks rosy for a whole other reason than desire. "No?" Disbelief sharpened her echo. "Why not? I want you. You want me. Isn't this what you've been working toward since you hired me?"

The lava boiled with fury. "You think I hired you because I want sex." It wasn't a question. "Let me be crystal clear: I've never paid for sex and I never will, directly or indirectly. Don't think I need to concoct a plan as elaborate or expensive as hiring you—at *three times* your rate—to get what, as you so astutely pointed out, we both want."

Farrah hugged the covers to her chest. Uncertainty and

defiance slid across her features. "Then what are we doing here, Blake? I know you. It's been years, but I *know* you, and there's more going on than you needing a designer. You could've hired anyone else in the city for less than what you're paying me. If you don't want sex, what the hell do you want?"

From the moment they'd laid eyes on each other at the Aviary, they'd been playing games. Cat and mouse. Push and pull. Truth or dare.

Blake was sick of playing games.

So he chose truth.

"I want you."

"That's what I'm offering."

"Not your body." Blake closed the gap between them once more. The rug muffled the sounds of his footsteps, and he could hear Farrah breathe, fast and shallow. "I want *you*. All of you. Heart, body, mind, and soul. I want what we had." His voice thickened. "I messed things up between us in Shanghai, and I'm so fucking sorry. I was young and stupid, and if I could do it all over, I would. But I can't. All I can do is stand in front of you and ask for another chance. I know I broke your heart, but if you let me, I'll spend the rest of my life putting it back together."

There it was. All his cards laid out on the table for her to see.

Blake hadn't had the guts to say those words out loud before, but they'd been there, waiting to spill forth at the first command, for five years.

Now, they hovered in the air, waiting for a verdict.

Farrah was the judge, jury, and executioner, and as Blake spoke, her breathing picked up until her chest heaved with each intake of oxygen. Her face was smooth and still as a pane of glass, but a hurricane brewed in her eyes. Emotions flickered through them at such a rapid pace Blake couldn't pin them down.

The seconds stretched into eternity, prolonging his torture.

Blake couldn't swallow past the lump in his throat. Every nerve of his body stood on alert while his heart paced in his chest, faster and faster until he wanted to throw up from the anticipation.

"I can't give you that." Farrah's rejection sliced through the space between them, turning Blake's confession into desolate scraps of confetti that fluttered into a heap on the ground. The glimmer of foolish hope in his heart crumbled into ash, filling his airways and choking him. "I can give you one night. That's it. Take it or leave it."

CHAPTER 17

One month later

THE SUN BEAT DOWN ON FARRAH WITH FIERCE INTEN-
sity, scalding her skin and causing rivulets of perspiration to
snake down her face. The heat was merciless, almost angry, as if
punishing her for her heartless behavior.

Not heartless, smart, she corrected herself. What she did in
Syracuse a month ago was smart, safe, and logical. As the saying
goes, *Fool me once, shame on you; fool me twice, shame on me*.

Farrah wasn't going to let Blake fool her again with his pretty
words and promises of forever. She'd made that mistake once,
and it almost broke her beyond repair.

But if she had done the right thing, why was she so miserable?

"Thank god. I was dying out there," Olivia said when the
hostess waved them into the restaurant. Leyla was the hottest
new brunch spot in town, and it didn't take reservations, which
meant you had to wait at least an hour for a seat on the weekends. Olivia hated lines more than she hated wrinkled shirts, but

Farrah knew she'd make an exception for food. "It's so freakin' hot today."

Farrah murmured in agreement as she followed the hostess to their table.

"Who's this mystery friend that's supposed to meet us?" Olivia examined the single-page menu. "They better be good, considering we waited in line for an hour and they're not even here yet."

"Uh, well, you know him."

Olivia lifted an eyebrow. "Really?"

"He's right there."

Farrah waved at her friend and braced herself for the fallout. Olivia turned, then whipped around to face Farrah again with fury oozing out of every pore.

"Are. You. *Kidding me?*"

"Remember Ken?" Farrah said quickly. "I forgave you for that."

"That's different! That was an innocent mistake on my part. He's perfectly respectable in the office. I didn't know he was such a jerk outside the office. But *this*, this is an act of utter betrayal—"

"Hey." Sammy stopped next to their table. He looked even more handsome than usual in a pale blue button-down that set off his tan and a pair of dark denim jeans.

His face lit up with surprise and anger at the sight of Olivia. He was too much of a gentleman to say anything, but the displeasure wafted from him in waves.

"Hi!" Farrah chirped. "So glad you could make it. Take a seat."

Sammy bypassed the empty seat next to Olivia and sat beside Farrah.

Both he and Olivia pinned Farrah with steely glares.

Hmm. Maybe tricking them into brunch with each other wasn't the best idea.

But Farrah was sick of the animosity between her friends, and she wanted them to make up already. It'd been years since their breakup.

She realized the irony of the situation, given her refusal to give Blake another chance, but that was different. Sammy and Olivia's breakup had been mutual, and one of them hadn't confessed they still had feelings for the other.

Allegedly still had feelings. Farrah wasn't going to take Blake's words at face value.

"I'm so happy we're together again." Farrah tried to get the conversation going. "It's like old times." Minus the rest of the group, but that was a minor detail.

"Just like old times." Sarcasm dripped from Olivia's voice.

Farrah kicked her under the table and winced when Olivia kicked her back. They glared at each other.

Farrah tried her luck with the more *reasonable* person at the table. "Sammy, how was your meeting?"

Sammy had texted her when he returned to New York a few days ago—this time, hopefully, for much longer than three days.

He'd had a "casual coffee" with a potential business partner this morning, which was why he couldn't wait in line with them. It was a Sunday, but Farrah swore half the deals in the city took place during "casual" weekend meetings.

"It was good." Sammy's shoulders remained stiff, but his grudging tone indicated he was well on his way to forgiving Farrah for the ambush. "We signed the deal."

"That's great!" Farrah almost knocked over her coffee in her excitement. "Sammy's opening a pop-up bakery at Convention," Farrah explained to Olivia. Convention was a trendy Soho storefront known for its revolving calendar of pop-ups. Every four months, it transformed into a new restaurant, bakery, or café headed by a Michelin-starred chef or food celebrity. The variety and star power made Convention catnip to Manhattan's fickle culinary elite. "New York's finally getting a Crumble & Bake! For four months at least."

"Great." Olivia downed her mimosa in one long swallow. "Congratulations."

"Thank you," Sammy said.

Their coldness hardened into invisible icicles that hung between them like swords waiting to drop.

There was a momentary thaw when they ordered their food, but when it came out and they dug in, they lapsed into silence again.

"Where are you staying in New York?" Farrah was determined to get the conversation back on track, no matter how difficult her friends were being.

"Williamsburg. My sister's friend has a house there, and he agreed to let me rent a room at a discounted price." Sammy cut into his eggs Benedict. "The pop-up doesn't open until next month, but I have to get everything ready."

"Why is everyone opening branches in New York?" Olivia sipped her second glass of freshly poured orange juice and champagne. "First Blake, now you."

"Well, New York's a pretty big market," Sammy deadpanned.

Farrah choked back a laugh.

Olivia ignored his answer and addressed Farrah. "Speaking of Blake, how's the design project going?"

The mirth disappeared. "Fine."

As far as the project went, Farrah couldn't have asked for a smoother rollout. She'd rented a storage space to house the furniture shipments trickling in—as well as the chest they'd bought in Syracuse—until the contractors finished the wall tiling and floors. As long as there were no delays or mishaps, she should finish the apartment in time for the *Mode de Vie* shoot.

Her relationship with Blake, if you could call it that, was another matter. After she gave him her ultimatum in the B and B, he'd walked out of the room without another word. She didn't know where he went, but she'd pretended to sleep when she heard the door creak open past midnight.

The next morning, they'd checked out and driven back to the city. Blake dropped her off, and that was that. Neither said a word during the four-hour drive, and Farrah hadn't seen or heard from him since.

Her gut twisted. Had she been too harsh on him? Thinking back, her words had been a little cold, but she wasn't the one who'd lied and cheated. She had no reason to give him another chance.

Farrah gnawed on her lower lip until she drew blood.

"Have you seen him since Syracuse?" Olivia asked.

"No." Farrah stuffed a piece of french toast in her mouth, so she didn't have to provide a longer answer. Olivia knew Blake and Farrah had stayed in the same room in Syracuse; she didn't know about them nearly having sex or about Blake's confession. Out of all the things Farrah had expected him to say, asking for a second chance had *not* been on the list. She'd thought he wanted a wild night of sex. Maybe a casual fling. Not a sequel to their doomed relationship.

Farrah forced herself to swallow. The toast tasted bitter.

"Good. The project will be over soon, and you won't have to see him again." Olivia flicked her gaze toward Sammy. "He's bad news."

"No, he's not," Sammy countered. "He's made mistakes, but he's a good guy."

That was Sammy—loyal to a fault. To *all* sides.

"Please." Olivia snorted. "He lied and cheated. Not my definition of a *good guy.*"

"He didn't—I mean, he did, but you don't know the whole story." Sammy appeared to regret his outburst the instant the words left his mouth.

Farrah and Olivia snapped their heads in his direction.

"What do you mean, whole story?" Curiosity lit up Olivia's dark eyes. "What do you know that we don't?"

"Nothing. That just slipped out." The color of Sammy's face matched that of Farrah's dragon fruit smoothie.

"Bullshit. I know a cover-up when I see one." When Sammy didn't budge, Olivia switched tactics from vinegar to honey. "Come on, you're among friends," she cajoled. Apparently, the thrill of a good secret was enough to make her put aside her animosity toward her ex.

All the while, Farrah's heart jackhammered against her rib cage. She shouldn't care, but a tiny hopeless part of her was desperate for anything that'd prove Blake was telling the truth.

Pathetic.

Sammy shifted his gaze away from Olivia's sweet smile. "It's not my place to tell."

"It's your moral obligation to tell. This is Farrah. One of your oldest friends." Olivia waved her hand over Farrah like she was showing off a prized pony. "Blake is back in her life, and if you have something to say that could prevent him from hurting her again, you better say it."

Sammy muttered something under his breath that sounded like, "She's not the one I'm worried about."

Olivia frowned. "What?"

"Nothing."

"Sammy." Farrah placed a hand on Sammy's arm. "Please."

She had no desire to dredge up the past, but it was already peeking out from the box she'd buried it in. Might as well let it loose so it could expend its energy before she locked it up again.

Sammy sighed. "Like I said, it's not my place to tell. But don't be so hard on Blake, ok? He's been through some shit. And if he wants to tell you…" He drummed his fingers on his knee. "The next time you see him, ask him about the night you lost your necklace."

Farrah's hand flew up to her pendant. It was the last gift her father gave her before he died. Blake was the only person who knew about its significance unless he'd told Sammy, which he had no reason to. "What does my necklace have to do with anything?"

Sadness crept into Sammy's eyes. "It has to do with more than you think."

CHAPTER 18

WHEN IT RAINED, IT POURED.

After a months-long streak of golden luck, Blake's professional life started shitting on him as much as his personal one.

His restaurant manager ran off to Greece to chase a girl he'd fallen in love with at a wine tasting and sent Blake an email from Santorini, apologizing profusely but making it clear he wasn't coming back to New York anytime soon.

There was a plumbing issue in the bar's second-floor bathroom that cost an arm and a leg to repair.

And *Mode de Vie* canceled his feature spread because they'd landed a last-minute exclusive interview with the notoriously press-shy Crown Prince of Eldora and his fiancée—an American flight attendant and newly minted fashion icon whom the prince's family reportedly loathed.

Blake didn't care so much about *Mode de Vie*, although it would've been great publicity for the bar. He did, however, care about Farrah, who'd worked herself to the bone trying to pull his apartment together for the shoot. She'd never said it, but he knew how excited she'd been about making her magazine debut. He'd caught her Googling a list of interior designers who'd appeared in *Mode de Vie* when she thought he wasn't looking.

Now, he had to tell her it wasn't going to happen.

"What's the status on hiring a new restaurant manager?" Blake asked Patricia, who tapped away on her phone as though her life depended on it.

"We've narrowed it down to three candidates. You have interviews scheduled with them next week," Patricia replied without looking up. "I also confirmed an interview with *City Style* to replace your *Mode de Vie* shoot. It's not the same caliber, but it has decent readership among our target audience."

"Is it going to be shot at my house?"

"No. It'll be in their studio. They never do on-location shoots for personal features."

Blake sighed. "Okay, thanks." He checked his watch. Almost 8:00 p.m. He'd been up since five in the morning. Awake since three. His head swam with exhaustion, but he'd promised Landon he'd meet him for drinks at the Egret. He'd been so knee-deep in shit and self-pity, he hadn't seen his best friend in weeks. "Let's wrap it up. Get some rest."

"I'm going to send a few more emails first."

"Patricia."

"Blake," she mimicked. His chief of staff rolled her eyes at his glare. "Fine. I'll leave after I send *one* more email. Good enough for you?"

"You should be glad I'm such an understanding boss," Blake grumbled. "Otherwise, I would've fired you a long time ago."

"You'll never fire me. I'm the best chief of staff you could have."

Dammit. She was right.

After another reminder about not working too late, which Patricia waved off, Blake exited Legends and took the subway uptown. Since it was a Tuesday, the Egret wasn't too crowded, and he spotted Landon chatting with Justin at the bar right as he walked in.

"Sup." Blake plunked his ass on the seat next to Landon and tilted his chin in greeting before addressing Justin. "Why is it every time I see you, you're not working?"

"Do you see anyone else sitting at the bar, jackass?" Justin whipped his towel at Blake. "Besides, last time you were here, I *was* working. So much so you lasered me in half with your eyes when I was slower than usual to bring you your beer."

"It had nothing to do with the beer."

"What did it have to do with?" Justin smirked. "Wait. Let me guess. Asian, long dark hair, lips that look like they're made for s—"

"Finish that sentence and your face will meet my fist," Blake growled.

The bartender seemed unfazed. "Maybe not because you clearly need to get laid. You're wound tighter than a British lord with a stick up his ass."

He wasn't wrong. Blake's night with Farrah in Syracuse had left him with a cracked-open chest and balls bluer than a Smurf. His right hand helped, but not much. He could go out and find a willing body to sink into for the night, but every time he contemplated the option, it sounded as appealing as sticking his dick in a hornet's nest.

Farrah had, for all intents and purposes, ruined him for other women.

"One day, J, someone will hand your ass to you and you'll deserve every second of it," Landon clapped Blake on the back. "Bring the uptight one here a burger and a whiskey. On me."

Within an hour, the bar filled up, which Blake didn't mind. It meant Justin had something to do other than butting into his conversation.

"Everything's going to shit." Blake stared at the amber liquid in his glass until it blurred before his eyes. "I swear, it's karma."

"For what?"

Blake shrugged.

As usual, Landon read his mind. "That wasn't your fault. It was an accident. Cleo, the police, your family...no one blames you."

I do. "Her dad does."

"Her dad's a jackass."

Blake's eyebrows shot up. Landon almost never cursed. Too uncouth for the $500 million heir.

He grimaced the second the thought crossed his mind. *I'm the jackass.* Landon may be rich, but he wasn't one of those stuck-up, my-shit-don't-stink types. They met when Blake accidentally kicked a soccer ball in Landon's face when they were seven. Blake's mom apologized profusely, and Landon's nanny freaked out, but Landon just laughed and bet Blake he couldn't beat him in a one-on-one match. Blake did—the first time around. Landon beat him the second time. They'd been best friends since.

"Don't give me that look," Landon said. "You of all people know how impossible Cleo's father can be."

True. Cleo's father made Blake's dad look like a basket of fuzzy newborn golden retrievers. He'd nearly ripped Blake's head off and fed it to his rottweiler when he found out Blake had impregnated his only daughter before marriage.

"I don't want to talk about Cleo's father or anything related to Austin," Blake said, even though a ticket confirmation for his flight home was burning a hole in his inbox. He'd caved and bought a flight home for his dad's birthday after all—not because he had a particular desire to see Joe, but because he owed it to his mom and sister. "I have enough present shit going on without digging up past shit."

"Fair enough." Landon twirled his glass on the counter. "Speaking of present shit, how're things with Farrah?"

Blake cracked a half-hearted smile. "Shitty."

"Tell me what happened."

Blake hadn't planned on detailing his humiliating night to his friend, but the whiskey loosened his tongue, and before he knew it, he'd spilled everything.

Landon listened while a kaleidoscope of surprise and disbelief played across his face. He didn't say anything after Blake finished, but maybe that was because a certain bartender butted in before he could.

"You *turned down sex* with her?" Justin's voice sliced between them. "What is wrong with you?"

Blake turned to see his friend-slash-royal-pain-in-the-ass staring at him with his mouth agape as he wiped the same spot on the counter over and over, apparently too stunned by Blake's bad decisions to notice the water ring two inches to his left.

"How are you back already?" Blake demanded. "The place is packed now."

"My shift ended ten minutes ago. I'm staying for shits and giggles."

Blake grimaced. "Please don't say *shits and giggles* ever again. You're a grown-ass man."

"This grown-ass man will say whatever he wants." Justin tossed his towel aside and winked at his replacement, a curvy redhead with a pierced lip and no-bullshit attitude. Two minutes later, he was up in Blake's face again from the other side of the bar.

"We need a new go-to bar until Legends opens," Blake told Landon, who smirked in response. "Preferably somewhere with bartenders who keep their nose out of other people's business."

"Having my nose in other people's business *is* my business."

Justin yawned. "Anyway, since I'm off duty, I'm speaking to you as a friend. You're an idiot. You should've had sex with her."

"I don't want a friend with benefits. Actually, not even a friend with benefits. She said, 'One night.'" Nausea churned anew in Blake's stomach. He hadn't bothered answering Farrah's ultimatum. He couldn't. Instead, he'd put on that ridiculously small shirt the B and B owner's son lent him, walked downstairs, and drowned his sorrows with wine. Not his first choice, but that was what they had, and at that point, he would've drunk rubbing alcohol to forget what happened in their room. He didn't return to said room until well past midnight, when Farrah was already sound asleep.

"Uh, yeah. That's your golden ticket, man." Justin groaned at the confused look on Blake's face. He turned to Landon. "You get it, right? Back me up here because our man is thicker than a concrete wall. I can't believe he's a successful businessman."

To his credit, Landon tried to stifle his laugh. Too bad he failed.

"I think what Justin is trying to say is, Farrah didn't say she wants nothing to do with you. She said she *only* wants to have sex with you. There's a difference."

Blake frowned. "I don't follow."

Twin blankets of exasperation fell over Landon's and Justin's faces.

"Why do you think friends with benefits relationships never work? Because someone always ends up catching up feelings. Personally, that's why I never do them." Justin smiled at a gorgeous passing blond, who smiled back. "One-night stands for me only. But I digress. You can tell Farrah you're down for just sex, then work on turning it into more. You can't do that if you shut down your only hope of seeing her on a regular basis."

"What he said." Landon jerked his thumb at Justin.

"Turn it into more after one night?" Skepticism coated Blake's words.

"Yep. If you can't do it, that's a problem I can't help you with," Justin said, oozing sympathy. "Sucking in bed—figuratively, not literally—is a common affliction amongst ninety-five percent of the male population. Excluding yours truly, of course. I gave you the strategy; I can't give you the tools too. You're either born with it or—fuck!" He cursed when Blake's fist slammed into his arm.

"Screw you," Blake said. "I'm ten times better at fucking than you are."

"You wish, Ryan. I've sampled every zip code in Manhattan and most in Brooklyn, and I've had no complaints."

"Classy," Landon said, tone dry. "But unless you both want to whip out your dicks for a measuring contest in the middle of a bar, I suggest we keep the conversation on track. Blake, J's right. It's easier to turn something into something than nothing into something." He frowned. "That made sense, right?"

It did, in its own twisted, screwed-up way.

Blake's friends were hardly "Dear Abby" material, but they made good points. Besides, their earlier advice of playing hard to get—as juvenile as it had been—worked. Sort of. At least it broke down enough of Farrah's walls for her to admit wanting him.

Hazy memories from the past curled around Blake. The heat, the passion, the breathy screams as Farrah fell apart in his arms. Hell, their make-out session in Syracuse almost set the room on fire, and they'd only hit second base.

For all the years, confusion, and secrets between them, Blake and Farrah's chemistry could still blow the doors off a nuclear lab.

Turn one night into multiple nights.

Blake could do that.

He hoped.

CHAPTER 19

FARRAH'S HEELS CLICKED AGAINST THE MARBLE FLOOR as she strode toward the elevator bank in Blake's building. The contractors had finished the floors and tiling last week, and she'd hired a company to move the items from the storage unit into the apartment so she could start her favorite part of the design process: arranging the furniture and decor and bringing her vision to life.

The elevator dinged on the twenty-seventh floor. Earlier that day, she'd overseen the assembly and arranging of the large furniture items—the sofa, the bed, the dining table—before she ducked out for a quick dinner, but she wanted to double-check everything before she wrapped up today so she could jump right into work tomorrow.

Farrah fished the spare key Blake had given her to use for the duration of the project out of her purse and let herself in. The apartment smelled of new furniture and lemon-scented wood polish.

Blake had decamped to a nearby hotel while he waited for the project to finish, so Farrah hadn't seen him at all during her comings and goings.

She brushed away the niggle of disappointment in her stomach and focused on the task at hand.

She was so engrossed in examining the furniture, she didn't hear Blake's bedroom door open.

"It's looking good."

Farrah screamed and spun around while picking up the nearest item that could double as a weapon—a white ceramic vase with navy blue coral design, to be exact. Her heart slammed against her sternum as panic crashed over her in waves.

Three years of living in New York and she had yet to be mugged or accosted in any way—unless she counted the aggressive elbowing of irate New Yorkers on the subway during rush hour—but Farrah wasn't about to go down without a fight.

"Whoa. Don't shoot." The person held up their hands, and the fog of adrenaline cleared enough for Farrah to notice the familiar head of blond hair and knife-sharp cheekbones.

She lowered the vase, waiting for her pulse to return to normal before she hissed, "Jesus, you scared me. What are you doing here?"

Farrah caught a shadow of Blake's dimples before they disappeared. "It's my apartment."

"I thought you were staying in a hotel."

"I am. I came to pick up more clothes." Blake gestured at the black duffel bag sitting at his feet. "Turns out, I'm not a great packer."

"Blake Ryan admitting he's not great at something? That's a first."

"I have more than enough redeeming qualities to make up for such a minor fault."

Her mouth tilted up into a smile.

Then she remembered what happened between them the last time they saw each other, and the smile disappeared.

Blake watched her with guarded eyes. "The apartment does look good. I wish *Mode de Vie* had panned out so the world could see it."

Farrah swallowed the lump of disappointment in her throat. Blake had called and broken the news a few days ago. Their first conversation since Syracuse, and a short one at that. As much as she'd freaked out about what might happen after being mentioned on a platform as large and influential as *Mode de Vie*, she hated seeing the opportunity slip between her fingers, especially since she had yet to receive a single callback for an interview.

Hundreds of job applications and not one follow-up, not even from the small design firms. Farrah even checked to make sure her emails were sending correctly. It didn't make sense. New York was a tough job market, but she had a stellar résumé. She should've at least received a phone screen.

The earnings from Blake's project would tide her over for a while, but if she didn't find stable employment soon, she'd be saying goodbye to the Big Apple and hello to LA smog in less than a year.

"Thanks." Farrah shoved her rising panic into her deal-with-it-later drawer. "It's not done yet. Give it another week. I just came by to double-check everything before I leave for the night."

"You don't have to rush now that the magazine scrapped the shoot."

"I'm not. Timeline worked out that way."

Silence descended. Farrah rubbed her thumb over her pendant, seeking comfort in its cool familiarity. Sammy's words echoed in her mind.

The next time you see him, ask him about the night you lost your necklace.

She could. The curiosity burned her from the inside out, and it wasn't like things could get any more awkward between her and

Blake. At the same time, she was terrified of the answer. Whatever it was, it was bound to tilt her world off its axis, and she'd had enough changes in her life these past few months, thank you.

Like they said, *Don't ask questions you don't want the answers to.*

"We should talk about what happened in Syracuse." Blake stepped closer.

Run, her sensible self warned, but something glued her feet in place.

Running wouldn't do her any good anyway. Blake was a black hole, a raw force so powerful he could suck her in whether she was four feet or four worlds away.

"There's nothing to talk about." Farrah focused on Blake's jaw instead of his intense eyes. It was strong and square, covered by a light layer of stubble that made him look even more like a Calvin Klein model than usual.

It should be illegal for guys to keep their good looks after they break a girl's heart.

If the universe were just, it would dish out one major physical flaw per heartbreak for the offender, like a giant oozing wart on the forehead or something. The flaw would serve as both a punishment and a warning.

Sadly, the universe was not just, which explained how Farrah ended up in her current predicament.

"I disagree," Blake said smoothly.

"Too bad."

His lips quirked up in a smile and sent the butterflies in her stomach in a tizzy.

Butterflies, Farrah decided, *are the Benedict Arnolds of the animal kingdom.*

"I have a proposition for you. Well—" He paused. "More like a response to your proposition."

"I didn't proposition you."

"You kissed the hell out of me and begged for more. I'm pretty sure that's a proposition."

Farrah's cheeks flamed. "I'm done with this conversation," she declared with as much dignity as she could muster, given how damp her panties got at the mental image Blake's words elicited.

She turned to leave but didn't make it two steps before Blake was behind her, his scent filling her nostrils and his breath brushing her ear. "Is the offer still on the table?" His voice threaded itself around her like a long, sensuous ribbon.

Goose bumps peppered her skin, and Farrah clenched her thighs to ease the hot throb of arousal.

Blake didn't touch her, but she could feel him all around her. His touch on her skin, his taste on her lips, his muscles rippling beneath her hands as he thrust himself into her. Fantasies so vivid, they blurred the line between dream and reality.

She fought back a moan. "Yes."

They both knew she knew what offer he was talking about. It would've been disingenuous to pretend otherwise.

The word barely left her mouth before Blake spun her around and his lips crashed against hers. Farrah reacted instinctively. She locked her arms around his neck and pressed herself flush against him. Her soft curves slid into the hard, lean lines of Blake's body as easily as pieces in a puzzle. It was as if they were made for each other.

A part of Farrah wondered if she was making the right choice. Another, much larger part didn't care because she couldn't stand it anymore. The knot of frustration inside her waiting to burst; the tension that threaded her to him, ensuring he was on her mind even if he wasn't in her presence; the promise of the things he could do to her. Her body responded to Blake in a way it never had for anyone else, and Farrah was sick of denying herself the pleasure of being back in his arms.

It's just sex.

Blake grasped the backs of her thighs and wrapped her legs around his waist, never taking his mouth off hers as he navigated them toward the bedroom. Farrah would've been impressed by his deft multitasking except her mind had gone hazy and she couldn't focus on anything except the throbbing in her core and the scrape of her hard nipples against her bra.

god, it really had been too long since she'd had sex. Farrah could hardly remember the times when she couldn't orgasm with a guy, not even Blake, because she was *this* close to combusting and they hadn't even taken their clothes off.

"Wait," she gasped right before Blake lowered her on the bed. "No sheets."

The contractors assembled the bed this morning, but Farrah hadn't had time to dress it up yet.

"Fuck the sheets." Blake nipped at her neck, swirling his tongue over her needy flesh. This time, a moan did escape her mouth. "We'll deal with it later."

Farrah was tempted, but... "This is a ten-thousand-dollar Hastens mattress."

"Ten thousand dollars?" His shock rippled down his spine. "That's obscene."

"You signed off on it." She'd presented him with a detailed list of her suggested furnishings for the apartment, *with* their prices, before she ordered anything.

"Don't take this the wrong way." Blake's fingers skimmed the edge of her panties, which were already drenched with arousal. "But I don't want to talk about furniture right now."

Farrah muffled her laugh against his skin. "Bathroom," she ordered. She may be so turned on she couldn't breathe right, but she wasn't so crazy she'd ruin a brand-new Hastens.

She didn't have to ask twice.

Blake picked her up again and carried her into the bathroom, his fingers tugging impatiently at the zipper of her dress as he did so. He waited until the black silk pooled on the floor before he set her on the counter and shed his shirt and jeans.

Farrah sucked in a sharp inhale. god, he was beautiful. No matter how many times she saw him, she couldn't get over it. Broad shoulders tapering down to a flat stomach and narrow waist, lean hips, long powerful legs, and sleek muscles encased in golden skin, not to mention the thick bulge behind his black Calvin Klein briefs. Michelangelo himself couldn't have sculpted a more perfect piece of art.

A lazy smile crossed Blake's face as he drank in her unabashed appreciation. "Like what you see?" he drawled. Confidence seeped from every pore, mixing with raw sensuality and potent masculinity to create an irresistible cocktail that Farrah lapped up like a kitten with cream.

"Very much." She ran her hand over his chest, reveling in his warm strength. She could feel the erratic rhythm of his heart beneath her fingertips. "But I'd like it better if you took those briefs off."

There'd been a time when saying such a thing out loud would've mortified her, but she wasn't a girl anymore. She was a woman who knew what she wanted, and she wanted Blake.

Blake chuckled. "Soon. But first, I want to feast."

He unclasped her bra and tossed it to the side without so much as a glance. He palmed her breast and rubbed his thumb over her nipple, sending a jolt of heat through her belly. He lowered his head to her other nipple, sucking and licking and blowing cool air on the warm, sensitive skin.

Farrah arched into him, wrapping her legs around his waist once more and drawing him closer until his erection rested against her most sensitive flesh. She braced herself on the counter and ground against Blake with abandon, desperate for the one thing only he could give her, while he devoured her breasts. Her body was a live wire, dancing with a thousand nerve endings on the verge of exploding.

Blake kissed his way down her stomach and hooked his fingers into the waistband of her panties. Her legs quivered in anticipation, but there was one thing Farrah needed to clarify before she lost her senses altogether.

"Blake." His name came out as a breathy whisper.

He looked up at her, his eyes glittering with lust.

"This is just sex." Farrah needed him to understand that. This was their one night. Nothing more, nothing less.

Another emotion swirled behind those sapphire blues, but when she blinked, it was gone.

"I know."

Then Blake yanked her panties down her legs, dipped his head, and proceeded to make her lose her goddamned mind.

CHAPTER 20

BLAKE COULDN'T HIDE HIS SELF-SATISFIED GRIN AS Farrah bucked against his face, her moans growing so loud they rattled the new bathroom windows.

He slid his tongue between her folds and savored her sweet, musky taste. It was an aphrodisiac, made just for him, and he couldn't get enough. A sweet swirl, a drag of his teeth, a flick of his tongue—each action resulted in a noise that sent flames of lust racing through his veins and straight to his dick.

Farrah gripped the counter with one hand and grasped his hair with the other, pulling so hard it hurt, but the pain only made him want her more. Her panting groans grew in length and intensity. The muscles in her thighs stiffened, and he knew she was about to explode. Blake considered prolonging her orgasm, pulling back and bringing her to the edge and pulling back again until she begged him to let her come, but he was so hard he might shatter if he didn't bury himself inside her in the next two minutes.

He drew her clit into his mouth once more and sucked hard, flicking his tongue over the tender bud as he did so, while he slammed his fingers deep inside her until they reached her sweet spot. Farrah screamed a wild, breathless scream that reverberated through the bathroom and sang through Blake like the world's most erotic symphony. Her hips bucked against his face over and over, as her orgasm quaked through her. She thrashed so hard, he had to pull his fingers out of her dripping core and pin her hips down with both hands lest she slide off the counter. Meanwhile, his hungry mouth devoured her, lapping up her juices, not wanting to miss a single drop. To his surprise, Farrah came again, even harder this time.

Blake waited until her last shudders subsided and she collapsed in a heap against the wall before he raised himself off the ground, so they were at eye level. *Fuck, she was gorgeous.* Her hair fell over her shoulders in a tousled cloud of midnight silk. Her flushed cheeks and red lips had him throbbing with desire, and her eyes, heavy-lidded and hazy with postcoital bliss, peered out at him from beneath thick dark lashes.

"I think it's time for me to return the favor." Farrah's throaty promise sent another shot of lust straight to his groin.

Blake didn't resist when she slid off the counter and made quick work of his briefs, but when she kneeled, he grasped her arms and pulled her back up.

Farrah's brow furrowed.

"Not tonight," he said. "I need to fuck you. Right now."

She didn't say it, but she didn't need to. It was written all over face. *Tonight is the only night we have.*

The burst of anger came out of nowhere. It knotted in Blake's stomach, fed by desperation. He wanted to grab Farrah's shoulders and shake her. Make her see what was in front of them. But he couldn't, so he settled for closing the distance between them until her back hit the counter and his hard arousal pressed against her soft center.

"Tell me how you want it," he growled. "Sweet and slow, or hard and rough?"

Farrah's eyes flickered with excitement. Her chest rose and fell in short pants of breath. "Hard and rough," she whispered.

A feral smile slashed across his face. "I was hoping you'd say that."

She cried out as he spun her around and bent her over the sink. He fished his wallet out of his jeans pocket and took out a condom—he always had one on him, just in case—and sheathed himself in it before he returned to the tantalizing sight of Farrah's glistening arousal.

"Spread your legs wider," Blake commanded.

She obeyed without hesitation.

Blake grabbed her hips, pressing his thumbs into her soft flesh, and leaned over until his breath tickled her ear. "Is this what you really want?"

"Yes," Farrah whimpered. The whimper turned into a full-on cry when Blake slammed into her, burying himself to the hilt.

"Jesus," he hissed. "You're so tight." Tighter than a fist, hotter than an inferno, and so damn wet he almost lost it in one stroke like a prepubescent boy.

Blake tightened his jaw, trying to regain control before he started moving.

Farrah whined and squirmed against him.

"Impatient," he teased. He reached around to stroke her swollen clit, taking great satisfaction in the shudder that rippled through her body.

"Fuck me." She gave the command this time, and Blake obeyed the way she had for him. He couldn't have waited any longer even if he wanted to.

He withdrew until just the tip of his cock remained inside her, then drove forward again in a vicious thrust that pitched her forward.

Blake pounded into her mercilessly, letting her moans and throaty screams drive him harder, deeper, faster.

This wasn't making love. Farrah didn't want that, and frankly, neither did he. What he wanted was to bury himself so deep she'd never forget him, to fuck her so hard he imprinted on her, to take her so high she'd realize they were meant for more than one night.

Blake angled himself so his dick rubbed against sensitive spot inside her with each downward stroke. He watched them in the mirror—her eyes closed and mouth slack with arousal, his own mouth set in a grim line as he made her take all of him, over and over, until there was no doubt in either of their minds that she was his, at least for tonight.

He fisted her hair and tugged it back just as he sent her jolting forward with a savage thrust. Farrah's eyes snapped open. His name flew from her lips in a strangled cry as she quaked around him, her third orgasm of the night rolling over them both like an out-of-control train. She twisted and writhed, her body desperate to convulse, but Blake forced her to hold still and ride out her climax without mercy.

Just as her shudders eased, he slammed into her again. And again. And again. He didn't know how long they stayed in that bathroom, but it was only when Farrah pleaded exhaustion after her sixth or seventh orgasm that he unleashed his iron grip on self-control.

Blake spun Farrah around to face him. His mouth descended on hers, hungry and desperate. She returned the kiss with fervor—her nails digging grooves into the skin on his back, her tongue chasing his as she moaned helplessly into his mouth. Blake accepted her surrender, the only surrender she would give him.

He increased the pace of his thrusts until Farrah's sweet taste and tight heat sent him over the edge. The orgasm he'd been holding in all night burst forth with a ferocity that had him seeing stars. Farrah said she was spent, but once again, she surprised him with another explosion, her cries mingling with his as they free-fell into oblivion and collapsed into each other's arms.

Blake closed his eyes, savoring her warmth and etching it in his mind before he withdrew from her. He rolled the condom off and tossed it in the trash.

He swept a cautious gaze over Farrah's face, trying to gauge her feelings now that the high from their sex session had worn off. She looked content and satiated, but he couldn't read her expression beyond that.

"How are you feeling?" He brushed a sweaty strand of hair from her face. An ache swirled in his chest. They used to lie awake all night, talking about their dreams and fears and wishes for the future. What he wouldn't give for one of those nights now.

"Amazing." Farrah grinned, her eyes sparkling. "That was amazing. Just what I needed."

Blake's hand froze. One by one, the pleasant aftershocks of his climax turned into petrified stone and dropped into the pit that had opened up in his stomach.

It's what we need.

One night to get each other out of our systems.

This is just sex.

He knew that. Hell, he'd agreed to it less than an hour ago. Still, he thought...

Blake's jaw clenched. "I'm glad." He dropped his hand from Farrah's face and avoided her gaze as he pulled on his briefs and jeans. "It worked, then."

A beat of silence. "What did?"

Blake forced himself to look at her, even though the sight of her face twisted the knife in his heart that much deeper. "You fucked me out of your system."

Farrah inhaled sharply. Her eyes glistened with wariness and something else he couldn't pinpoint. "Blake…"

"I'm happy to be of service." He smiled so hard his cheeks hurt. "One night, right?"

A part of him—a stupid, foolish part—hoped she'd refute him. Tell him she wanted more than what she'd been willing to give.

But that hope was a balloon waiting to be punctured.

"Right," Farrah whispered.

The air leaked out, slowly but surely, until the balloon was just a crumpled heap of what used to be.

Farrah gathered her clothes off the floor and got dressed. She stopped in the doorway to look back at Blake, indecision scrawled all over her face, before she left and took the jagged pieces of his heart with her.

Blake stood rigid, unmoving, until he heard the front door close. Only then did he allow his shoulders to sag. He lowered his head and rested his forearms on the counter, too tired to hold himself up.

He could still smell her. Taste her. Hear her. And when he looked at himself in the mirror, he appeared older somehow, as heartbreak seeped through his skin and hardened him from the inside out.

Turn one night into multiple nights.

He'd taken a gamble.

And he'd lost.

CHAPTER 21

One week later

"THIS IS THE PERFECT NIGHT." FARRAH NIBBLED ON A chocolate square and sighed in bliss. Chocolate made everything better. "It's so good to see you guys."

"I'm *so* happy to be here." Courtney Taylor squeezed Farrah's arm, her blue eyes twinkling with delight. "Spokane is nice, but it bores the shit out of me."

"Why don't you move back to Seattle?" Farrah couldn't imagine someone as larger-than-life and outgoing as Courtney living anywhere but a big city, but the brunette had moved two years ago to Spokane, Washington, for a sales manager job at a small manufacturing company.

Courtney shrugged. A shadow of unease passed over her face. "I'm over Seattle."

Before she could elaborate, Olivia traipsed over with Kris Carrera in tow. They both held freshly poured glasses of merlot and cabernet sauvignon, respectively. "We're back! What'd we miss?"

"We were just catching up." Farrah grinned when she saw Kris's Prada sunglasses. The wealthy brunette was the only person she knew who wore sunglasses at night—and indoors.

She supposed Kris had good reason to hide her face, given she was engaged to A-list Hollywood star Nate Reynolds, and the paparazzi constantly chased them down. Nate was in town filming his latest movie, and Kris had decided to accompany him and surprise Farrah and Olivia. She'd convinced Courtney to come along as well so they could have a mini FEA reunion.

The four girls had been thick as thieves when they studied abroad together in Shanghai. They weren't as close anymore, since Farrah and Olivia lived in New York and Courtney and Kris lived on the West Coast, but whenever they saw each other, it was as if no time had passed at all.

Kris removed her sunglasses and scanned the cozy bar. "This place is ok." No one bothered them, though a few people snuck surreptitious glances at Kris. That was the good thing about New York—locals left celebrities alone, and there was no place more local, or exclusive, than Elysian, a wine and chocolate bar tucked deep in the West Village. "Decent wine and atmosphere."

Coming from Kris, that praise was akin to a Michelin star.

"Of course it is." Olivia tossed her hair over her shoulder. She was the one who'd picked the spot. "Have I ever steered you wrong?"

"Never." Courtney grinned, her earlier unease gone. "So, what are we doing after this? Clubbing? Bar crawl? Rave? Underground house party?"

Farrah winced. She'd loved partying with Courtney in Shanghai, and she was still down for a night on the town every now and then, but she'd reached a point in her life where she'd much rather curl up with Netflix and a pint of ice cream than get smushed by a pile of sweaty bodies in some pretentious club.

"Sorry, babe." A sly smile spread across Kris's face. "Nate's shoot finishes soon, and I'm planning to reward him for a hard day's work."

It didn't take a genius to figure out what kind of "reward" Kris had planned.

"And I have work due tomorrow morning." Olivia yawned.

"But it's Saturday tomorrow," Courtney protested.

"The world of finance never rests."

Courtney pouted. "Farrah?"

"Um." As much as Farrah loved her friend, the thought of attending a wild party tonight was as appealing as a root canal without Novocain. She couldn't think of a good excuse, so she went with the truth. "I'm not feeling up to it tonight. Sorry."

"Boo." Courtney's shoulders slumped before she perked up again. "Isn't Sammy in town? He'll go with me."

Olivia snorted, a sign of derisiveness that didn't go unnoticed.

"Don't tell me you guys still aren't speaking to each other," Kris said. "How can you stay mad at him? It's Sammy!"

"So?"

"So he's the most likable guy on the planet."

"You're not the one who dated him," Olivia grumbled. "You don't know what he said to me."

Farrah, Courtney, and Kris exchanged glances.

Do you know? Courtney mouthed to Farrah, who'd been in New York the same summer Olivia and Sammy broke up. The summer after FEA.

Farrah shook her head. She'd been distracted that summer by her internship and recent breakup with Blake, but from what she saw, things had been going swell between Sammy and Olivia until the tail end of August. Stony glares and cold rebuffs cut off Farrah's attempts to find out what happened.

After a while, she'd stopped trying.

"Also, Sammy isn't as perfect as you think it is. He won't even tell Farrah the truth about Blake." Olivia gulped her wine in a way wine was not meant to be gulped.

Farrah was so startled by the sight of Olivia breaking wine etiquette she didn't notice Courtney's and Kris's gazes focusing on her until their heat pierced her skin.

"What's the truth about Blake?" Courtney's eyes grew to the size of silver dollars at the prospect of juicy gossip.

Farrah had told Kris and Courtney about Blake's interior design project, but she hadn't mentioned Sammy's cryptic advice at brunch.

"I don't know." Farrah touched the pendant resting at the base of her throat. "Like Liv said, Sammy didn't tell me."

"He told her to ask Blake about her necklace the next time she saw him," Olivia clarified. "Big help that is."

Kris arched one sleek, well-groomed brow. "Did you? Ask Blake the next time you saw him?"

Not exactly.

Farrah thanked god for dim lighting and Asian glow—her cheeks were already flushed from chardonnay—because she couldn't stop the blanket of heat creeping its way from the top of her head all the way to her toes. Every time she thought about what happened in Blake's bathroom last week, her womb clenched, and wetness pooled between her thighs.

She'd never seen Blake like that. There were times he'd been rough in Shanghai, but the other night? He'd been an animal. Feral. Merciless.

And she'd loved every second.

Whether it was Blake or the pent-up frustration from a year without sex—or, most likely, a combination of both—Farrah had, oh, the top five orgasms of her life in one night.

It worked, then. You fucked me out of your system.

"Farrah?" Kris prompted.

Did she get him out of her system? She wasn't so sure.

Farrah thought one last fling with Blake would give her the closure she needed, but now her body craved him more than ever. It hungered for him to return, to fill her again, and when he wasn't there, it turned its ire on her, torturing her with its insatiable neediness until she wanted to cry from frustration.

Her plan to fuck him out of her system, as Blake so succinctly put it, had hopelessly backfired.

But it wasn't just her hormones. Farrah couldn't stop thinking about the look on Blake's face when she left. He tried to hide it, but she saw it clear as day: utter heartbreak. And even though he was the one who'd wronged her first, the sight wrenched her gut in a way it had no right doing.

"Farrah!" Kris's voice shattered Farrah's inner turmoil and caused her to jump.

As a result, Farrah knocked the half-empty glass closest to her off the table with her elbow. She watched in horror as the glass tumbled toward the ground in slow motion, ready to splinter into a million pieces, before Courtney's arm shot out and caught it at the last moment.

"All good." She placed the now quarter-empty glass on the table. "Just a small spill."

"Sorry." The heat on Farrah's cheeks intensified. She grabbed her napkin and was about to clean up her mess when their server swooped in.

"I'll take care of it," she assured the table.

"Sorry," Farrah repeated.

"You never answered my question." Kris's mouth twitched, as if she were trying not to laugh.

"What was it again?"

"Did you ask Blake about your necklace?"

"Um, no."

She didn't ask him the other night because she wasn't sure she wanted to know the answer, but now, sitting here with her friends from Shanghai, the curiosity ate at her.

Would it be so bad to find out the truth? Maybe it wasn't a big deal, and she was just hyping it up in her mind.

Farrah did a quick mental calculation. They were in the West Village, and Blake's apartment was a ten-minute walk away.

She'd finished the design project a few days ago. Blake had said (via text) he didn't need a final walkthrough, and she hadn't pushed him for one. He should've moved back into the apartment by now.

Technically, she told him one night of sex. She didn't say that was the last night they had to see each other. Besides, she had a valid question to ask him.

"Oh no," Olivia said. "I know that look. Your contract with Blake is done. Finito. You don't need to get involved with him anymore. Forget about the necklace. Sammy was probably making shit up."

"Sammy doesn't make stuff up. And you were the one who brought up the necklace," Farrah pointed out.

"Potato, potahtoe. My point is, leave Blake alone."

"Too late," Farrah mumbled.

"What?" Olivia frowned, then gasped. "No. You didn't."

That was the thing about best friends/roommates, especially one as detail-oriented as Olivia—they could read you like a large-print book.

"What's going on?" Courtney tilted her head. Her mass of thick brown curls cascaded past her shoulder and over her arm.

"Judging by Farrah's blush and Olivia's glare, our girl has boned Blake Ryan recently." Kris yawned and examined her flawless manicure.

"Wow." Courtney mulled the revelation over. "This is like FEA 2.0."

"No, it's not." The color of Farrah's cheeks matched her friend's merlot. "We had sex *once*. It's not like I'm in love with him."

Olivia and Courtney gasped at the admission; Kris sipped her wine with a smirk.

"I don't blame you. I saw him in *Forbes*." Kris yawned again. "He's still looking mighty fine."

"Excuse me, but have we forgotten what he did to her in Shanghai?" Olivia huffed.

The Filipina waved off the concern with a dismissive hand. Her Wollman-rink-sized engagement ring glittered in the dim lighting. "That was years ago."

"Love has made you soft," Courtney teased. "There was a time when you would've been first in line to pin Blake's balls to the wall."

Kris shrugged, not bothering to deny it.

It had come as a shock to all of them when Kris announced her engagement to Nate. She was the last person they'd expected to marry first. Kris—who'd deemed the male species uninteresting, unprincipled, and unworthy of her time—hadn't dated or hooked up with anyone during their year in Shanghai.

Then again, Farrah would break her rules for Nate Reynolds too. The action star looked like a taller, better-looking hybrid of Liam Hemsworth and Theo James, and from what she could tell, he treated Kris like a queen. Which was good, because Kris considered herself a queen, and not in the modern empowerment kind of way. More like a Harry-Winston-crown-wearing, everyone-bow-before-me kind of way.

Besides, Kris and Nate met the summer Kris returned from China. Five years of dating and jet-setting around the world together. They were already practically married, and their upcoming nuptials were just a formality.

"So." Courtney's blue eyes glittered with mischief. "How's Blake in bed? Has he learned any new tricks?"

Australia-sized red blotches blossomed on Farrah's face and chest. That was her cue.

"As much as I would love to discuss my sex life, I'm afraid I have to cut the night short. There's have something I have to do," she announced. "You guys will be in town until next weekend, right?"

"Yes," Kris said at the same time Courtney asked, "Something or *someone*?"

"We'll hang out during the week." Farrah ignored Courtney's question and Olivia's disapproving stare. "Liv, see you at home later. Try not to blow a gasket before then."

"That's going to be tough considering my best friend insists on tangoing with the devil." Olivia's brows knotted together. "Be careful, ok?"

"I will." Farrah slung her purse over her shoulder. "Love you guys. Venmo me the bill."

"She's totally going to bang Blake," she heard Courtney say as she left. "Speaking of bang-worthy guys, we should invite Sammy out. I miss him."

Olivia hissed. "Over my dead body."

"Hey, whatever you're into…"

Farrah's friends' voices faded. The door to Elysian jangled closed behind her as she poured herself into the sticky summer heat of late June New York. By the time she arrived at Blake's building, a thin sheen of sweat coated her skin, and her orange sundress clung to her chest and thighs.

The concierge recognized her on sight and waved her up without calling Blake, even though it was well past business hours.

Farrah was grateful for the extra time to change her mind, though it didn't say much about building security.

You're already here. Might as well go through with it.

She got off the elevator, heart pounding, and knocked on Blake's door before she lost her nerve.

Silence.

Maybe he wasn't here. It was, after all, Friday night.

Relief and disappointment fizzled in Farrah's veins. This was stupid. She should—

She heard low voices, then footsteps. A second later, Blake opened the door, his eyes brightening with surprise when he saw who was on the other side. His hair was damp, and he wore a soft gray T-shirt that molded to his sculpted shoulders and well-defined arms.

"Farrah? What are you doing here?"

Farrah's response died in her throat when another set of footsteps approached and a willowy auburn-haired beauty appeared by Blake's side. She wore an oversized black Texas Southeastern sweatshirt.

Blake's sweatshirt.

One of his favorites, if Farrah remembered correctly.

"Who's this?" The woman cocked her head and eyed Farrah curiously. With her high cheekbones, creamy skin, and golden-brown eyes, she should have been on a Times Square billboard, showing off the latest designer fragrance or expensive lingerie line.

Say something.

Except she couldn't. All Farrah could do was stand there and try not to drown beneath the wave of jealousy that consumed her.

CHAPTER 22

"WHY DON'T YOU HEAD OUT FOR THE NIGHT?" BLAKE suggested to his chief of staff. "I'll call you tomorrow."

"Of course." Patricia tucked a strand of hair behind her ears. "Have a good night."

"You too."

Patricia shot one last quizzical look at Farrah, who remained unmoving in the doorway, before she brushed past her and swayed down the hall.

Patricia had been here all night helping Blake sort through their shitshow of an opening. They'd settled on a new restaurant manager, but they still had issues with the plumbing and now their liquor distributor said their alcohol deliveries were going to be delayed. Something about the company consolidating two facilities into one and a backlog.

Blake would be more sympathetic if he weren't so pissed off.

You couldn't have a bar without alcohol. Period. That was the whole fucking point of a bar.

He and Patricia spent all afternoon scrambling to find another distributor who could deliver the quantities they needed on time for a reasonable price. They'd only stopped for a quick dinner break, during which he'd spilled wine all over her white shirt. He'd lent her the first top he could find—his favorite TSU sweatshirt—to cover up the stain until she could change.

They'd been wrapping up when he heard a knock.

He didn't know who he'd expected when he opened the door, but he most definitely hadn't expected Farrah.

Blake leaned against the doorframe, drinking her in. She wore a little orange dress that bared her shapely legs and made her look tanner than usual. Her cheeks glowed pink, a sure sign she'd been drinking. Or maybe the pink had something to do with the anger flashing in her eyes.

"Sorry for showing up unannounced," Farrah said stiffly. "I didn't realize you had company."

"She was leaving anyway. Come in." Blake eyed the thin line of her lips and the tense set of her shoulders. "Is everything ok?"

"Yes." Farrah surveyed his apartment. She paused on the two half-empty glasses of wine on his kitchen counter, and her scowl deepened.

"You look upset."

"I'm not upset."

"If you say so," Blake drawled, not believing her for a second. "What brings you here tonight?"

By now, he knew better than to hope for a love confession. With his luck, Farrah was here to tell him something went wrong with the bank and that she hadn't received the final payment for her design services.

Blake tensed his jaw and cleaned the wineglasses while he waited for Farrah to answer.

"I, uh, came by to see how you're liking your new apartment." Farrah twisted her necklace chain around her finger until the surrounding skin turned white.

He dried the glasses and placed them upside down on a towel before facing Farrah with raised eyebrows. "You came here on a Friday night to check on the apartment you designed?"

"Yes." Defensiveness crept into her tone. "How do you like it?"

"The same as I did when I signed on off everything," Blake said dryly. "I love it."

Decorated in an elegant, masculine palette of navy blue, gray, and white with gold accents, the apartment looked like something out of a magazine spread. But thanks to personal touches such as the wall of photos from every one of his bar openings—custom framed to include an engraving of the host city's name—and the shelf of knickknacks collected during his travels, it felt like home instead of a museum.

"Pat loves it too," he added.

"Pat?"

"The woman who was just here."

"Oh." Farrah pursed her lips. "Pat, is it?"

"Short for Patricia." Blake chuckled. "She hates it when I call her Pat, so I only do it when she's not around."

That was a fair compromise in his opinion.

"I see." Farrah's voice could've frosted glass. "How do you know each other?"

He tilted his head. Was that...jealousy he detected?

Blake watched Farrah's face closely as he responded, "We met at a bar and hit it off right away."

Technically true. He met Patricia at his Austin bar when she showed up for her interview, and he knew within five minutes that she was the perfect person for the job.

Farrah crossed her arms over her chest. Her expression didn't budge, but her eyes blazed.

Oh yeah. She was definitely jealous.

Blake smothered a grin. A spark of hope rekindled in his chest.

"Great. I'm glad the other night worked for you too, considering how fast you moved on." Farrah turned on her heels and walked away. "So much for that big speech you gave about wanting another chance." She muttered the last part under her breath, but Blake heard her—and it pissed him the hell off.

All traces of amusement fled. He closed the distance between them with two long strides. He grabbed Farrah's wrist and spun her around, pinning her against the wall and caging her in with his arms. His eyes blazed just as hers did.

Other than a sharp intake of breath, Farrah didn't react, but defiance and resentment shimmered beneath those chocolate pools glaring up at him.

A volcano of pent-up emotion bubbled between them, waiting to erupt.

"You mean the speech where I offered you my heart and you turned me down?" Blake gritted out. "*You* rejected *me*. You said you couldn't give me a second chance, only one night, and at the end of that one night, you walked away without so much as a goodbye. So, tell me, what goddamned right in this goddamned world do you have to be jealous?"

"I'm not jealous!"

"Dammit, Farrah!" Blake pounded the wall next to her, frustration leaking from every pore. Her eyes widened in shock. "Can you say what you really feel for once?"

"I did," she shot back. "In Shanghai. Look where that got me! I loved you. I trusted you. I gave my *virginity* to you. And you threw it all away like it was nothing." Tears hung on the ends of her lashes like tiny fallen stars. "Do you really expect me to give you a second chance just because you say you made a mistake? It doesn't work like that. You broke my heart."

The stars fell, dripping down Farrah's cheeks in a molten river of grief. Each one shattered Blake a little more until the spiderweb of cracks exploded and destroyed him from the inside out.

He wiped away her tears with his thumb as pain ate away at his anger.

"Don't you know?" Blake's voice cracked with regret. "It broke my heart too. Because everything I said that night was a lie. I didn't stop loving you. I never stopped loving you."

CHAPTER 23

I DIDN'T STOP LOVING YOU. I NEVER STOPPED loving you.

Farrah couldn't breathe. Couldn't think. Couldn't process.

All she could do was tremble and cling to the edge of the cliff, trying to save herself from what was sure to be another fall. Except this time, she didn't think she'd survive.

There were only so many times a girl could fall before something inside her irrevocably broke. The first fall split her in half, into before and after. Before Blake, after Blake.

She didn't want to know what would happen a second time.

"You're lying." Farrah's voice quavered—from hope or fear, she didn't know.

Blake's laugh was so bitter, she could taste it in the back of her throat. He pushed himself off her and stepped back, and she mourned the loss of his warmth even as her senses crept back into her foggy brain.

"god, Farrah. We were together for months. I loved you, in every way I could, for months. But all it took was a few words for you to believe it had all been a lie." The anguish in his eyes ripped her apart. For all the years and distance between them, for all the heartbreak that littered their past, his pain was hers. "How could you believe me? How could you have looked into my eyes and believed you were anything except my whole world?"

The tears fell again, a torrential downpour so strong she couldn't see past it. Farrah didn't bother wiping the tears away. "Because everyone leaves," she bit out. "My dad left. You left. And I'm always the one left holding the pieces."

She sank to the floor, her body shuddering with the force of her sobs. She wrapped her arms around her legs and buried her face against her knees, drowning beneath the waves of her grief. Farrah was damn good at bottling up her emotions, but that was the thing about bottles—there comes a point when they run out of their capacity to contain, and their contents gush forth, toppling everything and everyone in their path.

For Farrah, that point was now.

For years, she'd been wracked with guilt over her last words to her father before he died—*I wish you were dead*—but there was something else. A part of her, buried deep down inside, that resented him for not taking better care of himself after he and her mom divorced. For gambling with his health and passing his days as if he had nothing to live for when he had a daughter who needed him. Farrah couldn't help but wonder if her words had driven him over the edge. She didn't think he killed himself—his liver disease had developed over several years—but maybe her teenage viciousness had loosened his grip on what tied him to this world. Maybe, if she'd been a better daughter, he would've tried harder to stay.

Farrah squeezed her eyes shut and tried to calm her sobs. She hated crying in front of other people. She could count the number of times she'd done so on one hand, and four out of the five, it had been because of the man next to her.

Blake slid onto the floor beside her and wrapped both arms around her, holding her close. The erratic thump of his heart and the shivers in his body matched hers. He was both her storm and her shelter from the hurricane.

"I'm here." He stroked her back, and it felt so safe, so familiar, she cried harder because she couldn't bear the thought of losing this haven. "I'm not leaving. I'm right here."

Farrah raised her head and wiped her face with the back of her hand. She must look like a mess, all teary-eyed and red-nosed, but she didn't care. "What happened with my necklace?"

Blake's brows dipped.

"Sammy said to ask you about the night I lost my necklace. He said it'll explain everything," she hiccupped.

Blake swore softly. "Do you remember how you got your necklace back?"

"Sammy found it and returned it to me."

"He didn't find it. I did."

Shock stuttered her breath. "How—"

Blake's throat convulsed with a hard swallow. "I knew how much that necklace meant to you, so I searched for it while everyone was getting ready for the dance. I found it hidden in a pile of leaves off the main path. It must've fallen off and washed away in the rain. Sammy saw me on his way to get his phone from the auditorium. I gave it to him to give to you and told him to say he found it."

There'd been a giant storm that night. The worst storm they'd seen during their year in Shanghai. The mental image of Blake rummaging through the bushes, searching for her necklace in the pouring rain, wrapped around Farrah's chest like a vise and squeezed until she couldn't breathe. "Why would you do that?"

Blake smiled a sad smile. "Like I said, I never stopped loving you. But I didn't want you to know."

Dammit. Farrah was going to run out of moisture in her body before the end of the night. She blinked back another onslaught of tears and asked the biggest question of all. "Why? If you still loved me, why did you break up with me?"

Blake's eyes darkened with guilt. "Before I say anything, I want you to know—I'm not always a good person. I want to be. But I make mistakes." He drew in a deep breath. "When I broke up with you, I told you I got back together with my ex-girlfriend over winter break and that I still loved her. That wasn't true. Not really. We were both at a mutual friend's party—Landon's party, actually. Cleo and I grew up together. My parents always pushed me to date her, even though I never saw her as anything more than a friend. But I caved in college, and we dated for a year. I broke up with her right before I left for Shanghai. When I saw her again on New Year's, I wanted to make things right. We'd been friends for a long time, and I hated the way we ended things. She agreed to be just friends, even though I could tell she still had feelings for me. We drank the night away and..." His voice trailed off. "Well, we got hammered."

Acid sloshed in Farrah's stomach. She had a feeling she knew where this was going.

"The next morning, I woke up in one of Landon's family's hotel suites. I had no recollection of the previous night, save for a few random flashes here and there. I rarely black out from alcohol, but I went in with an empty stomach and I drank a *lot*. At first, I thought, no big deal. I was hungover as shit, but it's nothing I haven't experienced before. But then Cleo came out of the shower and..." Another hard swallow. "She said we slept together."

Blake watched her closely, like he expected Farrah to bolt any second.

She should. She'd known he'd cheated on her that winter

break—he said so himself—but it was excruciating to hear the play-by-play of how it happened, even if he hadn't meant to do it.

Nevertheless, something glued Farrah in place.

"Go on," she said dully.

"I came back to Shanghai, and I felt so fucking guilty for cheating on you and lying to you. I wanted to tell you the truth, but I loved you so much, and I couldn't bear the thought of losing you." Blake's voice cracked. "I know it's not an excuse, but I honestly don't remember that night. I have no idea what happened or how I ended up sleeping with Cleo. I just know the secret killed me inside. That was why I acted so weird the first few weeks after we came back. I'm not proud of it, but I thought I could hide it from you. Then Cleo called me and..." Blake's jaw clenched.

Farrah's pulse drummed in warning. "And?"

"She told me she was pregnant. With my baby."

The acid in her stomach turned to ice. Farrah's breath rose and fell in rapid gasps as she tried to process the information. Blake got his ex-girlfriend pregnant while he and Farrah had been dating and he *never told her.*

She scrambled to her feet, needing to do something, anything, to release the rage and restless energy coursing through her. "Why didn't you tell me the truth instead of feeding me bullshit about still being in love with your ex?"

Pain carved itself into Blake's face. "Because I didn't want you to know how badly I'd fucked up. Because I wanted you to have a clean break. My life was a mess, Farrah. I was about to graduate with no career prospects except a wild dream about owning a bar, and I was going to have a baby with a woman I didn't love. I didn't want to drag you into the shitshow. I was young and stupid and thought I was doing the right thing. You probably would've broken up with me anyway, but with your heart and compassion, I couldn't be sure you wouldn't try to save me. And I didn't deserve to be saved."

Farrah pressed her fists against the counter and closed her eyes, trying to imagine what her twenty-year-old self would have done. She hated cheaters. If Blake had told her the truth back then, she might very well have drop-kicked him in the balls and ran. But she also knew reason took a back seat when it came to all things Blake Ryan. She'd been in love with him enough that she wouldn't have been able to walk away as easily as she had, had she known he still harbored feelings for her.

"Where's the baby?" she asked.

Since they reunited, Blake hadn't said a single word about being a father. No pictures of children, no nothing.

Unease edged into her consciousness.

"We lost the baby." Blake's voice flatlined. "Cleo had a late-term miscarriage."

Farrah snapped her head up and around. Blake was still sitting on the floor, his features tight with guilt and heartbreak.

"I'm sorry," she whispered. This time, Farrah was the one who sank next to him and wrapped her arm around his shoulder.

It looked messed up from the outside, her comforting her ex over the loss of the baby he'd had with the woman he'd cheated on her with. But humans were humans, and Farrah wouldn't wish the pain of losing a child on her worst enemy.

"We couldn't make it work after that." Blake's muscles bunched beneath her touch. "We'd only gotten together again for the baby anyway, and it hurt too much to look at each other and remember what we lost. She moved to Atlanta, and I threw myself into my business. I never looked back. Except some nights when I..." His voice trailed off. "Anyway, that's the truth. One mistake I don't remember that fucked up everyone I cared about, including you." Blake's head bowed. "If you want to leave, I don't blame you."

The secrets they'd laid bare soaked into the walls, the floor, and Farrah's very bones. There'd been so much information thrown at her in the past hour, she'd need a high-powered super-computer to sort through it all.

"Kiss me."

Blake's head jerked up. Shock scrawled all over his face. "What?"

Instead of repeating herself, Farrah grabbed his face and pressed her lips to his. Blake's confession shocked her and pissed her off, and yes, she should hate him for keeping something as big as a freakin' pregnancy from her. But she also felt his pain, and of all the emotions she'd had toward him over the years, hate had never been one of them.

It was impossible to hate someone who'd burrowed them-selves so deep in your psyche, they were a part of you.

"Is this really what you want?" Blake's voice rasped down her spine.

Farrah nodded. Her brain was short-circuiting from the events of the night, and she couldn't think properly.

Good.

She didn't want to think. She didn't want to feel. She wanted to forget.

She could deal with the ramifications of tonight tomorrow, but for now, she needed what only Blake could give her.

Oblivion.

Blake and Farrah stumbled into his bedroom without break-ing their kiss. Their clothes tumbled to the floor, their hands roamed, and their mouths explored, hungry and desperate to escape the demons of their past.

This wasn't about love or lust; this was about losing them-selves in a place where nothing bad could touch them, if only for a while.

Blake slammed into her, and a cry fell from her mouth.

Sensation sizzled through her, burning all the decisions she had to make and memories she wanted to leave behind until there was nothing left but ashes.

"Promise me one thing," Blake said. "Promise you'll be here in the morning."

Farrah dragged his mouth back to hers and clenched around him until he groaned and resumed his thrusts.

She didn't reply to Blake's request.

Farrah didn't like making promises she couldn't keep.

CHAPTER 24

SUNLIGHT. WARMTH AND SOFTNESS. ORANGE BLOS-
som and vanilla.

Blake's idea of heaven—if it weren't for the damn alarm clock
shrieking on his nightstand like a nun who'd walked into an orgy.

He set his alarm for 7:00 a.m. on the weekends, a few hours
later than when he woke up on weekdays, because early mornings
were his most productive time of day. Blake loved getting all his
shit done before other people rolled out of bed. Fewer distractions, more focus, though he would've happily stayed in bed all
day today.

Yesterday drained him more than a five-hour training session
in the rain back when he played football. Raw emotion was a
bitch; it knocked you on your feet faster and harder than any
three-hundred-pound lineman could.

Blake cracked an eye open and slammed his hand on his alarm
clock's off button.

Finally. Silence.

He braced himself before turning his head. The pillow next
to him was empty.

He'd expected it, considering Farrah never replied when he asked her to stay through the morning. Still, disappointment curdled in his gut. Blake was about to let loose a curse that would have his mother washing his mouth out with soap when the bedroom door creaked open, and Farrah tiptoed in holding two cups of rich-smelling coffee.

Promise you'll be here in the morning.

And here she was, like a vision straight out of his dreams with her sex-tousled hair and one of his white button-down shirts barely covering her thighs.

Blake's stomach flipped. His earlier disappointment took a back seat to the desire to crush her to his chest and never let her go.

"You're awake." Farrah handed him a coffee, which he accepted with a grateful nod.

"You're here."

She lifted a shoulder, looking almost as surprised as he felt. "I figured there are some things we need to talk about."

"That's putting it mildly," Blake said, tone dry. He took a sip of his morning elixir—strong and black, no cream, no sugar, just the way he liked it—before setting it on his nightstand. "Let's talk."

Their conversation last night had ended with a question mark. Blake assumed—hoped—that Farrah's presence this morning meant she was willing to give them another chance, despite how badly he'd fucked up the first time around.

Granted, Blake hadn't told her the entire truth. She didn't know how Cleo miscarried or how selfish he felt, burrowing himself into her life again when she deserved so much better than him. But she knew all the parts of the story that pertained to her, and Blake would do anything to protect her from the darkest side of himself.

"I'll be honest." Farrah clutched her mug like it was her

shield and salvation. "I believe what you did was a mistake—that you didn't intend to hurt me—but you did. And I am so fucking furious you lied to me about something as big as getting your ex pregnant." She swallowed. "I am also so, so sorry about what happened with your baby, and I appreciate you telling me the truth yesterday, but I can't lie and say I trust you again."

Blake's heart shriveled in his chest.

"At the same time…" She blew a stray strand of hair out of her eye, indecision stamped across her gorgeous face. "I'm sick of living in the past, and there's something inside me that can't let you go, no matter how hard I try."

The shriveling stopped.

There's something inside me that can't let you go, no matter how hard I try. Well, he'd be damned.

"So." Farrah examined him, her gaze inscrutable. "It seems we have a conundrum."

"And I have a solution." Blake tossed the covers off and stood.

Yes, he was naked. No, he didn't care.

Blake didn't do false humility. He knew he could give Michelangelo's *David* a run for his money. Heck, he was better than *David*, because David's dick was kinda small. Blake's was anything but.

Farrah's breath hitched. "What's the solution?"

"We take it one day at a time. Get to know each other again. Be friends again." Blake removed the mug from Farrah's trembling hand and placed it on the nightstand next to his own. He rubbed a thumb over her cheek, and her eyes fluttered closed. "We don't have to date or do anything you don't want to do. But if you want sex, I'll make you come so hard you won't be able to see straight. If you want somebody to talk to after a shitty day, I'll be your listening board. If you want someone to cook you a nice meal…well, I'm not a great cook, but I'm great at ordering delivery." He smiled when Farrah choked out a laugh. "The point is, I'll be anything you need me to be. A friend with the full suite of benefits, so to speak. The only thing I ask in return is for you not to shut me out."

"You would do that?" There was a tinge of skepticism in her voice.

"I thought I made myself clear. I'd do anything for you." Blake lowered his head and trailed his lips down her neck until he reached the pulse fluttering beneath her skin like a trapped butterfly. "I'll wait as long as I need for you to trust me again."

"What if that never happens?"

"Then I'll wait forever."

A noise wrenched from her throat. "You always were good with words."

"They're not the only thing I'm good with." Blake's mouth made the lazy journey back up her slender throat to her jaw, her cheek, her nose...everywhere but her mouth, which parted with impatience at his languid pace. "Do we have a deal?"

Farrah blinked, then ever so slowly nodded.

"What do you want now?"

"You."

"You'll have to be more specific." Blake reached under her shirt and caressed her inner thigh. Farrah tilted her hips toward him, but he didn't respond to the invitation, choosing instead to draw lazy circles on her inner thighs.

She glared at him, and he responded with an innocent smile. Just because she owned him, heart and soul, didn't mean he couldn't have some fun with her.

"I want you to make me come. In the next five minutes," she added, probably as retaliation.

Blake was insulted. "Five minutes? You underestimate me."

He made her come in two.

Less than two, according to the accurate-down-to-the-second

clock on his nightstand, but he rounded up because he was humble like that.

While Farrah was still shaking from her high, Blake picked her up and tossed her on the bed for the second round. Except this time, he was going to use more than his fingers.

His dick strained at the thought.

"By the way," Farrah said, watching with hooded eyes as Blake sheathed himself with a condom. "As part of the deal, you can't hook up with that woman from last night."

"You mean Pat."

She pursed her lips. "Right. Pat."

Blake's mouth curled up into a sly grin. "You're cute when you're jealous."

"I'm not jealous," Farrah insisted, twin poppies blooming on her cheeks.

"No?" Blake knelt over her, caging her in with his body. "So you don't care that I spent all day yesterday with Pat?"

Farrah's face darkened. "I cannot believe you're talking about another woman right now." She tried to shove him away with no avail.

"I thought you said you weren't jealous," he teased.

"I'm not. But this is not the time to talk about being with someone else." Her bottom lip pushed out into a pout before her eyes lit up with a mischievous gleam. "Although if you can be with Pat, I can be with someone else too. Maybe that hot bartender from the Egret? What was his name, Justin?"

A dangerous growl rumbled from Blake's chest. "You're not going anywhere near him," he snapped. "Not unless you want a bad case of STIs."

Farrah smirked. "Who's the jealous one now?"

"Damn right I'm jealous." Blake pinned her hands above her head and lowered his head until their faces were inches apart.

"I don't share. Not when it comes to you. This is an exclusive arrangement, and if Justin so much as looks at you the wrong way, I will rip him apart with my bare hands."

Farrah's eyes flared. "Fine. But if it's exclusive, that means you can't see Pat again either."

"That's going to be hard."

The anger returned to her expression. She opened her mouth to argue, but he cut her off.

"She's my chief of staff. I'm about as sexually attracted to her as I would be to a ninety-year-old nun, and the feeling's mutual."

An audible gulp. "Oh."

"But it's nice to see you care so much. Now that that's settled..." Blake grinned and nudged her legs open with his knee. "Let's move on to something more fun."

The red on Farrah's cheeks deepened. "You know, you're really a cocky son of—" The rest of Farrah's sentence fell away when he drove her into her with one hard thrust.

"What were you saying about cocky?" Blake lifted one of her legs and propped it on his shoulder so he could drive deeper.

Farrah didn't answer. She clutched the sheets with white-knuckled fists, a steady stream of breathless cries falling past her lips as he buried himself so deep, he could've fucking tattooed himself on her heart. She was still wearing his shirt, which made it even sexier.

Blake leaned down and captured her mouth with his. His tongue slipped into her sweetness, stroking and licking and swallowing her sighs of pleasure until she came apart in his arms.

Farrah didn't know it yet, but he was going to reclaim her, piece by piece. Her friendship. Her trust. Her love. Her heart.

He wanted all of her, and this time he wasn't going to fuck it up.

But until that day came, Blake would settle for anything she was willing to give him because even a piece of Farrah was better than all of anyone else.

CHAPTER 25

"THIS IS LIKE OLD TIMES." COURTNEY PROPPED HER chin in her hand, nostalgia wafting from her in waves. "We're missing Leo and Luke, but seven out of nine ain't bad. Plus Nate, of course." She winked at the actor, who exuded movie-star charisma even in a faded green T-shirt and jeans.

"Thanks for the shoutout. I was beginning to feel like an eighth wheel," he quipped, encircling Kris's waist with one arm. Kris perched on his lap, dressed to the nines in a pleated white sundress, sky-high wedges, and a tangle of fourteen-karat gold necklaces.

Farrah wasn't sure a five-hundred-dollar designer dress was the best thing to wear to a barbecue, but that was Kris for you. The girl wore diamonds to the gym. Diamond studs, but still. Kris was allergic to dressing down.

"How's the movie going?" Sammy's tan popped against his white shirt, and his muscles flexed against his shirtsleeves as he flipped the burgers on the grill.

Farrah slid a glance toward Olivia, who stared at her ex-boyfriend and chugged her watermelon juice like she was trying to quench the Sahara.

A grin spread across Farrah's face.

Oh, Liv.

"There were a few issues with my costar, but it worked out," Nate said. "We wrapped up the New York portion of the shoot yesterday. We'll shoot the rest back in LA."

"Very cool." Sammy nodded.

"Hey, Liv, why don't you help Sammy with the burgers?" Farrah suggested. "You look bored, and he's manning the grill all by himself."

Sammy and Olivia both flushed red.

"I can handle it. Grilling isn't a team activity." Sammy shot Farrah a warning glance, which she ignored.

Consider it payback for Sammy keeping Blake's secret all these years.

Okay, fine, it hadn't been Sammy's secret to tell, but that didn't mean a thing to Farrah's petty side.

"She can help you pass out the burgers," Farrah said. "Efficiency. Liv's favorite thing."

I'm going to murder you in your sleep, Olivia's eyes warned.

I'll lock my door, Farrah retorted.

Her roommate slammed her drink on the table and stalked to the grill, where she and Sammy stood with matching expressions of discomfort.

Nardo Crescas clucked his tongue. "Farrah. Come on."

"I'm trying to help," she whispered. "It's about time Sammy and Olivia got over their little feud, don't you think?"

"A feud is defined as 'a prolonged and bitter quarrel or dispute.' Therefore, *little feud* is an oxymoron."

Courtney snorted while Farrah rubbed her temple. Some things never changed.

Nardo, Sammy's best friend from college and another member of their study abroad group, wasn't as scrawny as he used to be, and he seemed a smidge less uptight, but he still talked like he was trying out for the role of Human Encyclopedia. Farrah wondered if everyone at his job talked like that. Nardo was an economist at the Department of Treasury, and he wore the unofficial straight-man-in-Washington-DC uniform: khakis paired with a gingham button-down. Bonus points for the oh-so-intellectual black-framed glasses.

While everyone else had already been in New York, Nardo drove up from DC yesterday to celebrate Sammy's pop-up bakery opening, which had been a smash success. Crumble & Bake was the hottest new thing in town, and Farrah couldn't be happier for her friend.

By sheer luck, Sammy's opening coincided with Kris and Courtney's visit, and he'd decided to host an FEA reunion/pre-July Fourth barbecue at his Brooklyn brownstone rental. Luke was in Wisconsin and Leo was on a book tour in Europe, but otherwise, everyone in their Shanghai circle was present and accounted for.

Including Blake.

Farrah's mouth dried when he stepped into the backyard, a god among mortals with his golden hair and sinful body. Memories of what she'd done to said body that morning before they arrived at Sammy's house flooded her mind, and her face turned the color of Olivia's watermelon juice.

"Sam, the ice is in the kitchen," Blake said, clapping his friend on the back. He'd volunteered to run to the corner store for more ice earlier.

"Thanks, man." Sammy nodded.

Blake slid into the empty seat next to Farrah at the picnic table. "Hey." His dimples flashed.

"Hey." The velvety tips of butterfly wings brushed Farrah's heart.

She was treading dangerous waters. Her arrangement with

Blake was the stupidest thing she could've agreed to since he'd made it clear what he wanted: her. All of her.

And if she wasn't careful, she might just give it to him.

Sex aside, Farrah had forgotten how easy it was to talk to Blake. How safe he made her feel. How hard he made her laugh. All the things that made her fall in love with him the first time around had the potential to do so again, maybe even more, because she'd realized her feelings for him were the exception, not the rule. He was the only guy who could turn her inside out with one smile.

She didn't trust him, not completely. But he was inching his way deeper past her defenses, and one day, she'd have to decide whether to wave the white flag or go out in a blaze of glory.

One day. Not today.

"What are you doing after this?" Blake ran one warm, rough hand up her thigh, and her core wept in response.

They'd had enough sex to repopulate an army this past week. You'd think her body would be all tapped out, but no, she was soaking wet in the middle of a barbecue with her friends.

"I hope you're not expecting me to say you," Farrah whispered, tightening the leash on her self-control.

Blake chuckled, his gaze gleaming with lazy male satisfaction. "I see someone has sex on their mind," he drawled. "I was going to ask if you wanted to hit up the Brooklyn Botanic Garden—there's a special night exhibit running there through the end of the month—but I'm down for something kinky too." He paused. "We could do something kinky *in* the garden. That'll spice things up." His fingers hit the edge of her panties beneath the table.

Farrah swallowed and glanced around to see if anyone noticed. Kris and Nate were laughing at something on his phone, Courtney and Nardo were arguing about *Black Mirror*, and Sammy and Olivia were busy ignoring each other.

"We are not getting kinky in a garden." She grasped his hand and placed it back in his lap. Her hand brushed his impressive hard-on, and molten lava spilled into her lower belly. "And what do you mean, 'spice things up'? Bored already?"

Blake's eyes glittered like pristine glacial lakes in the sun. "Never."

A thick rope of unspoken words stretched between them.

Farrah faked a cough, cutting the cord. "You're not the garden type. Besides, this sounds like a date." Dates weren't part of the deal. They weren't *not* part of the deal, but she was too afraid to go down that path yet.

Blake shrugged. "Heard about it from Landon, thought it sounded interesting. Besides, you like gardens, and it's not a date."

"It's not." Skepticism turned what would've been a question into a statement.

"Nope. If it were a date, I'd bring you flowers, not bring you *to* flowers."

Farrah burst into laughter, and the grin on Blake's face widened.

"Here." Olivia plunked a burger in front of Farrah, interrupting her mirth. "Be grateful I didn't spit in it." She frowned at the man sitting next to her roommate. "Blake."

"Liv."

Farrah had told her friends about her arrangement with Blake because she didn't need the added stress of more secrets. Sammy had been thrilled, Kris indifferent, Courtney excited, and Olivia upset. She was the closest to Farrah and, therefore, the most protective. Not to mention, the girl had a memory like a steel trap. Time had smoothed the animosity Kris and Courtney held toward Blake, but Olivia remembered it well. She'd been wary, even after Farrah explained the real reason Blake broke up with her.

Nardo's eyebrows rose when he saw Blake and Farrah together

at Sammy's opening, but he hadn't said anything, so Farrah mentally lumped him in the "indifferent" camp.

A doorbell rang deep in the house.

"I'll get it," Sammy said. "Nardo, you mind taking over for me real quick?"

"No problem." Nardo cast a strange look in Olivia's direction while Sammy went to answer the door.

"Just so you know," Olivia told Blake, "if you hurt Farrah again, I'll string you up by your balls and drop you in the middle of an ax-throwing competition."

Blake's smile didn't budge. "Noted. Bonus points for creativity. Your Yale degree is wasted on finance instead of screenwriting."

Farrah couldn't resist another laugh as Olivia huffed at Blake's blasé response.

"I mean it." Olivia poked a finger at Blake's chest. "Orgasms only. No heartbreak allowed."

This time, Blake was the one who laughed while Farrah blanched in horror.

"Liv!"

"Don't worry," Blake said, draping an arm over Farrah's shoulder. "Orgasms are a guarantee, and heartbreak is not on the menu."

"Who's guaranteeing orgasms?" Courtney butted into their conversation.

Before anyone could answer, Kris let loose an expletive. "Who the fuck is that?"

Their heads swiveled toward the entrance to the house. Sammy had returned...with a gorgeous leggy blond in tow. The mystery woman had a face that could put Charlize Theron to shame, and she wore a stylish red jumpsuit that Farrah recognized from the latest issue of *Mode de Vie*.

"Hi, Nardo," the blond lilted.

"Hey, Jess." Nardo cast another wary glance at Olivia, who was frowning at the newcomer.

Sammy cleared his throat. "Guys, I want you to meet my girlfriend, Jessica. Jess, this is everyone." He introduced the group, tripping over Olivia's name.

Silence greeted his announcement.

Shock slid through Farrah's veins. *Girlfriend?* Sammy hadn't so much as hinted at a girlfriend before today.

Nate was the first to speak. "Nice to meet you, Jessica. I'm Nate." He reintroduced himself even though he was the last person who needed a reintroduction.

Jessica smiled. "I know who you are." No fangirling, no blushing. "Nice to meet you too."

"She just arrived in New York. She couldn't make it to the opening yesterday because she had a court case," Sammy explained.

"Oh. Are you a lawyer?" Kris's tone indicated she couldn't care less about the answer.

"Technology law, which is why the Bay Area is my stomping grounds. You can say a lot of things about Silicon Valley, but it's never boring." Jessica smiled.

Kris yawned. "Fascinating."

Farrah snuck a peek at Olivia. She'd wiped the expression from her face, but Farrah could read the tense set of her shoulders and the way she fiddled with her watch strap. Olivia was pissed.

Nate cleared his throat. "Hey, why don't we eat before the food gets cold? Hot dogs are on the grill, but the burgers are done. Let's dig in."

The clatter of plastic utensils and light chatter broke the tension, but an undercurrent of unease remained.

"Looks like I'm not the only person Olivia wants to drop into the middle of an axe-throwing competition," Blake murmured. "I thought she and Sammy have been over for a while."

"It's complicated."

Olivia was not the type who liked to discuss her feelings in public, so Farrah spared her friend the third degree for now.

Reminder: stock up on Ben & Jerry's before I go home.

"Complicated, I get. But you know what's simple?" Blake wiggled his eyebrows. "A nighttime walk through the Brooklyn Botanic Garden. Not a date, I swear. Just two friends with floral benefits, smelling roses and shit."

Maybe it was the sunshine, the giddiness of being surrounded by old friends, or Blake's boyish smile. Either way, Farrah threw caution to the wind.

What could it hurt?

"Okay," she said. "Let's go to the garden."

CHAPTER 26

THE NEXT MONTH FLEW BY. FARRAH STILL HADN'T landed an interview at any of the design firms she'd applied to, not even after she'd dropped off copies of her résumé and cover letter in person and called to follow up.

As a result, she'd started looking for more individual clients, à la her previous arrangement with Blake. It wasn't ideal—she wasn't ready to go full-time freelance yet—but it gave her a sense of purpose amidst rising panic over her career.

Meanwhile, Blake helped distract Farrah from her nagging worries. Their night at the garden, post-Sammy's barbecue, proved to be the first of many noncarnal activities Blake persuaded her to indulge in. Farrah didn't know how he did it, but she found herself picnicking in Central Park, taking day trips to Coney Island, and going on midnight strolls across the Brooklyn Bridge with the man she'd once sworn she'd never allow back into her life.

What was worse, Farrah enjoyed their nondates. Very much. Each one aimed some sort of special Godzilla ray gun at the butterflies in her stomach, causing them to grow larger and larger until they threatened to take over her entire body.

"How long are you going to be in Miami?" she asked, shivering as the night chill skimmed over her skin.

August was the hottest month in the city, but it was 11:00 p.m. and they were one hundred stories above the ground. Farrah wished she'd worn a jacket over her dress and sandals. Then again, she hadn't planned for their lunch date—er, nondate—to stretch this late into the night.

"A week. Lots of meetings and walk-throughs planned." Blake pulled her to his chest and rubbed her arms, flattening some of her goose bumps. Warmth trickled into her stomach and she shivered again, this time for a whole other reason than the cold. "Don't miss me too much." His voice contained his signature cocky, teasing lilt.

"You wish." Farrah buried her face in his chest and breathed in his crisp, citrusy scent. "You better bring me back pastelitos or I'll be pissed."

Blake's chuckle vibrated through her. "Noted. How's the job search going, by the way? Liv mentioned you've been dropping off your résumés in person?"

Blake and Olivia had reached a truce in the past month. Apparently, that truce had evolved from Olivia not killing him on sight to divulging information about Farrah's professional woes.

Farrah didn't want to hide her job search problems from Blake; she just found it embarrassing. She'd charged him a ton of money to design his apartment, and now she couldn't even get a phone screen from a reputable firm. Or any firm for that matter.

"Not great, but I'll keep trying." Farrah pulled back and tucked a strand of hair behind her ear. "In the meantime, I'm looking for more clients, so if you know anyone whose house needs an overhaul…"

"I'll let you know." Blake examined her with a sober expression. "I wasn't kidding when I said you have what it takes to go it on your own. Fuck these studios who aren't smart enough to hire you. They're a few knives short of a full set, and you're better off without 'em. You can use all that time you spend chasing down those idiots to start your own firm. You have the talent, and you have the contacts. Look how good a job you did on my place. Everyone that comes by loves it."

Farrah raised her eyebrows. "How many people come by?"

Blake ticked off his guests on his fingers. "You, Landon, Justin, Pat, Sammy, and…" He frowned. "That's not the point. The point is, there's no set timeline for chasing your dreams. There'll never be a day when you wake up and see a flashing neon sign that says, 'This is the day to go for it.' You have to make that choice on your own."

Farrah knew he was trying to be supportive, but annoyance heated her skin nonetheless. "I told you, I'm not ready. Stop pushing it." She turned away from Blake and walked toward one of the angled glass partitions. They were at the Edge, an outdoor sky deck suspended midair above Manhattan. Included in the price of admission: 360-degree views of the city and a healthy dose of vertigo for those who weren't fans of heights—Farrah included.

Her moodiness didn't deter Blake. He followed her, grasped her chin, and forced her to look at him. "Do you know many branches of Legends there are in the world today?" he demanded. "Twelve: Austin, LA, Chicago, New Orleans, Seattle, Houston, Dallas, London, Boston, Dublin, Barcelona, and Madrid. Fourteen, if you include New York and Miami. And I plan on opening many, many more."

"Congrats." Farrah tried to tear herself from Blake's grip, to no avail.

His fingers burned into her skin, and the intensity of his gaze scorched her soul. "Do you know how many I had five years ago? Zero. I would still have zero if it weren't for the girl who told me to fuck the haters and go for my dreams. She believed in me when I didn't believe in myself, and I wouldn't be anywhere near where I am today if it hadn't been for her. She made me into who I am, and I owe her everything."

Farrah's pulse careened out of control. An unseen thread stretched between them and tugged at her heartstrings every time he looked at her the way he was looking at her now, like she was the sun to his earth. She was sure Blake could feel her shivers travel across that thread and into his body because he was trembling too, his eyes as dark as the night sky that hung above them.

"I don't remember using the term *fuck the haters*," she rasped.

Blake's teeth flashed white in the darkness before he turned serious again. "Maybe not in those exact words, but the sentiment was there. You can do anything. Believe that."

The sincerity in his voice sent her pulse from careening to crashing straight over the cliff toward a place she never thought she'd go again.

"I know you're scared. I was too. I still am. Sometimes I wake up thinking I don't know jack shit about what I'm doing and terrified everything will crash around me. That feeling never goes away. But it's the ones who push past the fear that succeed." Blake released her and spun her around to face the city again. He rested his hands on her hips and his chin on her shoulder. "Remember the last time we stood on top of the world?" he whispered. "Macau. Courtney's birthday. We went bungee-jumping, and you were so scared you tried to back out multiple times. I thought the bungee operator was going to kill us."

Farrah's soft laugh mingled with the night air. "I remember. You gave a motivational speech worthy of Tony Robbins."

"Please. I'm better than Tony Robbins," Blake scoffed. "The point is, you faced one of your biggest fears and punched it in its ugly face. You can do that again. Whatever your fear is or however far you fall—you'll survive. And I'll be there to catch you."

Farrah's breath whooshed out of her. Manhattan lay sprawled at her feet, a glittering, tangled web of lofty dreams and promises. Some broken, some fulfilled, all searching for a sense of purpose in the unforgiving concrete jungle. Nothing except a pane of glass separated her from a thousand-foot tumble over the edge.

Despite the glass and Blake's secure grip around her waist, Farrah was terrified—because she was already falling. And no matter what Blake said, she wasn't sure she'd survive if she hit the ground.

Blake flew to Miami the next afternoon, leaving Farrah alone with her thoughts.

Her inner voices were like weeds—expected, fine in moderation, but if there were too many, they'd choke and paralyze her.

Olivia was on another date, and instead of stewing in the silence, dwelling on her dwindling career prospects, and agonizing over her feelings for Blake, Farrah called her mom.

"Follow up with the studios again if they haven't replied to you by Friday." Cheryl Lau's voice crackled over the phone. "Some people are so lazy, they probably haven't gotten to your résumé yet. You're a NIDA competition winner. You graduated top of your class from CCU. They should be beating down your door."

"I know, I know." Farrah painted a fresh coat of red polish on her big toe. She'd rather not spend money on professional pedicures until she secured steady employment. *Or you could start your own design studio*, one of her stray inner voices whispered. Farrah squashed it. "Where are you?"

She could barely hear her mom over the sound of waves and people chattering in Cantonese in the background.

"I'm in San Diego for the association's annual retreat." Cheryl sniffed. "So much drama. The membership chair's wife filed for divorce right before the trip, and he drank so much yesterday, he passed out on the beach. So stupid. He's lucky he didn't get mugged."

"Wow. You're living on the wild side," Farrah teased.

"Hmph. I should've stayed home. All people do here is gossip, gossip, gossip."

"You say that every year, yet you go on the retreat every year."

Her mom had a love-hate relationship with the local Chinese dance association she'd joined right after Farrah graduated high school. As in, she loved to say she hated it, but Farrah knew it was all for show. The association provided a much-needed source of entertainment and company for Cheryl, who'd lived alone since Farrah moved to New York three years ago.

Guilt prickled the back of Farrah's neck. She should call and visit more often. Even though her mom had a robust social life, Farrah worried she was lonely. Cheryl hadn't dated anyone since her divorce, and she was only in her fifties. Still plenty of time for a second chance at love.

"Well, I come for the food and dancing." Cheryl yelled at someone in the background, "Be quiet, I'm talking to my daughter!"

Farrah laughed. "It's ok. Enjoy your trip. I can call you later."

"No, it's fine." Cheryl hesitated. "You're coming home for Christmas, right?"

"Of course. I always come home for the holidays."

"Good, good."

Farrah's Spidey sense tingled at Cheryl's tone. "Mom, what aren't you telling me?"

"Nothing. I was just thinking." Cheryl cleared her throat. "Anyway, will you be bringing a boyfriend with you? A son-in-law would be the best Christmas present, but I have to vet him first. Moms can always tell if someone is a good egg or bad egg."

As subtle as a sledgehammer to the head. Cheryl's gentle nudges about settling down, getting married, and birthing lots of grandbabies had evolved into outright shoves, and Farrah was only twenty-five.

"There are no eggs, good or bad. I'm not dating anyone." Technically true. Right?

"No one?" Disappointment seeped through the phone into Farrah's ear. "Not even a date? You're young and attractive. Maybe you're not going to the supermarket often enough."

Ok, the egg analogy was getting weird. "I've been on *dates*." Farrah chewed on her bottom lip, wondering whether to disclose her sort-of dates with Blake. "I've been, uh, hanging out with Blake."

"Blake? The boy from Shanghai who broke your heart?"

Cheryl had been there, tissues and ice cream in hand, to comfort her daughter when Farrah returned home from Shanghai and collapsed into tears whenever she saw or heard something that reminded her of Blake—a movie they'd watched together, a song they'd danced to, her set of Kelly Burke limited-edition Pantone markers, which he'd gifted her for her twentieth birthday and which she couldn't bring herself to throw away until they ran out of ink.

"Yes." Farrah gave her mom a quick rundown of what happened, minus the sex part. She'd already told Cheryl about Blake's design project—she just hadn't named him as the client. "Before you say anything, I know I'm being reckless. Given my and Blake's history, I shouldn't even be talking to him. Right?"

"Not necessarily." Farrah knew her mom so well, she could hear her shrug over the phone. "He sounds like he's changed and wants to make things work. Besides, you were so smitten with him. Maybe this is your second chance." She sounded wistful. "Grudges are the worst thing to hold on to. No matter how bad someone hurt you, you can't heal until you forgive. Sometimes that means moving on. Other times that means giving things another shot."

Farrah tightened her grip on her phone. "You think I should give Blake another shot?"

Two months ago, she would've scoffed at the idea, but now, a strange warmth filled her at her mother's advice.

"I think you should do what your heart tells you. We can be so afraid of getting hurt, we lock it up in a fortress, but hearts are meant to roam free until they find what they're searching for. Let yours lead you to where you need to go."

CHAPTER 27

AFTER WEEKS OF HEADACHES, BLAKE'S BUSINESS WAS running on smoother ground again. He'd fixed the plumbing issues, found another liquor distributor who could deliver on time, and knocked his Miami visit out of the ballpark. Not only did he have the city officials eating out of his hand, but he'd found the perfect venue for Legends in the trendy Wynwood district.

The New York branch may not be open yet, but when business operated at the size Legends did, he didn't have the luxury of waiting until one project finished before he started on the next one. Blake worked on a fast-paced rolling schedule.

But as much as he'd enjoyed Miami's beaches and the thrill of seeing a business deal snap together, he would much rather be where he was now: in his kitchen, hands braced against the counter, while Farrah sucked him off like she was auditioning for a Hoover gig.

"Fuck." Blake's groans echoed in the marble space as Farrah worked him mercilessly. Tongue. Hands. Teeth. Taking him to the edge over and over again until she drew him all the way down her throat and pressed on his taint.

His orgasm ripped through him, brutal and unrepentant. His knees buckled, and he would've collapsed onto the floor had he not been squeezing the kitchen counter with a death grip. Blake was sure he shouted—loud—but he couldn't hear anything past the roaring in his ears.

When his vision cleared, he found Farrah staring up at him with a self-satisfied smirk.

"I should go on business trips more often." He lifted her up and sat her on the counter. She wasn't naked yet, but that was something they could remedy in a second.

"Hmm. Maybe. That was for the pastelitos." She tilted her head toward the box of flaky, guava-filled pastries he'd brought back from Miami. "An appropriate apology for running off and leaving me with BOB."

Blake's brows snapped together. "Who the fuck is Bob? What's his last name? I just want to talk." *And kill him. Don't worry—it'll be slow and painful.*

Farrah's eyes sparkled with mischief. "BOB. Battery Operated Boyfriend. Last name: Vibrator. I think he's getting sick of me, so it's a good thing you're back." She hooked her legs around his waist and swiped her tongue across his bottom lip, which made him harder than the marble slab she was sitting on.

Yes, already. When it came to Farrah, Blake's dick could run longer marathons than an Iron Man champion.

"I'm second place to BOB Vibrator? Bullshit." Blake's shoulders relaxed now that he didn't have some asshole to hunt down. "For one, I'll never get sick of you."

"Hmm. We'll see."

"We don't have to see. We know. At least, I do." Blake ran his hands up the sides of her thighs. "I can prove it."

"Tempting," she murmured. "But first..." She pushed him away and hopped off the counter. "Coffee."

Blake's jaw unhinged, and Farrah broke out into sunny laughter that filled the room with its warmth.

"Coffee can wait. You haven't gotten your turn yet." Not to mention, there was no way he could walk out of here with a hard-on the size of the Statue of Liberty.

"I have, which is why I need coffee," Farrah huffed. "We didn't sleep at all last night, and it's already…" She checked the clock on the microwave. "Nine thirty in the morning."

Okay, Blake may have been overzealous in making up for lost time yesterday. Farrah hadn't complained, far from it, but now that he looked closer, she did appear tired. Her lips drooped, and she attempted to hold back a yawn with no success.

"We'll get you coffee," Blake said with some guilt. "I ran out of coffee beans but there's a café downstairs."

"Perfect."

Blake got dressed, taking extra care to tuck his package so it didn't look like he was going to knock someone out with a baseball bat, and rode the elevator down to the lobby level, which boasted a coffee shop, library, screening room, and several conference rooms.

There weren't many people up and about on a Sunday morning, and they snagged a prime seat by the window after Blake paid for their drinks.

"I have good news." Farrah stirred her coffee until the heart-shaped latte art dissolved. "I signed another client."

"That's amazing news!" Pride coursed through Blake. "Who is it?"

"A model. Up and coming, but she just signed a big beauty contract and is looking to make her apartment feel more like home. She's not paying much, but anything is better than nothing."

"Still amazing." Blake squeezed her hand. "I knew you could do it."

Farrah's eyes softened. "Thank you. I—" She stopped short. "Oh my god."

Blake followed her gaze to the couple walking in with their arms around each other. The guy was around their age. Mid-to late twenties, decent-looking in a metrosexual douchebag kind of way. The woman was impeccably groomed but older than her boy toy by at least twenty years. She looked kind of familiar, but he couldn't place her.

Farrah's grip tightened on his hand, cutting off his circulation. "That's Kelly Burke." Shock dripped from every word. "My old boss. And that's her *godson*, Matt. The one who got the pro motion after the Z Hotels project."

So that was why Kelly looked so familiar. Farrah had idolized the woman and shown him a picture of Kelly—not to mention every hotel Kelly had ever designed—when they were together in Shanghai.

Blake watched as Matt whispered something in Kelly's ear, and the older woman giggled like a teenager. They hadn't noticed Farrah yet.

"Uh, he's just her godson, right? No biological relation? Because if so, that's pretty fucking disturbing."

"No relation. But still." Farrah's voice shook. "He's her best friend's son and her employee."

Blake's mouth set in a grim line. "Now we know why he got that promotion."

Matt noticed Farrah first. His eyes widened before he smoothed his expression into one of nonchalance. He removed his arm from Kelly's waist and whispered something else to her that caused her to home in on her ex-employee with laser eyes.

Kelly was pretty hot for a cougar. Shiny brown hair, curvy figure, and a subtle touch of Botox that kept her skin smooth and unlined. But she had snake eyes, dark and cold.

Blake hated her on sight.

"Farrah." Kelly glided over with Matt in tow. "I'm surprised to see you here."

"I'm surprised to see *you* here. With Matt." Farrah threw a pointed glance at Matt, whose ears pinked.

"He is my godson, and he lives in the building. I was helping him with…something in his apartment," Kelly said, cooler than the AC blasting from the vents.

Blake hadn't seen Matt around before, but all four of them knew what the "something" Kelly was talking about was.

"We miss you in the office." Kelly oozed insincerity. "Which firm are you at now?"

Farrah withdrew her hand from Blake's and took a gulp of her coffee. "I'm consulting at the moment. After KBI, I thought a corporate career might not be the best fit for me."

"I see." Kelly's smile slashed across her face. "Which firms did you receive offers from? I'm friends with many designers in the city. Perhaps I can get them to sweeten the deal, so you'll reconsider. You're so talented."

Despite her encouraging words, Kelly resembled a cobra, coiled to strike.

Beside her, Matt rubbed a hand through his hair. He, at least, had the grace to look embarrassed.

Farrah's face paled. Something sparked in her eyes—realization. Over what, Blake didn't know. "Thank you, but no thank you." She stood up. "We have somewhere to be, so I'll leave you two alone. Always a pleasure running into you."

Blake followed Farrah into the elevator, where she jabbed at the button for his floor so hard, he was surprised it didn't break.

"You were way nicer to them than I would've been," he said. "What assholes. I know someone who knows someone. If you want, they can make it quick."

His joke fell flat on its face.

Farrah stared straight ahead, her face set in stone. "It's her."

"What?"

"Kelly's the reason I haven't received responses from any of the firms I applied to." He detected a slight tremble in her shoulders. Not from nerves but from anger. "She blackballed me. god, I can't believe I didn't see it before. She's vindictive and petty enough to do something like this. There was a senior designer who worked at KBI when I first joined. Julie. She got a shout-out in some magazine's list of the fifty top up-and-coming designers in the city. Kelly couldn't stand it, even though she wasn't an up-and-comer nor eligible for the list herself. She fired Julie, bad-mouthed her to the entire industry—something about Julie stealing design ideas—and forced her to move back to Michigan. I was new and under Kelly's spell. I thought she was telling the truth. But now that I think about it..." She shook her head.

The elevator dinged. "Can she do that?" Blake didn't know much about the design world, but based on what he saw on reality TV, he didn't put it past Kelly to do the things Farrah said. People were crazy.

"She's the most influential and well-respected interior designer in New York," Farrah said flatly. "She sits on the board of NIDA. People believe everything she says."

"She's also banging her godson and employee."

"No hard evidence, and knowing Kelly, she'll cover her tracks." Farrah groaned. "It's true what they say. Never meet your idols because they'll disappoint you. I knew she wasn't the warmest person on the planet, but I never thought..." She rubbed her eyes as Blake opened the door to his apartment. "god knows what she's said about me."

"I'm sorry." Blake hated how helpless he felt. "I can talk to Landon. He's a big KBI client." At least, until he dropped their ass, which he'd do in a heartbeat. Blake got the sense Landon wasn't the biggest Kelly Burke fan himself.

"No." Farrah drew in a deep breath. "I don't want to bother him with small stuff. He has enough on his plate, and so do you. You have the New York opening and the Miami rollout... Don't worry about it. It's my life. I'll figure it out."

"Hey." Blake cupped her face in his hands. "It's not 'small stuff.' Like you said, it's your life. Your career. And I will help you in any way I can. Just say the word."

"Thank you." Farrah swiped under her eye. "Can we not talk about this anymore? I just want to eat pastelitos and watch bad reality TV. I'll deal with the Kelly stuff later."

"You got it."

The two spent the rest of the day gorging on pastries and Chinese takeout and watching *Love Is Blind* on Netflix. Blake had a shit ton of work to do, and today had been his least productive day in years, but as Farrah's hand curled around his on the couch—her first time holding his hand since they ran into each other again—he knew it was worth it.

CHAPTER 28

IF FARRAH TRIED HARD ENOUGH, SHE COULD USE THE Kelly-screwing-her-godson-and-employee info to her advantage and take down her old boss. Kelly wasn't married, but it would be a big enough scandal to tarnish her otherwise spotless reputation.

Farrah had been ready to do it. She'd even drafted anonymous emails to the gossip rags and Kelly's competitors, tipping them off on her salacious discovery. But she'd deleted them before ever hitting send.

She wasn't that kind of person. She didn't care about drama and revenge, and she refused to stoop to Kelly's level. Plus, Farrah didn't have concrete evidence that Kelly blackballed her, though that seemed like the most plausible explanation.

She believed in karma. If Kelly did screw her over, she'd get her comeuppance.

After an afternoon of wallowing, Farrah threw her energy into her new project, instead of plotting her old boss's downfall like a soap opera villain. Thank god Kelly's reach didn't extend to every single person in Manhattan. Farrah could find enough clients to tide her over if she hustled hard enough.

Yuliya, the model, proved easy enough to work with. Her studio apartment was small, and she needed an interior decorator more than a designer. Decorators focused solely on aesthetics; designers focused on aesthetics, space planning, and structural execution. It didn't take Farrah long to pull together a concept that had Yuliya squealing in excited Russian.

"You're back early." She looked up from her computer when the front door slammed open, and Olivia marched in wearing her new green wrap dress and strappy black heels. "Date didn't go well?"

Olivia had been on a record number of dates since the Fourth of July, though none of the poor men ever made it past date three.

"It was fine." Olivia kicked off her shoes and placed them between her black ankle boots and black sandals. The shoe rack in their entryway was, like everything else in the apartment, organized and color-coded to Olivia's exact specifications. "But men in finance are so boring. Just because I deal with financial models during the day doesn't mean I want to discuss them over bucatini alla carbonara."

Farrah's lips twitched. "Perhaps you should venture outside the finance world for dates."

"I hate hipsters." Olivia waved a hand in the air. "That's the entire New York dating pool—finance, hipsters, and vain model/fitness trainer types."

"You're generalizing."

"Generalizations exist for a reason." Olivia plopped onto the couch next to Farrah. "How was your night? Where's Loverboy?"

"*Blake* is on his way to Austin for his father's birthday."

"How filial." Olivia snatched a chip from the open bag of salt and vinegar Lay's on the coffee table. "Can't believe he didn't take you."

"We're not at that stage of our relationship."

"Relationship?" A wicked grin spread across Olivia's face. "I didn't realize you and Blake were in a *relationship*."

Farrah's cheeks warmed. "We're not. It was just a turn of phrase."

She didn't know what she and Blake were. Something changed between them two weeks ago, after they ran into Kelly and Matt. Officially, they were friends with benefits. But Farrah recognized the glow in her chest when she was around him.

She'd had the same feelings before, five years ago. She knew what they meant, even if she refused to say it out loud.

Farrah's phone rang. Blake's name flashed across the screen, and yep, there went her poor little heart.

Not good.

"Hey." Farrah hoped he couldn't hear her chest pounding over the phone.

"Hey. Just landed in Austin and thought I'd see how you're doing," Blake said, his voice rich and velvety amidst a background of boarding announcements and airport chatter.

Farrah bit back a smile. "About the same as I was doing this morning before you left for the airport."

"No pining? No shaking your fist at the moon, wishing I were there beside you?" He clucked in disappointment. "I'm offended."

She rolled her eyes. "I'm pining so hard, you have no idea. In fact, I'm staring at a picture of you right now, wondering how any human being could be so perfect."

"That's the spirit," Blake drawled. "What do you say, phone sex tonight? Don't want you to have to make do with only a picture when we can add my voice to the equation."

Farrah wasn't one hundred percent sure Blake knew she'd been joking, and she was even less sure *he* was joking.

"Did you call to proposition me for phone sex?" She swatted

at Olivia, who made an extremely unladylike gesture with her fingers at Farrah's question.

Very mature, she mouthed.

Olivia shrugged and smirked.

"That hadn't been on my agenda, but it is now." Blake's voice faded out before it regained strength. Must be the cell signal. "Actually, I called to ask if there's anything you want from Austin. As far as I know, there aren't any pastelitos here, but there's a café with a kick-ass house-made coffee blend."

Farrah's stomach turned to warm goo. "You don't have to get me anything."

"I want to. So, coffee? I'd surprise you, but when it comes to food and drink...better safe than sorry."

"Coffee sounds good," she said through the lump in her throat.

"Great. I have to go—my sister's giving me the stink eye for ignoring her." Blake lowered his voice. "Phone sex later tonight. Text me when you're wearing that little black lace teddy of yours."

"Good night, Blake."

He laughed.

Farrah hung up and stared at the ceiling with a ridiculous grin on her face.

"Oh, babe." Olivia sighed. "You're a goner."

Farrah didn't deny it. They both knew it was true.

CHAPTER 29

THE GOOD PARTS OF BLAKE'S AUSTIN VISIT: HIS MOM and sister, amazing barbecue, and a hot-as-hell phone sex session with Farrah.

The bad parts: everything else.

The trouble started at Joe Ryan's fiftieth birthday party, which was standard fare for their small Austin suburb of Cedar Hills: burgers, chips, and sweaty glasses of lemonade piled on their rickety picnic table; guests milling around in short-sleeved polo shirts and shorts, their skin pinking beneath the scorching summer heat while they gossiped about the latest suburban scandal; and live music courtesy of the Ryans' next-door neighbor's son, who aspired to be a country-rock star.

After a mind-numbing conversation with the Harpers about the best lawnmower models, Blake escaped to the kitchen, where his mom and sister were whipping up a fresh batch of finger foods. Well, his mom was; Joy was scrolling through her phone and munching on nachos.

Blake arched an eyebrow. "Being useful, I see."

"Oh, shut up." Joy stuck her tongue out at him. "You're not exactly Mr. Helpful either."

"Mom, do you need help with anything after I refill the chips?" Blake asked with a wide smile. He pushed the bowl of nachos out of Joy's reach and ignored her indignant cry.

Helen Ryan laughed. "Oh, no, thanks, hon. I appreciate the offer, but I remember what happened the last time you tried to help me cook." She gave him an affectionate pat on the cheek. "You're very sweet, even if you only offered to help to spite your sister."

Hey, an offer was an offer.

Besides, how was Blake supposed to know the difference between baking soda and baking powder? He'd been seventeen.

"Ugh, don't encourage him, Mom." Joy stretched across the counter to reach the chips; he moved them farther away, earning himself a scowl. "Just because he's home for the first time in months, doesn't mean you need to spoil him. He's the worst."

"You're the worst."

"Am not."

"Are too."

"Children! Can we not?" Helen scolded. "You're adults. Act like it."

"She started it," Blake said at the same time Joy protested, "He started it."

Their mother shook her head. "And they say children grow up," she muttered. "Joy, take more lemonade out. And, Blake, take this to your father. It's his favorite." She handed him a plate of football-shaped bacon cheese balls.

Blake grimaced. He'd spoken three words to his father since he arrived yesterday: *hi* and *happy birthday*. Joe didn't seem keen on striking up a conversation with his only son, and the feeling was mutual.

Helen picked up on his reluctance. "It's his birthday," she reminded him. "Try, ok?"

"Okay," he grumbled.

"All right. Love you, sweetie." She squeezed his free hand. "It's so nice to have you home."

Blake softened. "Love you too."

He really did feel guilty about not coming home more often. Honestly, other than the undercurrent of tension between him and his father, it wasn't so bad. He'd spent yesterday helping his family tidy up the house and clean out the garage—grunt work, but he found the mindlessness soothing—and binge-watching *Too Hot to Handle* on Netflix with Joy. The show was so bad, it was almost good. Plus, his mother could cook like nobody's business and had been stuffing him with his favorite foods since he stepped foot in the house.

"You are such a kiss ass," Joy said as they left the kitchen's sweet AC for the sticky heat of their backyard.

"You're just jealous I'm Mom's favorite." Blake popped a cheese ball in his mouth. There were a ton left; his father wouldn't miss one.

"Please. Everyone knows I'm the most lovable Ryan. Anyway, good luck with Dad." Her voice was sweeter than the pitcher of lemonade she placed on the picnic table.

He narrowed his eyes. "If I could disown you, I would. In fact, I'm doing that right now."

Joy clutched her heart with mock distress. "But your life would be so boring without me."

"Negative."

"Go." She pushed him toward Joe, who was holding court with his poker buddies by the oak tree in the corner. "Mom says you and I act like children, but it's actually you and Dad." She tapped a finger to her chin. "Huh. There seems to be a common denominator."

"Disowned!" Blake shouted over his shoulder. "And forget about staying at my place if you ever come to New York."

Joy merely laughed in response.

Blake's humor faded and his mouth settled into a grim line as he approached Joe. Was it normal for sons not to want to talk to their fathers? Probably not.

But he'd promised his mom he would try.

"Hey, Dad," he said, breaking up the older man's conversation about the upcoming football season. "This is for you."

Joe accepted the plate without looking at Blake. "Thanks."

Tension hung thick in the air between them.

"Blakey boy! Haven't seen you around in a while." Max, a short, stocky man with a big beer belly and an even bigger mouth, clapped a meaty hand on Blake's shoulder. He was Blake's least favorite out of all his father's friends. "Too good for us common folk now that you made it to the big time?"

Blake's jaw tightened, but he smoothed it over with an easy smile. "I have a new bar opening up in New York, so I haven't had time to visit as much as I would like."

"New York, huh?" Max smirked. "The Big Bad Apple. Guess our little suburb must seem boring compared to Times Square and whatnot."

No self-respecting New Yorker would willingly visit Times Square, a.k.a. tourist central, but Blake didn't bother explaining that to Max. "Austin's not a small city."

"I'm not talking about Austin. I'm talking 'bout Cedar Hills. Big difference between the city and here." Max chewed on an ice cube. "Hey, what'd you end up getting your old man for his fiftieth, anyway? Big birthday. New house? New car? You got the money."

"You'll find out soon enough. Don't want to ruin the surprise," Blake said coolly. He'd gotten his father a watch—a custom-engraved, five-thousand-dollar watch, which he was sure would end up collecting dust in the back of a drawer. Joe never used any of the gifts Blake bought him.

In truth, Blake would've been happy to buy his parents a new house. The Ryans lived in a comfortable but old split-level, and they had to have repairs done every year. But Joe and Helen had called it home for decades and refused to move out, so Blake dropped the issue.

Not that Max needed to know any of that. He wasn't worth Blake's time.

"Sure, sure." Max chuckled. "Hey, you think you can get me a discount at Legends? Friend of the family and all that."

"Sure." *Over my dead body.*

"Speaking of Legends, we should go there for the NFL kick-off game," Phil, another of Joe's friends, mused. "It's a great bar."

This time, Blake's smile was genuine. "Thanks."

"Eh." Joe munched on his food. "Why bother driving all the way downtown when we can watch it at your house like we always do? You just got a new TV too."

Blake's blood heated, blistering his insides.

Are you fucking kidding me?

His father didn't want to go to his openings? Fine. Didn't want to go to his bars at all? Fine. But to stand there and discourage his friends from supporting his son's business *in front of his son*? Not fucking fine.

"Legends is a twenty-minute drive away, and it has TVs too," he said. "Not that you would know. You've never been to one."

The group fell silent. Even the wind stopped blowing.

"Uh, I'm going to...get another beer." Phil backed away.

"I'm going to take a dump," Max announced.

One by one, Joe's friends fled.

"What the hell was that?" Joe's left eye twitched, a sure sign he was angry.

"I could ask you the same thing." Blake vibrated with controlled fury. "Talk shit about me all you want behind my back, but you could at least pretend to support me in front of your friends."

"Stop being so sensitive," Joe said dismissively. "It's not like you need the money."

"It's not about the money."

"Then what is it about?"

Blake should stop. It was Joe's birthday, and he didn't want to ruin it for everyone else. But once you unscrew the cap on years of pent-up resentment, it's impossible to hold it back.

"It's about you never supporting me," Blake hissed. "Not when I quit football, not when I started my business, not ever. It's about you being so damned resentful you couldn't live out your NFL dreams through me that you can't stand me succeeding at something else. Let's face it, you wanted my bar to fail so you could rub it in my face. Most of all, it's about you being a shitty-ass father."

Joe's face paled, then flushed so red, an onlooker would think he was having a heart attack. A vein pulsed in his forehead, but he didn't confirm or deny the accusations. He didn't say a damn thing.

Someone else, however, did.

"Blake." The soft gasp behind him sent ice trickling through Blake's veins.

He swallowed hard and turned to see his mother and sister staring at him with horrified expressions. Joy's mouth hung open, while Helen's eyes brimmed with tears.

Blake's outburst probably hadn't been what Helen meant when she'd said *try*.

Fuck.

Joy sent Blake on a supermarket run so he could "cool off and pull his head out of his ass." Blake accepted the errand without a peep. Anything to get away from his father's stony silence and his mother's tearful eyes.

Now, if only he could get away from the hard knot of guilt in his throat.

Blake should've kept his mouth shut. As good as it had felt giving Joe a piece of his mind, it was his father's birthday, and the entire neighborhood had been at the party. They'd be gossiping about the Ryan father-son blowout for months. Not to mention, he'd ruined the weekend for his mom and sister.

"Fuck." Blake glared at the contents of the freezer aisle. His shopping cart contained enough food and snacks to sustain a four-person household for a year, but he grabbed an extra box of strawberry-kiwi popsicles (his sister's favorite) and mint chocolate ice cream (his mom's favorite) anyway.

He also swung by the beer aisle and picked up a six-pack of Budweiser. He told himself it was as much for his own sanity as it was for his father, even though Blake preferred Stella.

Satisfied he had everything he needed, Blake turned the corner to pay and bumped into another shopper.

"I'm sor—" His apology died in his throat.

You know that saying, "Things can always get worse"?

It was true.

Because as much of a shit-tastic day as Blake had been having, nothing could've prepared him for running into the person before him.

Her name fell from his lips in a stunned whisper.

"Cleo."

CHAPTER 30

GREEN EYES BLINKED UP AT HIM, HAZY WITH SHOCK.
"Blake?"

Cleo Bowden.

His ex-girlfriend. Ex-fiancée. Ex-mother of his child.

It had been four years since Blake had last spoken to her. Their last conversation had been stilted and awkward to the point of physical pain. It'd been right before Cleo transferred schools and moved to Atlanta. Her grandparents lived there, and her parents thought it would be good for her to get away from the bad memories. Cleo had been a shell of herself, withdrawn and in pain. Blake had been spiraling, consumed by guilt and self-hatred.

Two broken people who should've never been together, united by tragedy.

"I didn't know you were in Austin," Blake managed to say.

Did his family know she was back in town? No. If they did, they would've told him. Plus, they'd lost touch with Cleo a long time ago. It'd been too painful for the Ryans and the Bowdens to be around each other, knowing there was one less person in their family.

Because of me.

"I moved back a few months ago." Cleo looked good. Glowing, even. Her face and figure had filled out since their college days, but the catlike eyes and dark ringlets remained the same. "After, well…" She gestured at herself with a blush.

It took Blake a minute to figure out what she was pointing to. When he did, his heart stopped.

Cleo wore a long, flowy dress that camouflaged it well, but now that he looked closer, it was unmistakable. A baby bump.

"I'm sorry." A hint of sympathy crept into the doctor's eyes as Cleo gripped Blake's hand so hard he flinched. *"I'm afraid you'll no longer be able to have children."*

"H-how?" Blake didn't believe in miracles, but he'd heard the doctor with his own ears. The car accident had rendered Cleo infertile. Too much damage to her fallopian tubes. Yet here she was, basking in the glow only expecting mothers had.

The whole situation was surreal.

"IVF. In vitro fertilization. The first time didn't work. Second time did, against all odds." Cleo's eyes swam. "Kind of a miracle, huh?"

"Yeah." He squeezed the word past the lump in his throat. "Congratulations. I'm happy for you." Blake meant it. One of the things that'd haunted him most from that night was knowing he'd fucked up Cleo's future and dreams of starting a family.

Some of the guilt in his stomach eased. There was a shit ton left, but he felt just the tiniest bit lighter. "Who's the father?"

Cleo's ears pinked. "My accountant. I know what you're thinking," she rushed to add. "But he's sweet. Stable. I could use stability in my life." She tucked a strand of hair behind her ear, and the diamond on her finger flashed beneath the lights. "We got married last summer," Cleo explained when she saw Blake's questioning glance. "We moved to Austin after I got pregnant because my parents wanted me close, and they couldn't move to Georgia because of my dad's job, so here I am."

"That's great."

There was a beat of silence before they both issued awkward laughs.

"Man, this is crazy." Blake rubbed a hand over his face. "I'm glad to see you're doing well. I've...well, I've always wondered how you were doing."

Blood. Metal. Screams.

His ears rang with faded memories.

"I was in a dark place for a while," Cleo admitted. "I took some time off school too. There'll always be a part of me that—" She swallowed. "Anyway, losing a child is not something you ever get over, but I've found my peace." She searched his face. "And you? How are you?"

"I'm ok."

"Heard you're the king of the sports club world now." Her mouth tilted up in a small smile.

"Hardly," Blake said, even though he kind of was.

"Don't be humble. You never were good at it," she teased. Cleo fiddled with her shopping basket. "Listen, Blake. I've had a lot of time to think over these past few years, and there's something I need to tell you. Something I should've told you a long time ago."

Guilt flitted through her eyes, which didn't make sense. What did she have to be guilty about?

Blake had been the one behind the wheel. He'd been the one who'd insisted they drive to Cleo's place after he and his father had some ridiculous argument, even though it'd been storming so hard, you couldn't hear yourself over the rain. He'd swerved to avoid a deer, smashed into a tree, and killed both their son and relationship in one go.

He hadn't done it on purpose, but the guilt had weighed on his conscience every night since, especially when Blake remembered his prayer. He'd woken up at 3:00 a.m. one night before the accident, drenched with sweat at the thought of unexpectedly becoming a father at age twenty-two, and sent a silent missive to the heavens.

Please make this all go away.

A week later, the accident happened.

Blake hadn't been thinking miscarriage. He hadn't been thinking at all. He'd just been panicked and exhausted, and even though he wasn't a super religious person, he couldn't help but wonder if the accident had been god's way of punishing him for his shitty, selfish, off-the-cuff prayer.

"Can you meet me at our old place tonight?" Cleo glanced around. "I don't want to talk about it here."

Their old place—the playground they'd frequented as teenagers, back in the good old days when they were nothing more than friends. They used to stay up through the night, swinging on the swings and staring at the sky, musing about what their futures would look like.

Neither had expected things to turn out the way they did.

"Of course." Curiosity burned a hole in Blake's stomach. Before he could ask her for more information, the scent of Old Spice assaulted his senses.

Blake winced. He only knew one person who wore Old Spice.

"Blake Ryan." Daniel Bowden's scowl could've melted stone. "Didn't know you'd crawled back into town."

"Dad," Cleo hissed.

"Cleo, go meet your mother at the checkout counter."

"Dad, leave Blake alone. We just ran into each other."

"Now, Cleo!"

She gritted her teeth but did as he bid. Playground, eight o'clock, she mouthed behind Daniel's back.

Blake blinked his agreement.

Once Cleo was out of earshot, Daniel jabbed a finger at Blake's chest. To most people, he was an intimidating man—six feet four inches of corded muscle and fiery energy, all of which he aimed at his daughter's ex.

He'd liked Blake well enough when he'd dated Cleo. Hated him when he broke Cleo's heart. Fucking *loathed* him after the accident.

It'd been a rapid and ugly fall for the relationship between Blake and his ex-future-father-in-law, and if there was one thing Daniel Bowden was good at, it was holding grudges.

"Mr. Bowden—"

"Shut up," Daniel growled. "And stay away from my daughter. I don't want you talking to her. I don't want you even *looking* at her. You've hurt her enough. She's finally found someone who treats her right, and I will not let you screw that up."

"I wasn't plan—"

Daniel continued like Blake wasn't speaking, and his next words turned Blake's blood to ice.

"You've been toying with her emotions since you were old enough to vote, and I won't let you mess things up for her again. Because that's what you do. You screw up people's lives. The world sees a golden pretty boy, but I see you for what you really are: a black star, a heartbreaker, and a selfish bastard. You hurt everyone around you and, what's worse, you can't help yourself. It's just what you do."

The full moon hung round and heavy in the sky; in the distance, a dog howled, and the swings creaked in the quiet night, adding to the horror-movie atmosphere draped over the empty playground.

Empty except for Blake and Cleo, who sat side by side on the swings.

Their old teenage stomping grounds.

How simple life had been back then, when all they'd had to worry about was where to apply to college and who they were going to prom with.

"Forgive my dad," Cleo said. "I don't know what he said to you, but I can imagine. He's a little overprotective."

"I don't blame him." Blake threw her a lopsided smile like Daniel Bowden's words hadn't carved themselves into his heart with a sharp, poison-tipped pen.

It was never the lies that were lethal. No matter how scandalous or widespread, lies fell short of piercing the armor of righteousness because you knew—even if no one else did—that what your enemy was saying rang false. No, it was the dark truths that were most dangerous, the ones you couldn't admit to yourself until someone said them out loud for you. They forced you to face your demons, the ones you'd hoped would stay locked up forever. But once they were out, there was no putting them back.

They were there to haunt you for the rest of your life.

"He's gone overboard since…you know." Cleo's lashes swept down. "Thank god Peter—my husband—and I have our own place, or I'd go nuts. Anyway." She laughed nervously. "Enough about my dad. That's not why we're here." Guilt crept back into her eyes, along with a healthy dose of nerves. "Like I said, I have something I want to tell you."

"Me too."

She blinked. "What?"

"Before you say anything, I have something I need to tell you." Blake sucked in a breath. Oxygen filled his lungs, and he forced the words out before the air left his body. "What happened the night of the storm—"

Pain slashed across Cleo's face. "Blake, don't."

He pushed on. He had to say it and get it off his chest.

Otherwise, his guilt would crush him, inch by inch, until there was nothing left. "It was my fault. All of it. I know you said you don't blame me, but I prayed for something like that to happen. I mean, not a car accident, and certainly not for you to get hurt. But I asked for god to make it all go away and—" His throat constricted. "I'm sorry. I've been running all these years, avoiding you, because I couldn't face you. I couldn't face what I did. I'm the reason you miscarried. I killed our son."

A sob escaped Cleo's throat. She pressed her fist to her mouth and shook her head. "That's what I should've told you," she said, her voice wretched with agony. "He wasn't your son."

CHAPTER 31

SOMETHING WAS WRONG.

Unease dug into Farrah's bones, weighing her down until she sank beneath a tide of doubts and nerves.

Blake had returned from Texas a week ago. He'd texted her to cancel their date for the night after his return, and she hadn't heard a peep from him since.

Farrah tried to shrug it off, but she felt the depth of his absence to her core. She missed him—the sparkle in his eyes, the richness of his laugh, the heat of his touch.

If it were anyone else, the silence wouldn't be a big deal, but Blake never went MIA this long. At the very least, he would call or text her to say good night.

The last time he'd been this incommunicado had been in Shanghai...right before they broke up.

You're being paranoid.

Farrah nibbled on her cardboard-tasting pizza. Her taste buds must've taken the day off while her mind spun intricate stories of why she hadn't heard from Blake. Each story branched off into a new, more horrifying path until they formed a cobweb

of paranoia that choked off the possibility of dwelling on anything else.

She hated feeling this way again. Hated that it was because
of Blake—again. Last time, she'd made the mistake of waiting to
confront him and stewing in her own anxiety. She wasn't going
to do that this time.

"Do you want more wine?" Olivia raised their half-empty
bottle of sauvignon blanc.

Farrah shook her head. "All yours. You need it more than I do."

Olivia had a new manager at work, and she did not get along
with him—to put it mildly. She'd come home every day the past
week ranting about how incompetent, misogynistic, and sexist
he was—a rare slip of form for a woman who'd handled Wall
Street's old boys' club with admirable aplomb the past four years.
If Olivia lost her cool like this, that meant the new manager must
be a special form of horrible.

It had been Olivia's idea to de-stress with an outdoor movie,
so here they were, plunked on a blanket in the middle of Brooklyn
Bridge Park while Patrick Swayze and Jennifer Grey mamboed
their way across the screen. Grapes, cheese, wine, and a large
grease-stained pizza box separated the roommates, and the
Manhattan skyline—a cinematic masterpiece in and of itself—
glowed golden behind the projector.

"Thanks." Olivia filled her plastic cup to the brim. "Let me
know if you change your mind. Is Blake still pulling the Casper act?"

"He didn't ghost me." Farrah took another bite of pizza
before she gave up and tossed it into the empty box. She debated
texting Blake, but her past five messages had gone unanswered,
as had her phone calls. One more and she may as well register
herself in the national stalker database, if there was such a thing.
"Legends New York is opening in two weeks. He's busy."

That's what she told herself anyway.

She would've worried about Blake being sick or kidnapped or something had behind-the-scenes videos of him not been splashed all over the official Legends Instagram account in the run-up to LNY's opening.

He was alive and well and, apparently, avoiding her. But Farrah didn't want to jump to conclusions without knowing the full story, so she kept that theory to herself.

"You're probably right." Olivia dropped a grape into her mouth.

Farrah arched a surprised brow. Despite Blake and Olivia's truce, her friend still wasn't Blake's biggest fan. "I thought you hated Blake," she said.

"I don't *hate* him. Well, I hated him a little after he what he did to you," Olivia amended. "But we were friends once. Besides, people change, and he's crazy about you. I can tell by the way he looks at you."

Farrah's heart flipped. "You don't know that."

"I do, and I know the feeling's mutual. Don't deny it," Olivia said when Farrah opened her mouth to protest. "I was there when you fell for him the first time. I was also there for every guy you've dated since him. And there's only been one person who made you look at him like he hung the stars in the sky."

The ache in Farrah's chest had nothing to do with the cold, greasy pizza she ate earlier.

"I just got over him," she murmured. "Before he dropped back into my life."

"Bullshit." Olivia slammed her empty cup onto the blanket. "You've never fallen out of love with him. Your first love is like a tidal wave. Your head can break above the water, and you might even make it to shore, but the slightest nudge and you're in the deep again. Now, that's not true for all people, but it is for you and Blake. You are each other's oceans."

If that were true, the waters were rocky as hell. They crashed against the edges of Farrah's confidence, chipping at it, eroding it, until she floated adrift in a sea of uncertainty. Was she making too big a deal out of Blake's silence, or did she have every right to worry?

"Liv, the poet." Farrah threw a grape at her friend in an attempt to dispel the heavy emotions Olivia's observations stirred up. "You should get an MFA instead of an MBA."

It worked. The conversation about Blake ground to a halt as Olivia snorted and tossed a grape back. "Ha! No way. I don't do lovey-dovey literature. That's why I read erotica. They gloss over all the bullshit and focus on the good part: the sex."

"Hmm." A teasing smile tugged at Farrah's lips. "I remember a time when you were very much in love."

"You better not be talking about Sammy." Olivia poured herself another cup of wine and chugged it. "That turned out to be a disaster."

Farrah's smile widened. "I didn't mention Sammy. You did. You should stop by to see him, you know. His pop-up is crazy popular, but he'll make time for you."

Olivia's eyes narrowed into slits.

Luckily, someone interrupted them before she could strangle Farrah.

"Farrah?"

The throaty, familiar voice slid through the humid summer air, followed by a cloud of Chanel No. 5.

Farrah's eyes grew to the size of saucers when she saw Jane, her old supervisor at KBI, picking her way through the crowd toward her.

She scrambled to her feet. "Jane! What are you doing here?"

"Same as you. I can't resist me some Swayze, though it appears I missed half the movie. I just got here and saw you, figured I'd say hi. It's been a while." Jane surveyed Farrah. "How are you doing? Where are you working these days?"

Jane couldn't know about Kelly blackballing Farrah. Kelly was subtle about her sabotage. She planted her rumors in a few key ears and let them spread the gossip for her. Plus, Jane viewed Kelly the same way Farrah used to: as a sometimes-ruthless industry icon whose talent outweighed her shortcomings.

There was also zero chance Jane knew about Kelly and Matt's relationship, or she wouldn't be so calm. If there was one thing Jane despised, it was office romances, especially between a higher-up and their subordinate.

"I'm giving the consultant route a try," Farrah said. There was no point in spilling Kelly's dirty secrets. Even if Jane believed her, it wouldn't do anything except stir up drama.

"Oh." Jane's brow creased. "Any chance you'll come back to KBI? We miss you and you were—are—an excellent designer."

Yeah, if I want Kelly or Matt to poison my coffee on my first day back.

"I don't think so. I appreciate the offer though." Farrah smiled. Jane had been a mentor to her since she was an intern, and she missed the other woman's advice and humor. "We should get coffee one day. No work talk."

Jane beamed. "I'd love to."

Farrah introduced her to Olivia, and they chatted for another minute before Jane returned to her friends, and Farrah sank back onto the ground. Good thing she and Olivia were sitting at the back of the crowd, or she would've gotten pelted with popcorn for blocking other moviegoers' view of Johnny and Baby's final dance.

"She seems nice," Olivia said. "Too bad she's not the top dog at KBI."

"Yeah." Farrah fiddled with her skirt.

When she first quit KBI, she'd been intent on joining another firm. She liked having a stable paycheck, and she still had so much to learn about the industry. But after Blake's and Yuliya's projects, she realized how nice it felt to set her own hours and have full creative control over her vision (except for the client's input). Sure, the business side of things gave her a major headache—taxes and bookkeeping were the work of the devil—but she was doing pretty well for herself, all things considered. Yuliya had even recommended her to one of her magazine editor friends, and Farrah was in the midst of closing the deal.

So why didn't she go all- in on the independent route? What was she afraid of?

Whatever your fear is or however far you fall—you'll survive. And I'll be there to catch you.

Here was the crazy part: Farrah believed Blake.

Even though he hadn't contacted her in a week. Even if her brain swarmed with conspiracy theories about his absence.

She didn't know how or when it happened, but she trusted him. Not only about what she was capable of, but about…everything. Blake was dangerous, as any person who had the power to break you was, but he was also her safety net. The person she turned to when she needed comfort and support.

Maybe it was the sincerity in his eyes when he promised he'd do anything to help her after they ran into Kelly and Matt. Maybe it was the way he pushed her to be a better, stronger version of herself. Or maybe it was just him—the way he filled her soul and made her belicve in love, in fate, and in destiny, not only as abstract concepts but as something real. Tangible.

Whatever it was, Blake had, once again, breached her defenses. She should've known it was only a matter of time—once Blake Ryan set his sights on something, he didn't stop until he got it.

And he got her.

Hook, line, and sinker.

CHAPTER 32

FARRAH WENT TO SEE BLAKE THE NEXT DAY.

She was tired of waiting for him to reach out, and she needed clarity before her paranoia drove her crazy. It didn't help that she was still reeling from her realization of how easily he'd burrowed himself inside her heart a second time.

Then again, he'd never left.

But when Blake swung open his door, Farrah wondered if she'd made the wrong decision.

Because the man standing in front of her? She didn't recognize him.

He had the same golden hair, crystal eyes, and sculpted muscles, but his playful, cocky smile was missing in action, and he surveyed her like she was a stranger.

Blake, normal Blake, never looked at her like that.

Don't jump to conclusions.

"Hey." Farrah flashed an easy smile even as her heart thumped in warning. "Haven't heard from you in a while so thought I'd swing by."

"Sorry." He stepped aside to let her in. "I've been busy."

"I figured."

The smell of booze assaulted her the instant she walked into the apartment. Farrah wrinkled her nose. What the—

Her eyes widened when she saw the pile of empty beer and whiskey bottles on the kitchen counter. She whipped her head toward Blake, who watched her reaction with curious apathy.

He didn't appear drunk. No slurring of the words, no unsteadiness on his feet, no redness in his face. Then again, Blake was the type who could be hammered and you wouldn't know it unless he threw up or passed out.

"What's going on?" The unease in her stomach spread. "Is everything ok?"

Blake had been fine when he left for Texas. Something must've happened, either with his bar or his family. He didn't have a great relationship with his father.

Something flickered in his eyes. "I'm fine, but I'd rather be alone. It's a whiskey-and-me kinda night. No intruders allowed."

His cool, dry delivery made his words sting even more.

"You'll drink yourself to death."

Blake shrugged.

Frustration curled in her gut. "What happened in Texas?"

"What makes you think something happened in Texas?"

"You left as your normal self and you came back—" Farrah stopped before she said something that'd put him on the defensive. "Is it your dad? Did he say something?"

"It's not my fucking dad." Blake's eyes sparked. Finally, a hint of life. "He's the least of my problems."

"Then what is it?" she asked softly.

"None of your business." His jaw clenched. "I mean it. Leave now."

Her chin angled at a stubborn tilt. "Not until you tell me what's wrong."

"Dammit, Farrah." Frustration leaked into Blake's voice and broke his icy facade. "Stop being so stubborn. This is for your own good."

Indignation sparked in her chest. "Then stop treating me like a child. Tell me what's going on and let me decide for myself. I'm a grown woman. I can decide what's good for me or not."

"Fine. You want to know what happened in Texas?" Blake closed the distance between them, and Farrah gulped at the sheer pain radiating from him. She wanted to grab him, press him tight to her chest, and never let go—not until that pain disappeared. "I realized you were smart not to trust me." He brushed his thumb over her bottom lip. "You never should've accepted my job offer, even though I insisted. You should've taken one look at me that day at the Aviary and walked the hell away."

A vise wrapped around her throat and squeezed. This conversation wouldn't end well. Farrah could feel it in her bones. But there was no way to go but forward, even if it meant falling off the cliff. "Why?"

"Because I'm not a good person. I'm a selfish bastard, Farrah, and when I want something, I'll stop at nothing to get it." Blake's eyes brewed with regret. "I wanted you, more than anything, and I pursued you, even though I knew I didn't deserve you. Even though I knew I'd hurt you one day. So this is your chance to leave before that happens."

Too late. He was already hurting her, slicing her open piece by piece. With his words, with his bitterness, with his belief that he wasn't good enough.

This was the part of Blake most people didn't see. On the surface, he was confident and self-assured, but underneath the polished veneer lived a boy filled with doubts and insecurities, who was afraid he'd never be able to live up to the expectations the world had of him.

Farrah loved both parts equally—if he would let her.

"You're a good person to me," she whispered.

"For now." Blake rested his forehead against hers, his face taut with torment. "You don't know the thoughts that run through my head. The things I've done. I always end up hurting the people I love, and the scary part is, I almost never do it on purpose. It just happens. Walk away from me now, Farrah, before you're in too deep, and I break your heart again."

The backs of Farrah's eyes burned. "You say I don't know the thoughts that run through your head? Tell me. You say I don't know the things you've done? Show me. Let me in, Blake. Don't push me away."

A frustrated groan rose in his throat.

Blake wrenched away; his warmth disappeared, and merciless cold rushed to fill the void. Its icy needles stabbed at Farrah's skin until they pierced all the way to her heart.

"I can't." The emotionless mask was back.

"You said you loved me." Farrah gave it one last shot. "You were the one who asked for a second chance—and I gave you one. You said you'd changed, and I believed you. You want me to trust you again but how can I do that when you yourself don't trust me enough to let me in?" Her gaze drilled into Blake's, willing him to back down, to open up, to do anything except stare at her with those vacant eyes. "Blake, it's *me*. You can tell me anything."

The seconds ticked by.

Farrah's breath stuck halfway down her throat, unsure where to go given the apprehension gathering in the air.

"I do love you." Blake's voice cracked. "That's why I'm letting you go."

The breath released as a sob.

Stupid. Stupid. Stupid.

She should've known better, but she did it anyway.

Farrah had fallen in love with Blake, again. And he broke her heart, again.

This time, it wasn't because of his cruel words and heartless dismissal. She believed him when he said he loved her and when he said he thought she deserved better.

No, what hurt was knowing Blake's love wasn't enough. It wasn't enough for him to let her in, and it wasn't enough for him to fight for her. He loved her, yet here he was, letting her go.

He thought it was noble? She thought he was a fucking coward.

Blake was taking the easy way out instead of allowing Farrah to see the darkness within him. Even though she *wanted* to see it. Darkness didn't scare her. A part of her reveled in it because it was only under the cloak of darkness that people dared show their true selves. Everything—the good, bad, and ugly—came out at night. But contrary to popular belief, those ugly parts didn't detract from a person. No, they made them whole, and there was nothing in this world more beautiful than completeness, nothing more breathtaking than knowing someone loved every last bit of you—including the pieces you hated about yourself.

If the sun never sets, the stars will never shine.

But Farrah would never be able to show Blake the beauty of darkness. He wanted all of her but refused to give her all of him, and she could tell by the stubborn set in his jaw and the flintiness in his eyes that there was nothing she could say that would make him change his mind.

If she told him she loved him, that would only make him retreat further.

Something else brewed in her gut next to the hurt: anger.

"That's your final answer, then?" Farrah's voice was lava, hot with fury until it cooled and hardened with a thick hard crust. "You're letting me go because you quote-unquote 'don't want to hurt me'? Without even telling me what brought this all on? Without even trying to make it work?"

Blake didn't answer. Other than a convulsion of his throat, he just stood there like a beautiful, emotionless statue, carved out of marble and cold to the touch.

There was nothing left to say.

Farrah stepped around him and twisted the doorknob.

Stop me.

The hallway's plush carpet muffled the sound of her footsteps as she walked toward the elevator.

Trust me.

She pressed the down button, her eyes burning so wildly, the flames engulfed her entire body, and she tasted ashes in her mouth.

Fight for me.

But Blake never did.

CHAPTER 33

THE NEXT MONTH BLED BY IN A STRING OF MISERABLE mornings and starless nights.

Blake tracked the passing of time not with a calendar but with the shards of his heart. One day, one piece added to the world's most fucked-up hourglass, until he had nothing left to give.

His life had fallen apart yet again, and without Farrah's light, all that seeped through the cracks was an ugly, dark ooze. It contained everything Blake hated about himself—his deepest fears, his worst memories, his most selfish acts and shameful thoughts.

When he'd returned from Texas, he'd had two choices: tell Farrah the truth about Cleo's pregnancy, including the fact that he'd never actually cheated on her, or let her go.

The first was the one he'd been so tempted to take. But it was also the selfish choice because even if Blake hadn't cheated on Farrah, he'd never deserved her in the first place.

Plus, Cleo's father had been right. Blake did screw up people's lives. He hurt the people he loved, even when he didn't want to.

His mom. His sister. Farrah. Cleo. Even his dad, if his dad could hurt.

If Blake stayed with Farrah, he'd hurt her again. It was inevitable, his curse.

So he'd let her go—even if it meant losing himself in the process.

"Hey, man. Congrats on the opening." Landon strode up to Blake, dressed in a black Hugo Boss jacket and jeans. The dress code for LNY's opening night was dressy casual, and the guests had followed it to a tee. "This party is killer."

"Thanks." Blake slapped on a smile because that was what everyone expected from him. There was no room for darkness tonight, only the lights that blazed throughout the bar and the stars in attendance. Socialites, celebrities, and business moguls alike drifted through Legends, and judging by their laughs and chatter, LNY was a massive hit—three stories of entertainment and escape that had already generated so much buzz, they couldn't keep up with the media requests.

The first floor was classic Legends: a sports bar swathed in the same upscale, down-home decor that made the brand such a hit in other cities. Antler chandeliers swayed over oak tables with leather booths, and huge flat-screen TVs lined the paneled walls, broadcasting every type of competitive sports game you could think of. The gigantic projection screen and eight rows of stadium-style seating in the corner were reserved for the biggest sports events: NBA playoffs, the Super Bowl, the World Cup, and the Olympics.

If someone would rather play than watch games, they could immerse themselves in the rec room heaven that was the second floor, which boasted pool tables, Ping-Pong tables, dartboards, air hockey, foosball, beer pong, shuffleboard, board games, and even a miniature bowling alley.

The third floor was a step up—literally and figuratively—in terms of luxury, featuring a craft cocktail bar that morphed into a nightclub after 11:00 p.m. It boasted the hottest DJs, the best alcohol, and a fifteen-foot-tall champagne tower.

LNY was everything Blake had dreamed of. It marked the transition of Legends from your typical sports bar chain to a sports bar *and* nightlife franchise that took the company and brand to a whole other level.

Tonight was the VIP opening; tomorrow was the grand public opening, and it'd be even bigger. But Blake couldn't summon the rush he usually got when he saw his visions come to life.

Instead, all he could focus on was Cleo's voice, echoing in his head in a nightmare.

"We never had sex. You were wasted, and I brought you to one of the hotel suites to sleep it off. But I was too drunk to drive home myself and all the other rooms were full, so I stayed the night. We didn't do anything. But you didn't remember what happened when you woke up, and I was so angry with you I lied.

"You were one of my oldest friends. I'd been in love with you since we were fifteen, and you broke my heart. You ran off to Shanghai and left me behind. You humiliated me! To make matters worse, you went and fell in love with some girl you'd known for only a few months. You picked her over me. Me. The person who's been there for you your entire life. I waited for you. I waited and waited, until you were finally there, and you did the most unforgivable thing you could've done: you gave me hope.

"You never should've dated me, Blake. I would've gotten over you eventually. But you brought me flowers, and you kissed me, and you told me you loved me. You made me fall so hard for you, I couldn't get up, and then you left me there. Alone. That's why I was angry at you. Even if I said I was ok with us being just friends, I wasn't. But it was the only way I could keep you in my life, so I lied."

Blood rushed in Blake's ears. A familiar cocktail of emotions oozed through his veins—fury, guilt, shame, shock, remorse. All present and accounted for, like perfect students that never missed a class or an opportunity to torture him.

"You ok?" Landon's brow furrowed with concern. "You've been acting strange since you returned from Texas."

"I'm fine." Blake sucked down the rest of his whiskey and grinned his thanks at a TV actress who congratulated him as she passed by. "Just tired."

He should've been an actor. He could give Nate Reynolds a run for his money.

"I went to a bar that night. I was still so pissed at you, and seeing you... Anyway, I had too much to drink again, and I slept with a guy I met at the bar. I don't remember if we used protection—I wasn't on the pill anymore—but a few months later, I found out I was pregnant." Cleo's lower lip trembled. *"It had to be his. He was the only person I slept with after you left for Shanghai. But I didn't even know his name, and I couldn't tell my parents that. It's bad enough I had sex before marriage. If they found out I had a one-night stand and got pregnant by some guy I didn't know, they would disown me."*

Blake's hands tightened around his empty glass.

He wanted to hate Cleo. He had hated her for the rest of that weekend, when the tension from his outburst at his father's party hung heavy in the Ryan household and he'd retreated into his thoughts instead of dealing with the fallout. He'd had to mourn his son all over again, only this time, he'd been mourning the loss of what he thought had been his. Something he'd held as truth, that had defined his life for half a decade, upended in minutes.

Would Cleo have told Blake the truth had the baby been born? Did it matter?

"You made sense. At least we knew each other. We grew up together, and we dated. Everyone thought we'd end up together

anyway." Tears tracked down Cleo's face. *"I'm so sorry. I was young and stupid and panicked. The secret has been tearing me apart for the past five years, but I had no idea how to tell you. It didn't seem right to do this over the phone, or that was the excuse I gave myself. But when I ran into you earlier today, I saw that as a sign.*

"I hope you can forgive me one day, and that we can have closure. I said it before and I'll say it again—I don't blame you for my miscarriage. It devastated me—us—but it wasn't your fault. It was an accident. This isn't to guilt you into forgiving me, but hopefully, it'll give you the peace you need. We've both been through so much. I think it's time we finally let go of our past and move on."

As much as Blake wanted to continue hating Cleo, he couldn't. Partly because they'd both been at fault—him with the accident, her with the deceit—and partly because he'd been relieved. The scales had evened a bit (though it still tipped heavier on his side), and he hadn't cheated on Farrah. It may have seemed like a small detail in the grand scheme of things, but not to him.

But Farrah would never know because his need to save her from him outweighed his relief.

"Where's Farrah?" It was like Landon read his mind, except he didn't know about Blake and Farrah's split or what happened in Texas. Blake had been too busy and too miserable to hash out the details with his best friend or anyone else. "I haven't seen her all night."

"She couldn't make it." Blake's smile hurt. That was the thing about fakeness—it made everyone around you feel better but ate at you on the inside.

"She ok?" Landon's worried expression didn't budge. "She wouldn't miss a big night like this."

No, she wouldn't.

Not unless Blake forced her to.

"As far as I know." Blake was dying for another drink.

He'd done the right thing, letting Farrah go before she got in too deep with him again. It didn't matter that it destroyed him to do so; all that mattered was doing the unselfish thing for once.

"Is it just me, or is it really fucking hot in here?" Sweat beaded on Blake's forehead. The air thickened, choking him. He needed to get out of here, but it was his party. He couldn't leave.

His head pounded in rhythm with his pulse.

Thud. Thud. Thud.

"There are a ton of people here." The concern on Landon's face escalated. "Maybe you should—" He stopped short. "Whoa. Is that who I think it is?"

"Yeah, Pat spoke to her publicist, and she agreed to—"

"No, it's not a celebrity. Blake. Look." Landon's eyes gleamed with a strange excitement.

Blake looked.

And looked again.

His jaw dropped.

What the hell were they doing here?

"Blake!" Joy waved at him and pushed her way through the crowd, channeling Tinker Bell with her green dress and blonde waves. "Surprise!"

Behind her trailed Blake's mother, looking starstruck by all the celebrities surrounding her, and a man Blake never thought he'd see step foot in one of his bars: Joe Ryan. His father.

CHAPTER 34

HE'D ENTERED THE TWILIGHT ZONE.

That was the only explanation Blake could come up with for his current predicament: sitting in his office at LNY on opening night, across the desk from his father.

His father. Here. In New York. Wearing a suit of all things.

Joe never wore a suit unless he was going to a funeral.

Maybe this was Blake's funeral, come too little, too late. He'd already been in hell for the past month.

"Quite a party you got out there." Joe looked wildly uncomfortable in his formal outfit. No doubt Blake's mom put him up to this. His father would never wear a tie of his own volition.

Blake steepled his fingers beneath his chin. He hadn't spoken to his father since their argument on Joe's birthday. "What the hell are you doing here?"

Perhaps not the nicest way to start things off, but his patience ran a short fuse these days.

Joe's eyes sharpened. "Watch your tone."

"Or what? You'll send me to time-out?" Blake leaned forward and planted his hands flat on his desk. "I'm a grown-ass man, Dad. I have my own business and my own money. You don't scare me anymore. *You can't tell me what to do.*"

"Did I come in here telling you what to do?" Joe roared. "You think you'd be more goddamned grateful, considering your mother, sister, and I flew all the way out here for your big night. You know I hate airplanes!"

"One night out of how many? A dozen?" Blake sneered. "I've invited you to every opening, and this is the first one you've ever attended. You didn't even show up for the Austin celebration, and that was right in your goddamned city, so excuse me if I'm not falling all over myself because you're here."

His ugliness boiled to the surface, grateful for a target to take itself out on.

Hell, Blake's personal life was already in shambles. He might as well continue the trend and take a match to his already-frayed relationship with his father.

Watch everything burn and get all the agony out of the way in one fell swoop.

"I can't talk to you when you're like this." Joe stood and loosened his tie with sharp, angry jerks. "I don't care what your mother says."

A glint on his wrist caught Blake's eye. "What is that?"

His father glowered at him. "What's what?"

Blake jutted his chin toward the item that had captured his attention. He'd asked a silly question because he knew what it was. It was a gold Patek Philippe timepiece with a brown alligator strap and the number 50 custom-engraved on the back of its case.

Blake knew because he'd bought it for his father's fiftieth birthday.

Discomfort filled Joe's face. "It's a watch."

"It's the watch I gave you for your fiftieth. You're wearing it."

"Of course I'm wearing it," Joe snapped. "It's a watch. What else am I supposed to do, eat it?"

"You've never used any of the presents I've gotten you in the past."

The golf clubs Blake had bought for Joe's forty-eighth birthday, collecting dust.

The rare whiskey he'd bought for his forty-sixth birthday, unopened.

The birthday cards he drew when he'd been too young to buy presents, tossed.

"How would you know? You don't come home often enough to know what the hell I use."

Blake's nostrils flared. "Don't try to guilt-trip me. That bottle of whiskey was still unopened last time I checked, and I was home two months ago. Four *years* after I gifted it to you."

"It's a nice whiskey. I'm saving it for a special occasion."

"The golf clubs?"

"I used them until Rick moved away. He's the only one of my friends who played." Joe scowled. "Why the hell are we talking about this?"

"Because." Blake curled his thumbs around the edge of his desk. The smooth oak seared into his skin until he was sure he could see the wood grains etched across his fingers if he released them. "Nothing I give or do is good enough for you."

Shock glittered in Joe's eyes. He stopped fussing with his tie and collapsed into his seat again. "Is that what you think? That you're not good enough?"

"You've never given me any indication otherwise," Blake said bitterly. "The only thing I'm good at is football, remember?"

His father's reaction when he'd told him he wanted to start a sports bar all those years ago had burned itself into its memories. *You know nothing about running a business. A sports bar?*

C'mon. There are a million sports bars out there. Take it from someone who's been around a lot longer than you have, Son: stick to what you're good at. You're good at football. That's it.

Joe grimaced.

"I guess only being an NFL superstar is good enough for you. All this"—Blake swept his arm around his large office—"doesn't mean shit. You will always hate me for not living out the dreams you couldn't live yourself."

Joe had played college ball too, until a torn ACL forced him to quit before he could go pro. He'd turned to fitness coaching as a consolation career, but from the moment Blake threw his first perfect spiral at age seven, he'd piled expectation upon expectation on his son until Blake buckled beneath the weight. Joe relived his glory through Blake until it came time for the thing he wanted most: the NFL. Blake quit before the draft and squashed his father's dreams of a pro-football career by proxy.

"I don't hate you," Joe bit out. "You're my son."

"Only by blood." Blake flashed a sardonic smile. "You could barely stand to look at me. Not even on your fiftieth birthday."

"It's because I'm ashamed, ok?" Joe exploded. "That's why I can't look you in the eye!"

Had Blake not been sitting, he would've tumbled to the floor. Shock swelled in his throat, cutting off his air supply.

Joe's mouth flattened into a grim line. "I'll admit, I was pissed when you quit football. You were a unique talent, Blake. One in a million. I thought you were throwing your future away for a pipe dream. I didn't hate you for it; I was worried about you. Figured you needed some tough love to help you pull your head out of your ass before you were stuck, miserable, and in debt." His lips twisted into a wry smile. "Luckily, you proved me wrong. But when you invited me to the opening…" He tapped his fingers on his thigh, looking uncharacteristically nervous. "It seemed wrong to celebrate and act the role of proud father when I had been such a...well, less than stellar one. I'd tried to hold you back every step of the way, and you succeeded despite me, not because of me. I didn't want to leech off your success—not when I had nothing to do with it. So I stayed away. It's not because I hate you. You're my son. I could never hate you."

Blake couldn't have been more stunned had Joe ripped off his face to reveal one of those squid-like alien heads from *Independence Day*. Every interaction he'd had with his father over the past five years—and there hadn't been many—flashed through his mind. Part of him resisted Joe's explanation. It was easy to resent Joe because that was all Blake knew. They hadn't had a "normal" father-son relationship since Blake thought girls carried cooties.

Yet Blake could tell by the look in his father's eyes that he was telling the truth. He also knew how much it must've cost him to utter those words out loud. Joe Ryan was a proud man, and he didn't admit to his faults often, if ever. His logic may be twisted and fucked up, but it made sense—to him.

"Then why are you here now? What changed?" Blake eyed the bottle of scotch on his shelf longingly. He could use a stiff drink, if only so he didn't pass out from shock. There were few things as disorienting as having what you'd always considered a truth be flipped upside down.

First Cleo, now my dad. That's twice in one month. I'm setting a damned record.

Joe scratched his chin with an awkward frown. "I thought about what you said at my party. About me being a shitty father."

Guilt twisted in Blake's gut. "I didn't mean to blow up on you on your birthday."

"Seemed like it was a long time coming," Joe said dryly. "Ya know, I honestly didn't think it would bother you that I told Pete to host the kickoff at his house instead of Legends. It's what we've always done. But I guess I'm not the best at sussing that sort of stuff out." Another scratch of his chin. "I admit I haven't been... the best father over the years. I wanted to skip New York too, ya know. Wanted to keep avoiding the issue. But your mother and sister blew up at me. They took your side."

His mom went against his dad? The shockers kept coming.

"Anyway." The discomfort returned to Joe's face. "I figured it was time I stopped running and had a talk with you. Man to man. And I know this is the biggest opening you've had so far. You did a good job," he added gruffly. "A really good job. I'm proud of you."

I'm proud of you.

Blake had waited his whole life to hear those words come out of his father's mouth. Now that they had, his brain nearly exploded trying to comprehend them. Joe might as well have been reciting *Ulysses* in Latin.

A strange warmth dripped from Blake's heart to his stomach, where it pooled into a puddle of pride and disbelief.

"It wasn't all me." Blake cleared his throat. "My team did a fantastic job."

While he oversaw the strategy and vision, his team members were the ones who'd turned his vision into reality. They were the bedrock of Legends, and Blake treated them as such. He'd be nowhere without his team.

"That they did. Well, good talk. I'm going to head downstairs." Joe stood. He'd clearly reached his bonding limit for the night. "Lord knows your mother and sister get into all sorts of trouble when they're around margaritas."

Last Blake saw, Helen and Joy had been busy gawking at Zane, a famous male model and LNY's celebrity bartender of the night.

"Wait."

His father froze.

Blake licked his lips. "I got a new bottle of scotch yesterday." He tilted his head toward said bottle on the shelf. "Straight from Scotland. Want to try it with me?"

The olive branch stretched between them, taut with hesitation.

Joe's eyes traveled between the scotch and Blake's face. He settled into his chair again with a shadow of a smile. "I'd love to."

CHAPTER 35

"I CAN'T BELIEVE IT'S MIDNIGHT." FARRAH STIFLED A yawn. "At the risk of sounding like a grandma, the last time I stayed out this late was…"

With Blake.

She winced.

Farrah had done a damn good job of pushing Blake into the darkest corner of her mind, and she wasn't going to unravel that progress now. Not when she was on a date with another man.

"I don't remember," she mumbled.

Paul's eyes crinkled into a smile as he threaded his fingers through hers. "I'm honored you broke your late-night rule for me."

"It's not so much a rule as a coincidence," Farrah decided. "I coincidentally fall asleep around ten every night."

He laughed. "Regardless, I'm happy we stayed up. I had a great time."

Paul's sweetness killed her. They were on their third date. She'd met him on a dating app Olivia forced her to download to "get her mind off Blake," and he seemed like the perfect man—handsome, kind, and smart, the type who would never break her heart. But as much as Farrah enjoyed hanging out with him, their chemistry was more tepid than a two-day-old cup of coffee. When they kissed, she felt nothing. No fireworks, no butterflies, no racing pulse.

"Do you want to grab something to eat?" Paul asked. "There's a twenty-four-hour diner around here that's supposed to be good."

Farrah's exhaustion battled with her hunger.

Hunger won.

"Okay." Nothing eased her worries like a good burger and milkshake.

As they ambled down the sidewalk, Farrah's mind ran a mile a minute, trying to figure out her next move.

Should she break up with Paul or continue to wait, hoping she'd develop stronger feelings over time? They weren't *dating* dating, per se, but they weren't not dating either. She didn't want to string him along and prevent him from meeting someone else who could give him the love and attention he deserved.

But Farrah's selfish side feared what would happen if she let Paul go. It would open up a void in her life, and here was the thing about voids: they must be filled. Good, bad, it didn't matter, as long as there was something there to appease it.

Farrah had a sinking feeling she knew what would fill that void post-Paul, and she wasn't ready to face it. Not yet.

I'm a terrible person.

"Oh, wow." Paul sounded awed. "Is that who I think it is?"

Farrah followed his gaze and saw the so-hot-it-should-be-illegal male model Zane stumbling into a taxi with a pixie-faced actress known for playing quirky, offbeat characters in indie movies. But that wasn't what caught her attention.

No, it was the name of the bar they were stumbling out of: Legends.

Blake's bar.

She'd known Legends was near the venue where she and Paul caught a late-night stand-up comedy show, but the sight still threw her for a loop. The building might as well have Blake's face stamped on it, smirking down at her.

Farrah tightened her grip on Paul's hand. Tonight was Legends' opening party. She'd read all about it in the latest issue of *City Style*, which ran a multipage feature on Blake, his business, and his lifestyle as a handsome, successful bachelor in New York City.

She'd been ashamed to find herself leafing through Blake's feature at night, after Olivia had gone to bed, her heart aching at the sight of his smile and confident, relaxed posture. At least, that was what most people saw. Farrah noticed the touch of tenseness in his shoulders and the fact that his smile didn't quite reach his eyes.

For all his success, Blake was hurting.

It's none of my business.

If Blake wanted to run and suffer alone, far be it from Farrah to stop him.

"C'mon, let's go." She tugged on Paul's hand. "I'm starving."

They made it five steps before a deep, familiar voice stopped them in their tracks. "Farrah."

Her name drifted through the air, whispered with the reverence of one who had seen the ghost of a loved one.

Farrah was tempted to keep walking, but Paul gave her a gentle nudge. "I think he's talking to you."

Coincidence, you're a bitch. You know that?

Farrah steeled herself and turned around. All the breath rushed out of her lungs when she saw Blake standing there, looking so earth-shatteringly gorgeous she wished she had paints and a canvas so she could immortalize him for all eternity.

Blake wore a pair of dark blue jeans, a tailored black blazer, and a crisp white dress shirt that showed off his broad shoulders and trim waist. His tousled blond hair shone beneath the lights like a halo, but his eyes were pure sin: pools of blue crystalline that entranced you, sucking you under their spell without you realizing until it was too late.

He was a god descended from the heavens, Apollo made flesh, and no matter how much time had passed, Farrah's body reacted the same way it always did: whimpering, purring, straining, like a needy animal desperate to return to its owner.

Her mind, thankfully, shut it down before her knees turned to jelly and she collapsed on the sidewalk in a pool of lust and heartbreak.

"Hello." Her cold, formal tone displayed zero emotion. Farrah silently congratulated herself on the feat. "Fancy seeing you here."

"This is my bar," Blake drawled. His gaze flicked to her and Paul's entwined hands; a muscle ticked in his jaw. "You didn't attend the opening party."

He'd invited her months ago, before everything fell apart, along with Olivia and Sammy. Farrah didn't go tonight, so Olivia didn't either. Sammy took a quick trip to San Francisco to check up on his bakery there, according to Olivia, who shut down when Farrah asked her how she knew Sammy's whereabouts.

"I had something else to do." Farrah took perverse pleasure in the storm brewing in Blake's eyes. They weren't crystalline anymore; they were sapphire, dark and furious. Still beautiful but blazing with a raw, hot jealousy that sent shivers of triumph down her spine.

The dark part of her—the petty, vindictive part—wanted to break him the way he broke her. She wanted him to see what he was missing and drown in regret.

"I had a date with Paul." She inclined her head toward the

man next to her, who looked mighty uncomfortable. Farrah didn't blame him. The tension in the air was so thick, you could snap it in half. "I don't believe you've met. Paul, this is Blake, one of my old design clients. Blake, this is Paul, my boyfriend."

Paul wasn't her boyfriend—they'd only been on three dates—and she could feel him shift in surprise. He didn't correct her, though, bless his heart.

Guilt swirled in her gut at using him like this, but she'd deal with that later. Right now, Farrah could only focus on the displeasure radiating from Blake in waves, both at her clinical description of their relationship—*old design client*—and the word "boyfriend."

Like he had any right to be upset. He was the one who'd pushed her away without warning because she "deserved better." Well, here she was, deserving better.

Take that.

Yes, she was being childish. No, she didn't care.

"Nice to meet you." Paul released her hand to shake Blake's with an affable smile. "Blake Ryan, right? I read about you the other day. Congrats on your bar."

"Thank you." Blake bared his teeth in a smile. He grabbed Paul's hand so tight the other man flinched, but Blake kept his focus on Farrah.

"Guess who's inside right now?" His voice dropped an octave to soft and intimate, and her skin warmed in response. "My father. He came."

Surprise rushed through her. "I'm happy to hear that."

Farrah really was. She wanted Blake to find peace with his father. What she didn't want was for her heart to go all crazy on her, like it was doing right now.

"How do you know each other?" Paul's voice cut between them, and Farrah yanked her gaze away from Blake's.

She'd forgotten Paul was there.

The darkness returned to Blake's expression. "We used to date." He maintained his crushing grip on Paul's hand.

Paul's face reddened, and Farrah glared at Blake. He smirked in return.

"So how long have you two been dating?" he asked conversationally. The soft intimacy was gone, replaced by silk-covered steel.

"A month." This time, Farrah was the one who smirked when Blake's eye twitched at the implied meaning behind her words.

It took me no time to move on.

Not true, and she went on her first date with Paul two weeks ago. But Blake didn't need to know that. Besides, if you rounded up, fifteen days counted as a month.

"Good for you. It takes most people longer than that to find a decent rebound." Icicles hung from Blake's barb.

Paul finally yanked his hand away.

The sudden anger in Farrah's stomach skipped the simmering stage and went straight to full-on boiling. "There was no one to rebound from."

Blake's eyes sparked with challenge. "No? It didn't seem that way when you were moaning my name every night."

Thwack!

Pain blossomed in her palm.

Farrah stared at her hand, then at Blake's face, where a bright red palm print marred his perfect cheek.

His chest heaved; his jaw clenched so tight, she could hear his molars scream in protest. Other than that, no reaction to her slap.

It was the first time she'd slapped someone in her life.

"What the fuck!" Paul shoved Blake's chest. "What the hell is wrong with you?"

Paul never cursed.

Looked like tonight was bringing out the best in all of them.

"Paul, let's go." Farrah was tired, so tired she couldn't stand straight. "He's not worth it."

After a second's hesitation, Paul released Blake with a scowl. Blake didn't retaliate. He just stared at the other man blankly, like he wasn't sure how they got there.

Farrah and Paul left him standing there beneath the bright lights of his bar, a lonely king in front of his empire.

Once they were out of Blake's presence, the vindictiveness that'd sunk its claws into Farrah's skin melted away, replaced by shame.

"Paul—"

"Don't." Paul walked on the far side of the sidewalk, like he couldn't stand to be too close to her. "Let's talk after we've both had some rest."

They both knew how the talk was going to go.

Even though Farrah had debated ending things with Paul herself, she hated how this all happened. Paul was a sweet guy who did nothing wrong. He deserved better than to feel like a cheap rebound.

She stared at the ground, angry tears searing her eyes.

Once again, Blake Ryan had to ruin everything.

CHAPTER 36

"HE SHOOTS, ANNNND HE SCORES!" JUSTIN CROWED. He made a throwing motion with his hands as the ball swished through the net, breaking the tie and bringing his and Sammy's score up by two points. "Good job, man." He slapped hands with Sammy and grinned at Blake. "You're off your game today, Ryan."

"Whatever." Blake watched Landon fetch the ball with zero interest. He was a competitive person by nature, but today, he didn't give a shit who won their two-on-two basketball game.

"Whatever?" Justin's eyebrows shot up. "What crawled up your ass and died? You've been acting like a moody sonofabitch all day."

Blake glared at him. He regretted inviting Justin to join their game, and he regretted hiring him away from the Egret to Legends even more. Justin was a good bartender but a major pain in his ass, and now he had to deal with his smart mouth day in and day out. "Is that any way to talk to your boss?"

"Boss my ass," Justin said cheerfully. "Fire me if you'd like. I'm still right about the moody bitch part. Right?" He looked at Sammy and Landon, who shrugged in agreement.

Traitors.

"How was the grand opening?" Sammy lifted his shirt to wipe the sweat off his forehead. "Sorry I missed it. Had to deal with bakery stuff in San Fran."

A passing group of girls ogled his bare abs through the chain-link fence of the Tompkins Square Park basketball courts.

"It's cool."

"Really?" Sammy eyed Blake with suspicion. "Because you look like you want to snap my head off and feed it to those stray dogs."

"It's not because of you."

No, it was because of *him.* Paul Whatshisface, with the stupid blue jacket and stupider face. What kind of fucking name was Paul anyway? They lived in the twenty-first century, not 1900s England.

Of all the moments Blake could've chosen to step outside for fresh air, he had to choose that one. The one that ruined his night and month and the rest of his fucking year. He had to walk outside and see her. With him. Holding hands. Her *boyfriend.*

He should've hit the boxing ring today instead of the basketball court. Pummeling a punching bag, pretending it was Paul's boy-band face, sounded very appealing.

The rational side of Blake told him he had no right to be jealous. He was the one who'd let Farrah go and told her she deserved better.

The rational side of Blake could fuck right off.

"He's not lying." Landon unscrewed the cap of his Gatorade. "He's pissed at Farrah."

Blake gaped at his friend.

How the fuck did he know?

"I saw you outside Legends the other night." Landon took a swig of his sports drink. "When you ran into her and that guy she was holding hands with. You were so busy pissing all over your territory, you didn't notice me. Given that display, I'm guessing you two had a falling out."

"Seriously?" Sammy groaned. "What did you do this time? How is it possible for one person to fuck up so many times?"

"Shut up." Blake's blood pressure neared the red zone. He was this close to exploding from anger all over the basketball courts, and if he did, he was going to make sure every last piece haunted Paul Whatshisface's ass for eternity.

Try dating *anyone* when you had a ghost fucking you up at every turn.

"She slapped him," Landon added for Sammy and Justin's benefit.

"She did?" Sammy looked appalled and amused at the same time. "That's not like Farrah. What did you do?"

"Why do you assume it was my fault?"

"Was it?"

Blake scowled. Fine. He'd been an ass the other night. He'd been an ass the night he kicked Farrah out of his apartment too. He was just an ass all around.

But he hadn't expected to see Farrah with another guy so soon, not when his heart wasn't even finished breaking. He was responsible for his own torture, but dammit, couldn't she have waited at least a few months before moving on? Or better yet, a few centuries.

You deserve better.

Looked like she'd taken his words to heart.

If Blake were selfless, he'd be happy she'd moved on. But he wasn't, so he would settle for burning mental voodoo dolls of Paul in his free time.

"Of course it's his fault." Justin yawned and addressed his next statement to Blake. "I assume your genius plan to fuck your way back into her heart didn't work."

He didn't have time to blink before Blake grabbed him by the collar and slammed him against the fence. The chain-link rattled in alarm.

"It was *your* idea," he growled.

"Someone's got their panties in a twist." Justin didn't appear fazed by the semiviolent turn of events. "You should know better than to take my advice. You also need to take a chill pill and sign up for anger management classes. Stat."

"And *you* are begging for a shiner."

"Don't take it out on me because Farrah dumped your sorry ass."

Red flickered in front of Blake's eyes. He drew his arm back, ready to knock that smug grin off Justin's face before Landon yanked him off.

"Enough," he said firmly. "Let's talk about this like adults, not bickering children."

"Good thing you didn't hit me." Justin brushed his shoulders off. "I'm your employee. I could've filed for workplace assault."

Blake lunged at him again. This time, both Landon and Sammy had to hold him back.

"You're fired," he hissed.

"Okay." Justin smiled, cheerful as ever. Crazy mother-fucker. Blake was beginning to think he'd hired—and fired—a psychopath.

"Calm the fuck down," Sammy ordered, sounding like a different person from the easygoing, good-natured Sammy who Blake remembered from Shanghai. "Do you want to tell us what happened so we can figure out a solution, or do you want to fight like a temperamental child?"

Blake counted to three and exhaled sharply through his nose. "Let go of me."

"Only if you promise not to beat Justin to a pulp."

"I promise. Now let go," he gritted.

Once Landon and Sammy released him, Blake brushed his shoulders off and gave his friends an abbreviated version of what happened, minus the Cleo part. He didn't want to, but they'd hound him to the ends of the earth until he did.

By the time he finished, all three of their jaws hung open.

"Wait. Let me get this straight." Justin held up a hand. "You broke up with a girl you're *still in love with* because...you're afraid you'll hurt her one day? Are you fucking kidding me?"

Reliving the night of the breakup had sapped Blake of his energy, and he was too tired to snap at Justin. "It's complicated."

"No, it's not. It's simple. You. Are. An. Idiot. Of the highest degree." Justin shook his head in disgust. "Congratulations, Sir Idiot, you win the award for Most Fucked-Up Reasoning of the Year."

"Thank you, Sir Syphilis, your input means so much to me."

"I do not have syphilis. I get tested every two weeks."

Blake grimaced, trying not to think about how many women Justin had to sleep with to warrant such frequent testing.

"I agree with Justin," Sammy said. "Man up and tell Farrah the truth about what's got you all twisted up inside. Pushing her away because of a hypothetical is, in fact, idiotic. It should be her decision whether she stays or leaves."

She already left. And moved right the fuck on with someone who looked like a reject member of One Direction back when they were still a thing.

"She's better off without me," Blake muttered.

"Do you hear yourself?" Sammy threw his hands in the air. "Stop trying to decide what's best for her! She's in love with you, you freakin' doofus. You're in love with her. Don't make this so hard. *Figure it out.*"

"She's not in love with me. And I don't want to hurt her."

Sammy, Landon, and Justin groaned at the same time.

"Moron," Justin said. "I have a moron for a boss."

"You're fired," Blake reminded him.

"Thank god. Otherwise, your stupidity might bleed into me by osmosis."

"Blake." Sammy grabbed Blake by the shoulders and shook him. Actually shook him. "What do you think you did when you pushed Farrah away? You *hurt her*. We both know how stubborn she can be. She wouldn't have tried so hard to get you to open up if she didn't care. She gave you a second chance. She trusted you again even though you broke her heart the first time around. And how did you repay her? By letting her go instead of letting her in. You didn't even give her a chance to be there for you."

Blake opened his mouth, but no words came out.

"You done fucked it up this time." Justin yawned again. "Good luck finding another girl who'll put up with your shit."

"Shut up, J," Landon said.

Meanwhile, dismay crept through Blake's veins, slow and insidious, until it swallowed him whole. "I'm an idiot," he realized.

His friends let out another collective groan.

Landon pinched the bridge of his nose like he had a massive migraine.

Justin dribbled the basketball he'd grabbed from Landon, looking like he was on the verge of throwing it in Blake's face.

Sammy sank onto the floor and rubbed his eyes with a tired hand. "I need a drink."

The image of Farrah leaving his apartment flashed through Blake's mind.

FUCK.

CHAPTER 37

THE DOORBELL RANG, A LOUD, UNEXPECTED CHIME that caused Farrah to jump and knock her coffee to the ground. The ceramic mug hit the carpet with a loud thud.

She issued a string of curses that would make a sailor blush.

"Coming!" She checked to make sure none of the liquid had spilled onto her sketches. It hadn't, thank god. She would die if she had to start all over again.

Farrah had finished Yuliya's apartment and was now designing the magazine editor's Soho flat. The editor, a Frenchwoman so glamorous she gave a young Brigitte Bardot a run for her money, had relocated from Paris to take the editor-in-chief position at...well, Farrah wasn't sure. She hadn't asked. But it must be a high-profile publication if she could afford an apartment in Soho. Magazines weren't known for their lucrative paychecks.

The doorbell rang again.

"I said I'm coming!"

Farrah skidded across the apartment toward the door, wondering who it could be. Olivia was at work. Delivery guys left their packages in the lobby, and her neighbors never dropped by. Heck, she didn't know what half of them looked like.

She peered through the peephole. Her heart stuttered when she saw a familiar flash of golden locks and...was that a teddy bear? It was hard to tell, considering the object was so large it filled up half the peephole. Farrah could only make out what appeared to be a furry brown hand holding a red balloon.

Still, there was no mistaking that blond hair. She knew only one person with hair like that.

Farrah's sweaty palms slipped off the doorknob. She could pretend she wasn't home. But no, she'd already yelled and alerted him to her presence.

Damn.

Olivia was always berating her for giving away her presence before she saw who was on the other side of the door. Farrah had dismissed it as paranoia, but now she understood where her friend was coming from.

She took a deep breath, rearranged her expression into a mask of indifference, and opened the door.

Despite her vow to remain indifferent, Farrah couldn't help but gape at the spectacle in front of her. Blake *was* holding a teddy bear—a massive, adorable teddy bear that covered most of his six-foot-three frame. The teddy smiled at her, holding a shiny red heart-shaped balloon and wearing a white T-shirt that said, "I'm sorry, Farrah" in red script with a little heart beneath the words. Blake's other hand clutched the biggest bouquet she'd ever seen. The floral arrangement burst with purple hydrangea, lavender roses, lavender spray orchids—her favorite—and large green echeveria succulents.

Blake poked his head out from behind the fur and flowers. His cheeks dimpled nervously. "Hi."

Farrah slammed the door in his face.

"Farrah." A plea crept into his voice and seeped through the door, wrapping itself around her traitorous heart, which whimpered with excitement at how close its other half was. "I just want to talk."

"We have nothing to say to each other."

There was no way in hell Farrah was opening that door again. Her heart and her body were her enemies. Her mind was the only sane one of the trio, but majority rules, and she didn't trust herself in Blake's presence. No matter how many times he broke her heart, he had a way of melting her down like a candle beneath a hot flame.

Farrah was starting to think the organ pumping in her chest was a bit of a masochist.

"I have a lot to say," Blake protested. "Don't make me do it through the door. Your neighbor just passed by, and I'm pretty sure they think I'm a crazed stalker. They'll probably call the police."

"Good."

There was a shuffling sound, and just when Farrah thought he'd left, he spoke again. "I'm sorry, ok? I'm sorry I acted like such a jerk the other night, and I'm sorry for pushing you away. I'm sorry I keep fucking things up. I'm—" Blake's tone changed. "What are you looking at? Haven't you ever seen anyone apologize before?" he growled.

Farrah's mouth tugged up into a smile before she squashed it.

Someone said something in the distance, followed by the slamming of a door, and she heard Blake huff before his voice turned pleading again. "I'm sorry for everything. Please forgive me."

She was a cheap birthday candle, disintegrating into a puddle of wax.

Don't do it, her brain warned. *He has a way with words, but he can't be trusted.*

Do it, her heart urged. *He's right there! Go to him. You know that's what you want.*

Meanwhile, her body purred, choosing to show instead of tell by peppering goose bumps all over Farrah's skin and stoking the fire in her belly.

Farrah gritted her teeth. After an eternity of indecision, she flung open the door. "What are you doing here?"

"I told you. I want to talk."

"You didn't want to talk when you kicked me out of your apartment. You said I should walk away from you and that I deserved better. So what changed?" She tightened her grip on the doorknob. "Do I not deserve better anymore?"

Blake swallowed. "I messed up. I'm sorry it took me so long to realize it. But—"

"You were a complete asshole to me *and* Paul."

Blake's lips thinned at the mention of the other man. "He deserved it."

His foot shot out and wedged itself between the door and doorframe before she could shut it again. "I'm sorry, I'm sorry," he said quickly. "You're right. I was a complete asshole, but—" His jaw tensed. "Are you really dating him?"

No. Farrah and Paul never had their talk. He'd stopped contacting her after the night they ran into Blake, and Farrah didn't blame him. She'd been selfish and manipulative and used him to further her own petty agenda. She would've kicked her to the curb had she been in his shoes.

Not that Farrah was going to tell Blake this. He didn't deserve to know.

"I don't see how it's any of your business." Frost wrapped around each word. "You let me go, remember? I can date whoever I want."

Blake's shoulders drooped. "I know." He resembled a puppy who'd just been kicked, and dammit if her heart didn't squeeze at the sight.

Farrah tapped her foot against the floor. Finally, unable to take it any longer, she opened the door wider. "Come in. The last thing I want is to be my floor's subject of gossip for the next month," she muttered. "You already made enough of a scene."

Blake perked up at the small sign of her relenting. Confidence returned to his eyes, and he flashed her a dazzling grin as he breezed inside and placed the teddy bear and flowers in the living room. The bear was so large, it made the nearby armchair look like a piece of dollhouse furniture.

Farrah stroked the bear's soft fur. "How did you get this here? It's almost as tall as you."

Pink stained Blake's cheekbones. "Uber XL. They closed off your street for construction, so I carried it the rest of the way. I almost knocked over an old lady coming out of your building. I'm lucky I made it here alive—for someone who was probably born before World War II, she's quite aggressive with her cane."

Farrah couldn't hide a smile at the mental image of Blake dodging a sweet old lady's cane while balancing a giant stuffed animal and flowers.

Blake saw it and pounced. "That's how sorry I am. I almost died for you." His teasing smile melted into a puppy-dog stare. "Can you please give me—"

"No." Her mirth disappeared, and she stepped back, the frantic little beats of her pulse dancing along her skin before he could finish his sentence.

She knew what he was going to ask her.

She wasn't sure she could deny him.

Despite everything that had happened, Farrah still loved Blake. She could build the walls around her heart so high they reached the heavens, she could arm it with a thousand soldiers firing flame-tipped arrows, and she could surround it with a moat filled with crocodiles, but if Blake persisted—if he got close enough—those defenses would crumble faster than a sandcastle at high tide.

Once, he was her greatest savior. Now, he was her greatest downfall.

The only way Farrah could protect herself was to keep him so far away, he couldn't touch even the outermost perimeter of her defense.

"Don't finish that question." Her words were bullets, shot point-blank at Blake's chest. "I made myself clear—our second chance is over. If you think a couple of gifts will change that, you're sorely mistaken."

"I know. I'm not asking you for another chance," Blake said softly. "I'm asking you for an opportunity to explain. I'll tell you everything. What happened in Texas, why I pushed you away. I'll tell you anything you want to know."

"It's too late."

They say the definition of insanity is doing the same thing over and over again and expecting different results. Unless Farrah wanted a nice long stint in an insane asylum, she needed to stop believing Blake. How many times was she going to let him hurt her until she got the hint?

Blake's eyes darkened. "Is it Paul?" He spat out the name like it was a rotten piece of fruit. "Are you in love with him?"

You've got to be kidding me.

Disbelief and anger replaced the humor in Farrah's laugh. "Get out of my house."

Instead of leaving, Blake moved closer. Farrah stepped back, he stepped forward, until her back hit the wall and there was nowhere left to go. He was all she could see, and his presence was so powerful, so all-encompassing, she drowned in it.

"What is it about him?" Blake demanded. "How could you move on so quickly? From me? From *us?*"

Farrah's blood hissed in her veins. "I'm serious, Blake. Get the fuck out."

"I need to know!"

"I'm not in love with him, you idiot!" she yelled. "I'm not even dating him! god, how dense can you be?"

Blake looked thunderstruck. "You're not?"

"No." Farrah shoved him off her. "We met on a dating app. I'd only known him for two weeks. That night you ran into us? It was our third date. Do you think I'm so fickle that I could turn around and fall in love with someone else just like that?" She snapped her fingers for emphasis.

The paleness of Blake's face could've given Edward Cullen a run for his money. "Does that—you fell in love with me again?"

Farrah wanted to bang her head against the wall. "I was always in love with you. Even when I thought I forgot you. Even when I thought I was over you." Her voice trembled. "From the day I met you, you chipped away at my heart, piece by piece, until you took the entire thing. And you never gave it back, you bastard."

Blake grasped her chin and tilted it until his eyes bored into hers. "And I'm not giving it back. Ever," he said fiercely. "It's mine, and mine is yours. A heart for a heart. It's only fair."

If only that were true.

A chill settled in Farrah's chest, fortifying her defenses and keeping her standing until she did what she had to do.

"Here's the difference between you and me," she whispered. "I saw you taking my heart, and I let you. I gave it to you unconditionally. You gave me yours in a locked glass box—beautiful, close enough for me to believe I could touch it, but every time I came close, you pushed me away. Because you didn't trust me, or you thought I couldn't handle it, I don't know. It doesn't matter. In the end, you kept the key, and you ran. Even though you said you loved me. Even though I was right here, all this time."

Blake trembled against her, tiny, barely imperceptible shudders that belied the stony set of his jaw. He ripped his hand from her chin and grasped her palm, pressing it flat against his chest. "There is no glass box," he said, the storm in his eyes intensifying into a hurricane. "*This* is my heart. Feel it. It's there, and it's beating. For you. Only for you."

Silence.

"We can make this work." Quiet desperation leaked from Blake's voice and crackled in the air. "I've fucked up more times than I can count, but tell me how I can make it up to you. You want the key? I'll give you the key. I'll give you ten keys. I'll give you the whole goddamned house! Just tell me what you want and it's yours."

"I don't want anything." Farrah slipped her hand out of his grasp, as calm as if they were sipping tea on a summer porch in the Hamptons. "You see, there's only so many times you can push a person away before they never come back."

"Farrah..."

"The key is useless because I've given up trying to unlock what's inside."

"Don't do this."

"You can keep my heart." She blinked up at Blake, trying to feel something beyond the numbness spreading through her limbs. She couldn't. "But I no longer want yours."

Until today, Farrah didn't think it was possible to see a person actually die inside. Now she witnessed it in slow motion as the light bled out of Blake's eyes, turning the crystal pools into flat, empty swaths of ice. His strong, muscular frame crumpled, and devastation lined his face. He was no longer Apollo but a fallen god, mortal and bleeding, and she couldn't bear to watch any longer.

Farrah closed her eyes. Apparently, there was a limit to her numbness.

Blake's laugh was short, rueful, and laced with pain. "For someone who claims never to have touched my heart, you have an uncanny ability to rip it out and tear it apart."

His footsteps stopped at the door. She felt rather than saw him look at her. "It's still yours, you know. It will never belong to anyone else. Not in this life, and not in the next thousand lives. You have my heart until the earth stops spinning and the stars turn to dust. You can love it or hate it or forget all about it. But it will always be yours."

CHAPTER 38

FARRAH THOUGHT SHE'D GOTTEN RID OF BLAKE.

She didn't hear from him for a week—unless you counted the endless stream of pleading texts, phone calls, and voicemails, which she ignored, though she couldn't bring herself to block him...yet.

Then he started showing up in person. Every damn day. Begging her to give him just five minutes. Ensuring she couldn't forget about him no matter how hard she tried.

Farrah's mouth pressed into a thin line when she saw Blake sitting on the stoop in front of her building, the same way he'd been doing for the past three weeks, even as she tried to ignore the sharp ache she felt at the sight of him.

She'd thought one of her neighbors would've called the cops by now, but he'd somehow managed to win them all over, even the grouchy old lady on the second floor.

Farrah didn't know what kind of sorcery he was practicing, but she wanted no part of it, no matter what her traitorous, fluttering heart said.

The closer she got to him, the more her chest hurt.

Don't look at him. Don't look at him. Don't look at him.

Blake scrambled to his feet when he saw her. "Give me a chance to explain?"

Farrah fished her keys out of her bag, determined to ignore him, but the question slipped out before she could prevent it. "Don't you have somewhere to be?"

Blake waited in front of her building every evening like a puppy waiting for its owner to come home. She assumed he came here straight from work. She didn't know how long he stayed, but Olivia came home once at eight and said she saw him outside, looking miserable. Farrah had lasted two minutes before she'd excused herself from the conversation and locked herself in her room, where she'd alternated between trying not to cry, cursing Blake out in her mind, and resisting the urge to run outside and fling herself into his arms.

"I do. Here." Blake flashed a small, devastating smile before his face turned serious again. "Farrah, please. I just need a few minutes."

"I thought I made myself clear the other day." Farrah's hands curled around her keys until the metal dug painful grooves into her palm. Her ears buzzed, and her heart slammed against her rib cage in a frantic, unyielding rhythm. "I'm not interested. You had your chance. You had *two* chances. Both times you pushed me away. So congratulations. You got your wish. I'm staying away. Now you need to do the same."

She tried to look Blake in the eyes to drive home her point but ended up staring at his forehead instead.

Blake's jaw tightened. "I'm not letting you go that easily."

A frustrated groan tore from her throat. *Why was he making this so hard?* "Stop. We both know this isn't going to last." She gestured between them. "One day, you won't be here. You'll leave. That's what you've always done when the going gets tough."

"Not this time." Blake's eyes burned into hers with an intensity that sent trembles up her spine. "I love you, and you love me. I'm not giving up on that."

"You already did." Farrah sucked in a deep, shaky breath and turned her head, afraid the mess of emotion in her throat would be reflected on her face. She needed to leave before she broke down. "You've always been good with words, but actions matter more, and yours told me all I needed to know."

She fled inside her building before Blake could rope her back in. A tear escaped, then two, then more than she knew what to do with.

Damn him, she thought bitterly.

Blake was right. She did love him, even after all he put her through, and he knew what he was doing by showing up here every day.

But he was going to stop. She was sure of it.

Except...he didn't.

Mid-December rolled around. The leaves had fallen off the trees, and holiday fever had swept the city, but Blake remained stubbornly, infallibly *present*, to the point where even Olivia felt bad for him.

"Maybe you should talk to him," Olivia said tentatively one evening, while Farrah was packing for her trip home for the holidays. Her flight was four days away, but after living with Olivia for so long, some of her roommate's tendencies—including packing early—had become her own. "It's been almost two months. I know you're hurt and angry, and you have every right to be, but he's trying. No guy waits that long—"

"Liv, don't." Farrah shoved a dress into the corner of her suitcase. She'd done a decent job of pushing Blake out of her mind—other than her heart splintering every time she saw him outside her building, of course. "I don't want to talk about it."

She'd managed to avoid discussion of Blake so far, even when Olivia complained about the teddy bear blocking half the TV in the living room. Farrah said she couldn't throw the bear out because it was gigantic, and there was no good way to dispose of it, but they both knew that wasn't true. Olivia, thankfully, hadn't called her out on her obvious lie.

It helped that there had been plenty of distractions this fall: namely, the Kelly-Matt scandal, which blew up right before Thanksgiving and sent shock waves through Manhattan. Kelly's best friend and Matt's mom, a wealthy, well-connected socialite who split her time between Chicago and New York, had flown in to surprise her son. She ended up being the one surprised—when she caught him in bed with Kelly.

The socialite killed Kelly's reputation among Manhattan high society. The gossip sites covered the sordid affair for weeks— *Design icon caught in bed with employee (and godson)! Wealthy heir ensnared by cougar!*—and in an attempt to save his own ass, Matt declared Kelly forced him into the relationship. He also spilled all her dirty secrets, including the tactics she used to get back at those she felt had wronged her. Among them: sending a PSA to all the design studio heads in New York, telling them not to hire Farrah because she was insubordinate and difficult to work with. Kelly claimed she'd been about to fire Farrah anyway before Farrah quit in a childish tantrum over not receiving a promotion.

Matt's accusations fell apart after a gossip columnist dug up the history of filthy, very much uncoerced texts he'd sent Kelly over the past year. He fled to Chicago with his tail between his legs; Kelly took an extended leave of absence from KBI and was reportedly hiding out upstate.

Meanwhile, Farrah had been inundated with messages from her former coworkers and interview offers from companies who'd been radio silent until news of Kelly's deception broke. She was glad she finally knew for sure what happened and that her reputation in the industry was no longer in tatters, but she couldn't help feeling bad for her ex-colleagues. A lot of them had to look for jobs elsewhere, given KBI's new client stream had slowed to a trickle.

Farrah herself hadn't replied to her interview offers yet. If this were a few months ago, she would've jumped on them in a heartbeat, but now, she wasn't so sure she wanted to work for someone else. She enjoyed being her own boss, and she was even getting the hang of the business side of things. Sort of.

"I'm just saying." Olivia's voice brought Farrah back to the present. "It's snowing like crazy out there. Blake's probably freezing."

Farrah's heart seized at the mental image of Blake standing outside, shivering in the storm. "He's not out there."

"It's seven. He usually doesn't leave until eight or nine."

"You said it yourself. It's snowing like crazy. No sane person would be outside right now."

"No sane person would wait outside their ex's building for two months straight, either," Olivia retorted.

Farrah resumed packing, but her heart wasn't in it. "When did you turn into a Blake apologist?"

"Since I saw how miserable you are. You can ignore him all you want, but if you really wanted to get rid of him, you'd have called the cops on his ass a long time ago."

"He's not breaking any laws," Farrah murmured.

"I'm sure you could make a case for harassment or something. At the very least, you could've tried. But you didn't." Olivia's tone softened. "Babe, you can't keep going on like this."

"I won't. I'm leaving for LA in a few days, and I'll be gone for a month. Once I come back, Blake won't be here." Farrah folded a denim jacket and stuffed it next to her dress.

"If you say so." Olivia pursed her lips. "I'm going to take a shower before this storm knocks out the electricity or something."

"It's not snowing *that* bad!" Farrah yelled after her, right as a fierce howl ripped through the air outside.

There was no way Blake was out there. Right?

Don't do it, Farrah Lin. Don't you dare.

With a groan, Farrah threw on a coat and shoes, grabbed her keys, and stomped outside. She was furious with Blake for being so persistent, with Olivia for putting the suggestion he might be outside in her head, and with herself for caring.

She opened the door to the building and flinched when a blast of icy air almost knocked her over. The ground was blanketed in thick, powdery snow, and the cold soaked through her layers of clothing until it clawed at her skin.

Farrah didn't notice. She was too busy staring at the figure shivering in the corner. He stood beneath an awning, but it was too small to prevent the snow from collecting on his hair and coat. There was an alarming blue tinge to his skin.

Her breath rushed out in a gust of shock and anger. "What the hell are you doing?" she demanded. "You're going to get yourself killed!"

Blake's eyes lit up. "You came outside." Then he frowned at the sight of her thin coat—she hadn't put on her parka for such a quick trip—and slip-ons. "You must be freezing."

Farrah wanted to cry. "*I'm* freezing?" She grabbed his arm and yanked him inside, trying to ignore the shower of sparks that erupted in her belly. The door closed behind them, shutting out most of the cold, but Blake continued shivering. No wonder—he was soaked from the melted snow. A messy ball of emotion clogged her throat. "What are you doing outside in this storm? Are you crazy?"

Blake lifted his shoulder with a slight furrow in his brow. "I told you I'm not going anywhere. Not until you give me a chance to explain."

Farrah wanted to scream. "You could've gotten hypothermia!"

"Worth it." His lips curved into a small smile. "At least you're speaking to me."

He was certifiably insane.

They could've argued all night, but pale blue still tinted Blake's skin, and if he didn't warm up soon, he really *was* going to catch hypothermia.

"You need to get out of those clothes, or you'll get sick," Farrah said. "And don't you dare make a sexual innuendo right now," she added when Blake opened his mouth to speak.

"Okay." The mischievous glint in Blake's eyes told her he may not be saying it, but he was thinking it.

Farrah's lips inched up before she caught herself. "Don't take this as anything more than basic human decency, but you can shower and change at my place."

Blake followed her silently into her apartment, where a freshly showered Olivia was reading one of her erotica books on the couch. Other than an arch of her eyebrow, she didn't look surprised to see a soaking wet Blake enter her living room. "Blake."

"Liv." Blake returned her greeting.

"I'm going to be in my room. All night," Olivia announced. She closed her book, stood, and left, but not before shooting Farrah an I-told-you-so look, which Farrah ignored.

While Blake took a shower, Farrah tossed his clothes into the laundry and fixed a cup of hot tea, all the while trying to sort through her tangled web of thoughts. How long had Blake been standing out there? It'd been snowing for hours. He was bundled up, but dammit, why hadn't he had the common sense to leave after the snowstorm intensified? Lord knows how long he would've stayed had she not gone outside.

A burning sensation spread behind Farrah's eyes. Her heart ached so much, her hand trembled and she almost spilled the tea all over herself.

The sound of the shower turned off, and Blake stepped out of the bathroom dressed in a pair of men's sweatpants and a purple Thayer University T-shirt. The blue tinge had subsided from his skin, thank god, but a dark scowl marred his chiseled face.

"Drink this," Farrah instructed, shoving the tea into his hand. "It'll warm you up."

"Thanks." Blake took the mug but didn't drink. Instead, his eyes bored into hers, as if searching for the answer to a question he hadn't asked yet. "Who do these clothes belong to?"

"Excuse me?"

"These clothes." A muscle ticked in Blake's jaw. "Don't tell me you just have men's clothing lying around."

She shrugged. "Maybe they're an old boyfriend's. Or a current fling's. I don't remember."

A growl emanated from his chest. "You don't have a current fling. I would've seen him—and killed him."

"I could've snuck him in the back." Farrah's smile was sweeter than pie. Never mind the fact that the back of the building was sketchy as hell and she would never use that entrance; she relished Blake's glower even as guilt nibbled at her stomach for making him suffer after he nearly froze to death.

The guilt won out, and she sighed. "The clothes belong to my cousin, ok? He visits sometimes and always leaves some of his shit behind. Not that you have any right to be jealous," she added, jabbing a finger at his chest. It was like poking a brick wall. "Plus, you didn't answer me earlier. What the hell were you doing out there?"

"Waiting for you." A glimmer of satisfaction replaced the jealousy stamped on Blake's face. "It worked. You came."

Farrah couldn't believe it. She was in love with a fucking idiot. "You have zero sense of self-preservation," she fumed. "You could've died!"

The burning sensation behind her eyes returned.

"I'm still alive. But it's nice to know you care," Blake teased.

A tear slipped out, and she wiped it away angrily. "Of course I care," she snapped. "I don't want anyone dying because of me."

Blake's expression morphed into one of alarm as more tears tracked down her face. "Hey, don't cry. I'm here. I'm fine." He drew her into his chest, and she let him, burying her face in his shoulder while he stroked her hair with soothing motions. "Shh. It's ok."

Sobs rolled through Farrah's body. It was beyond embarrassing, considering she was still supposed to be angry with him, but seeing him outside, shivering and soaked to the bone, had cracked the ice around her heart. She'd imagined, just for a second, what it would be like to live in a world without Blake, and the thought was so devastating she couldn't breathe.

For all his faults and misdeeds, Blake had always been her light, her rock, her center of gravity. Without him, the earth would surely fall off its axis and plummet into oblivion.

Another sob ripped through her before Farrah mustered the strength to shove him away and glare at him. "Don't you ever do that again, you hear me?" She hiccupped. "I don't know what you were trying to prove, but it was beyond stupid."

"Okay." Blake raised his hands in acquiescence. "I won't. But I don't regret doing it."

He was impossible. "Blake—"

"No," he said firmly. "Listen to me. You said actions matter more than words, and you were right. I screwed up by pushing you away in the past, by not trusting you when you trusted me, but that's not me anymore. I'm done running." He swallowed hard. "I know forgiveness might be too much to ask, but is there even the smallest chance you'd let me let you in? To show you I've changed, and that I'll be here, no matter how hard the snow falls or how much shit goes sideways?"

The ache in Farrah's chest grew. "I want to," she whispered. "I really do. But every time I look at you, I remember that night in Shanghai and that night in your apartment. You shut me out and didn't even give me a chance to be there for you. Twice. I can't just forget. Not yet."

The most painful part of loving someone was knowing you couldn't live without them but not being able to live with them, either.

Blake's throat convulsed. He hung his head and nodded. "I understand. I'll be here when you're ready."

He looked so sad, Farrah almost caved and threw herself into his arms again, but she forced herself to stand her ground—no matter how much doing so killed her inside.

CHAPTER 39

BLAKE STAYED THE NIGHT ON THE COUCH SINCE THE snowstorm continued to rage outside and Farrah still worried about him getting sick. The downside was, she didn't sleep a wink. Instead, she stared at the ceiling, fighting every impulse to curl up beside Blake and never let him go.

Yes, she loved him. So freakin' much. But she hadn't stopped hurting, and she wasn't ready to give him another chance yet.

Farrah left for LA a few days later, hoping the holidays would prove a decent distraction. She spent most of it bingeing on Netflix and In-N-Out burgers and conducting ill-fated baking experiments. Farrah's attempt to recreate Sammy's signature egg tarts resulted in misshapen brown confections instead of crispy, flaky shells filled with golden custard. One bite confirmed the egg tarts tasted exactly like they looked. Farrah and her mom threw out the batch, picked up a dozen real egg tarts from the nearest Chinese bakery, and never spoke of the incident again.

Farrah also met her mom's boyfriend.

Yes, boyfriend.

She'd nearly choked on a Hot Cheeto when Cheryl brought

it up, looking as nervous as a teenager asking her parent if she could go on a date for the first time. So that was why her mom had been so weird when she'd asked Farrah if she was coming home for the holidays.

Cheryl shouldn't have worried about Farrah's reaction: Farrah was thrilled. She was an only child, and they didn't have family in LA. She'd worried about her mom being lonely, even with Cheryl's dance association friends. Friend love wasn't the same as romantic love, and Cheryl was far too young to live out the rest of her days alone. She deserved happiness, especially after her brutal divorce from Farrah's dad.

Besides, Kevin, her mom's boyfriend, seemed like a nice guy. He and Cheryl were old classmates who'd run into each other again at a ballroom dancing competition, and Farrah could tell he adored her mom. He was divorced with no kids, soft-spoken with a surprisingly sarcastic sense of humor, and he had a stable, if boring, job as a database administrator. As far as middle-aged boyfriends went, he could have been a lot worse.

All of this *would* have been a distraction, had it not been for the letters.

Farrah didn't know how Blake had gotten her LA address, but she could guess, and she was going to have a stern talk with Olivia when she returned to New York.

The first letter was a precursor for what to expect. It arrived in a plain envelope, handwritten and unsigned.

I know you need time, and I respect that. But the door is open whenever you're ready. Read my letters when you feel like you might be able to give me another chance.

The second letter had been a simple card. Farrah had debated whether to open it, but in the end, curiosity won out.

When I was six, my family canceled a vacation to Disneyland because my sister got really sick, and I remember wishing, just for a second, that I was an only child.

The next day, she received a giant box of her favorite chocolates with a third note.

When I was fourteen, I stole my dad's credit card to buy porn online. My mom saw the charges and had a huge fight with my dad about it. My dad thought he'd been hacked, and I never told them the truth.

The gifts and notes kept coming, hand-delivered by messenger. A box of gourmet coffee beans from an Austin café—the ones Blake had said he would buy her as a souvenir:

When I was sixteen, I saw two of my "friends" shove a freshman in a locker. It wasn't the first time. They'd bullied him the entire year and made his life hell. I didn't take part in the bullying, but I didn't stop them either— because I wanted to fit in. Because I wanted to be liked. Because I was this close to becoming homecoming king, and I didn't want to mess it up. Beyond pathetic, I know, but I was young and stupid, and all I cared about was being popular. Well, I won homecoming king. The glory wore off in about two weeks. But the regret of not saying anything—of not standing up to those bullies who were my so-called friends—haunts me to this day.

A beautiful snow globe:

When I was twenty, I asked my childhood friend out on

a date, even though I didn't want to. I did it because my family wanted me to and because everyone said we were perfect together. I thought if I gave it time, I would love her the way I was supposed to. I quickly found out that wasn't the case, but I still led her on for an entire year. I saw her falling in love with me, and I didn't do anything to stop it. I broke her heart, then I left, but karma later found me anyway...

A framed black-and-white photo of the Shanghai skyline:

When I was twenty-one, I fell in love for the first time in my life. I didn't want to or expect to, but I did. She was beautiful, kind, smart, funny, sassy, talented...everything I could've wanted. I lived in fear of messing things up with her. Then, one day, I did. I broke her heart... but I also broke mine. Completely and utterly. Only she didn't know it then because I never told her. Instead of telling her the truth, I lied and said I had a girlfriend back home—even though I didn't, not really. I was afraid of what she would think of me if she found out the truth, which is ironic, considering I lost her anyway.

A beautiful infinity bracelet:

When I was twenty-seven, I ran into the woman I loved again. I never stopped loving her, but I was too afraid to reach out after we broke up because...well, if you can't tell, I have issues with hard conversations. I don't like them. I run from them. But being the angel she is, she gave me another chance—and I fucked it up again. I pushed her away, and I ran again. I drowned in misery for a while until I finally pulled my head from my ass long enough to realize what I should've known all along: trying to run from her is as futile as trying to sweep water back into the ocean. Everything I do, every thought I have leads back to her. She's angry at me right now, and I don't blame her. But I'm done running. For the first time in my life, I'm going to stay, and I'm going to fight. For her. For us.

None of the letters were signed. They didn't have to be.

"Are you sure you'll be ok?" Cheryl surveyed her daughter with concern. "We can stay home and watch bad TV if you'd rather do that."

"No, I'm fine." Farrah took a deep breath.

Blake's letters, combined with that crazy, stupid stunt he'd pulled in the snowstorm right before the holidays, had rattled her defenses, but she forced a smile on her face. Cheryl had spent most of the holiday break watching her read the letters, shove them into a shoebox under her childhood bed, and fight back tears. Farrah could tell her mom was worried. But it was New Year's Eve. She wasn't going to ruin it by being an emotional mess. "Have fun with Kevin. I have to go to Kris's party anyway. She'll kill me if I miss it."

Kris and Nate hosted a massive New Year's Eve bash every year at their Beverly Hills mansion, and Farrah wouldn't miss it for the world—not the least because she was terrified of what Kris would do to her.

Kris in love may have been nicer than Shanghai Kris, but she could still bite your head off with one well-timed barb.

"All right." Cheryl's concerned expression remained in place. She patted her daughter's hand. "You've had a tough few months, but it'll be a new year soon. Remember what I told you: no matter how bad someone hurts you, you can't heal until you forgive. Especially when you so clearly want to. Don't argue," she added when Farrah opened her mouth to do exactly that. "I'm your mother. I know how stubborn you are and how hard it is for you to trust. But I also know you wouldn't have kept all those letters and gifts if this boy didn't hold a piece of your heart. You want to give him another chance. What's stopping you? What are you afraid of?"

Farrah stared at her shoes. They were brand-new, bought just for the New Year. "I don't want to get hurt again."

"Aren't you already hurting?" Cheryl asked gently.

Farrah didn't have to answer; they both knew the truth.

Kris's party was incredible, per usual. Five hundred of LA's hottest, richest, and most famous feted New Year's Eve at her and Nate's gigantic mansion, alongside live entertainment from the world's top pop star and gourmet catering courtesy of the city's most expensive and sought-after chef.

Farrah sipped her champagne and tried not to fangirl when two of the male leads of a massive superhero movie franchise strolled by. One of them caught her eye and smiled, and her ovaries exploded.

It still boggled Farrah's mind that Kris knew most of her favorite celebrities, but as much as she was dying for a selfie or an autograph, she knew her friend would kick her ass for acting like a crazed stalker at one of her parties.

"Hey!" The hostess herself sailed over in a glittering gold gown that probably cost more than the average American's monthly rent. "How're you enjoying the party?"

"It's great, as usual. Thanks for inviting me." Farrah hugged her friend.

She and Kris had met up a few times since she'd landed in LA, but Kris had been so swamped with planning her foundation's Christmas gala, the New Year's party, and her wedding that they hadn't had time for any in-depth conversations.

Not that Farrah wanted her friend's opinion on Blake's letters or anything. Knowing Kris, she'd tell Farrah to create a voodoo doll of Blake and toss it into a bonfire sprinkled with the ashes of his letters and presents.

Kris Carrera didn't do sentimental.

Meanwhile, Cheryl's words swirled in Farrah's brain, muddying her thoughts further.

Aren't you already hurting?

Yes. But were there degrees of hurt? Was keeping Blake at arm's length better than letting him back in and having him walk away again? Was dull, perpetual pain better than experiencing the highest of highs only to drop to the lowest of lows?

Farrah's head pounded with indecision.

"Please. Like that's even a question." Kris rolled her eyes. "Sorry we didn't get a chance to chat before now. Nate—" She blushed. "Anyway, I was busy."

Farrah smirked. If she had any doubts about where Kris had snuck off to, Nate's mussed hair and cat-that-ate-the-canary grin confirmed it.

"Hey, Farrah." He greeted her with a wink as he sauntered past them. He didn't miss the opportunity to plant a quick kiss on Kris's lips.

Kris kept her cool, but her eyes sparkled with obvious love.

Jealousy sank its claws into Farrah's guts. She was happy for Kris, truly, but watching her and Nate's loving display was like exfoliating her still-raw wounds with salt.

Once Nate left to say hi to an R&B singer and his supermodel/foodie wife, Kris tilted her head and examined Farrah with an eagle eye. "Liv told me what happened with Blake."

Even when they lived across the country, her friends gossiped more than middle school girls.

Farrah shrugged. She did not want to spend the last hours of the year discussing her love life, or lack thereof.

"You look sad."

"I'm not sad." Farrah tried to take another sip of champagne only to discover her glass was empty.

Kris pursed her lips. "I don't like sad people, especially not at my party. It's not on-brand."

"I told you, I'm not sad." Farrah pasted on a smile.

"You're lying, as I suspected you would. But I've decided to try and be a nicer person this year so..." Kris hesitated, looking uncharacteristically nervous. "I did a thing, which Liv may or may not have put me up to."

Every warning bell in Farrah's head clanged. "What did you guys do?"

Instead of answering, Kris pointed her chin at something over Farrah's shoulder.

Farrah knew.

Even before she turned around, she knew what—or who— was behind her. The tingle on her skin, the racing of her heart... her body reacted before her eyes confirmed her suspicions.

Blake Ryan. Here. In LA, in Kris's house, standing not six feet from her.

He wore a tailored blazer over a white dress shirt, bow tie, and slim-fit black pants that showed off his lean, muscular frame in all its glory. His hair was just tousled enough to keep it from looking too perfect, and his lips quirked up in a small sheepish smile that did strange things to Farrah's stomach. He carried a small gift-wrapped box in one hand.

"Hi," Blake said softly. "Can we talk?"

CHAPTER 40

BLAKE'S HEART HAMMERED IN HIS THROAT WHILE HE waited for Farrah to react. She blinked up at him, her huge brown eyes unreadable. Her red jumpsuit clung to her curves and matched the color of her lipstick. She looked like a goddess of fire, and her heat incinerated him, burning through skin and bone to reveal the secrets he'd tucked away in the darkest corner of his psyche. Tearing them out of their hiding place and handing them to Farrah, one by one, had been akin to tearing out pieces of his soul.

But as painful and anxiety-inducing as writing his previous notes had been, they didn't compare to the one Blake clutched in his hands.

Kris cleared her throat. "I'm going to check on the other guests. If you want privacy, you can use the library." She tilted her head toward the door to Blake's right before leaving.

Gratitude bloomed in Blake's chest. He hadn't expected Kris to help him. They hadn't spoken in years, and she hadn't exactly left Shanghai with a great impression of him. He supposed he had Olivia to thank for Kris's reluctant assistance.

Olivia had taken pity on him after seeing him wait outside her and Farrah's building for months and offered to help. She'd tipped him off to the fact that Farrah would be at Kris's NYE party and convinced Kris to add him to the guest list.

According to Olivia, Farrah wouldn't return to New York until mid-January, and he couldn't wait that long. He was already dying a little more inside each day as it was. So he flew home to Austin for Christmas, where he had a long, hard talk with his family about Cleo. They'd been shocked but had taken the news of Cleo's lies better than he'd expected. They'd mostly worried about whether he was ok, which touched a part of him he hadn't known existed.

The past was the past, and Blake could finally put it behind him.

Now, there was only one major piece of his life he needed to fix.

"Let's talk in there." Farrah brushed by him and walked into the library; Blake followed, his body taut with anticipation.

He'd landed in LA last night and spent most of today pacing his room, working out in the hotel gym to rid himself of restless energy, and taking care of business stuff. It was New Year's Eve, one of the biggest nights for the nightlife industry. During the past few months, Blake had kept on top of his company via email, phone calls, and day meetings, but he'd delegated site visits— including for the Miami rollout—to Patricia. It'd been the only way he could pursue Farrah without disappearing for days at a time every few weeks.

Farrah leaned against the marble fireplace and folded her arms across her chest. "What are you doing here?" She was shaking—or maybe that was his hope talking.

She still cared about him. Her freak-out when she found him in the snowstorm proved that. To be honest, Blake wasn't sure why he'd waited outside so long. All he knew was, he was desperate to get back into her good graces, and if that meant he had to freeze his ass off on the slim chance that the love of his life might come out and talk to him…well, that was a risk he'd been willing to take.

And it had worked.

Now, if only he could break through her final wall.

"I came here for you," he said simply. "And to give you this." Blake held out the gift in his hand. Farrah stared at it like it was a cobra waiting to strike.

For a second, he thought she wasn't going to take it. But then she walked over and plucked the wrapped box from his palm. Her orange-blossom-and-vanilla scent slammed into him with dizzying impact, and he had to shove his clenched fists into his pockets so he didn't crush her to her chest and kiss her until they couldn't breathe.

Blake's gaze didn't stray from her face as the crinkling of gift wrap replaced the silence. Farrah sucked in an audible breath when she saw what lay beneath the matte gold foil.

An engraved heart-shaped locket, nestled inside a tiny glass box.

"There's something inside the locket." Blake fished the key to the box out of his pocket and pressed it into her palm, savoring the soft warmth of her skin against his before she pulled away. "My final letter. You don't have to read it now. I just…" He trailed off. "I wanted to deliver this one myself." He watched her, his pulse jumping beneath his skin. "Have you read any of my other letters?"

Farrah's nostrils flared. "Yes," she admitted.

Funny how one quiet word could hold so much power. Blake's heart soared in his chest, and he tamped down a grin.

Read my letters when you feel like you might be able to give me another chance.

Maybe Farrah had just been curious, but he was going to take any win he could get.

He watched, afraid to breathe, as she opened the box with

trembling hands. She retrieved the sheet of paper tucked inside the locket, folded into the smallest of squares.

In it, Blake explained everything—the truth behind Cleo's pregnancy; the accident; his run-in with Cleo and her father when he'd been in Austin; how Daniel Bowden's words had ingrained themselves into his brain, exploiting every fear he had about the kind of person he was.

He shared the deepest, darkest thoughts he had over the years, the ones that convinced him of what a shitty person he was—the excitement and panic of being a father, the resentment over being forced to parent at such a young age, the guilt over his role in the car accident, and most shameful of all, the relief. It had been a flicker that lasted less than a millisecond, but the tiny frisson of relief Blake felt at not having to spend the rest of his life with someone he didn't love plagued him long after he and Cleo parted ways.

In that millisecond, he'd been sure he would go to hell because only monsters would be relieved over a loss so horrific. It didn't matter that the relief played an infinitesimal part of his larger reaction, that it'd been quickly drowned out by overwhelming grief and pain. The fact it'd existed at all was his greatest disgrace.

Blake's pulse ticked in rhythm with the clock on the mantel.

Tick. One eternity. *Tick.* Two eternities.

All the while, a universe of emotions played out across Farrah's face—shock, horror, sympathy, pain, and sadness — which crashed into a crescendo when she lifted her head to meet Blake's eyes

"This is all true?" she whispered.

"Yes." The word rasped over his dry tongue. "You can check the sources if you don't believe me. Landon knows what happened. My family too. But the parts about how I felt—" Blake's throat processed a hard swallow. "That's all me. I've never told anyone the things I told you in these notes. I've spent so much of my life being the sun—the homecoming king, the football star, the successful businessman—that I was terrified of what would happen once the sun sets and night falls. So I ran. I ran every time darkness closed in, every time I had to have a hard conversation or face up to my shit. When I quit football, I ran to Shanghai because I didn't want to deal with the fallout. When I found out Cleo was pregnant, I ran from you and lied because I was too scared to find out how you'd react to the truth. I thought it would be easier if you believed I never cared at all." Blake's mouth twisted into a wry smile. "I told myself it was because I wanted to give you a clean break, but in reality, I was a selfish bastard who didn't want to complicate things for myself.

"After we lost the baby, I could've reached out to you. You were all I ever thought about. Every single fucking night. But I was in such a dark place, and even after I crawled out of that pit, I felt so guilty about what I did—or what I thought I did. I didn't deserve you, and I didn't want to upend your life again after so many years. Then you fell into my lap again like an angel from the heavens, and I thought, *This is it. This is a sign we're meant to give this another chance.* And we did—*you* did, even though you didn't have to. But once again, when the going got tough, I pushed you away and ran because I didn't want you to see what a twisted, fucked-up mess I really am inside. I said I didn't want to hurt you, but really, I didn't trust you enough to believe you'd stay once you found out what kind of person I really am, and I am so freaking sorry. You trusted me, and I didn't trust you. So I let you go."

Blake's voice thickened. "But here's what I realized. I'm tired of running. I know it's hard to believe, given my history. That's why I waited for you all those months, and I'll continue to wait for as long as it takes. You need time, I get that. But these letters...I wanted you to see the real me. To give you the choice I should've given you a long time ago. You can stay or you can leave, but know this: if you aren't by my side, it doesn't matter how bright the sun shines. I'd rather live in eternal darkness with you than live in eternal sunshine without you. So here I am, asking you to give me another chance. This time, it's all of me. Every scar, every flaw, every fucked-up thought, and every dream I've ever had. It's yours. I don't want to run anymore, but unless you look me in the eye and tell me you don't love me, I will chase you to the ends of the earth until the sun fucking explodes. You are it, Farrah Lin. You always have been. You always will be."

The paper fluttered from Farrah's hand to the floor. She closed the distance between them until she stood so close, Blake could count each individual eyelash and see the teeny-tiny mole above her upper lip. He breathed her in, drunk on her scent, even as his nerves raced full speed down his spine.

"You're not a terrible person, Blake," she whispered, cupping his face with one hand. "Those dark, selfish thoughts you have? We all have them. It doesn't make you a monster. It makes you human."

Blake wanted to argue. A sick part of him wanted to prove he *was* a terrible person, that he didn't deserve any of the good things in his life. But he was coming to the realization that that part of himself was his own guilt and insecurities talking, and that in order to move on, he had to forgive the person who needed it most: himself.

Farrah took a tiny step back, and it was all he could do not to yank her close again.

She didn't break their gaze as she clasped the locket he gave her around her neck.

"You know a lot of things about me, Blake Ryan, but here's what you don't know. I never fell out of love with you, not even after Shanghai. I told myself I did, but it was a lie. This is my truth: you are my One Big Love, my fairy tale, my Hollywood romance. I want all of you the same way you want all of me. Every scar, every smile, every dream and nightmare. I've been falling all this time; I just needed you to stop running long enough to catch me. Also..." Farrah leaned in, her breath tickling his lips. "I think darkness is beautiful. And I fucking love sunsets."

Blake didn't get a chance to respond before her lips crashed against his, his mind went blank, and instinct took over.

Their hands roamed, their bodies rubbed, and their tongues tangled in a sultry dance, one he wanted to last forever.

"Does this mean I get another chance?" he panted, just to be sure.

"Last chance. Don't fuck it up," Farrah warned, her cheeks rosy and eyes glazed with lust. But the undercurrent of seriousness was there.

"Trust me. I'd rather chop off my arm than fuck it up." Blake nipped at the sensitive spot below her ear, and her resulting shiver rolled through him, hardening him to the point of pain. "You're stuck with me, babe. Think of me as your very own super sexy, super talented superglue."

Farrah's laugh pealed through the air. "Talented, huh?" Her mouth curled up into a naughty grin, and he almost came right there. "Prove it."

Thirty seconds later, their clothes were on the floor, the emergency condom Blake always kept in his wallet was on, and he'd slammed Farrah up against the wall.

"Kris will be pissed if we defile her library," he warned.

Farrah hitched a shoulder up. "She'll get over it."

"Damn right she will."

Blake tightened his hold on Farrah's hips and plunged into her, covering her mouth with his and swallowing her cry of surprise and pleasure. Perspiration slicked their bodies, and he hoped to god Kris had soundproof walls; otherwise, every A-list celebrity in Hollywood was getting an audio experience they hadn't signed up for.

Not that he cared. All Blake cared about was the woman in his arms.

Five years, two continents, multiple heartbreaks.

They'd been through some shit, but there was not a doubt in his mind that this was where they belonged.

Together.

He slammed into Farrah, his fingers digging into her thighs as he willed himself not to come.

Not yet.

Sweat beaded his forehead, and his breath rushed out in short, heavy pants.

Farrah tightened around him and screamed, a breathless wail of pleasure that crashed over him like a wave of molten lava, setting every nerve ending on fire until he couldn't take it anymore.

Blake's orgasm exploded through his body as he drove into her one last time, its fury so raw, so powerful, he would've collapsed had Farrah's limbs not locked around his torso. Bright lights speckled his vision, and aftershocks rippled through him until he regained control of his senses.

Once he did, he heard Kris fuming through the library doors. "I'm going to kill them. This was *not* what I meant when I said privacy. Now I have to hire a crew to disinfect the entire room."

Blake and Farrah looked at each other and burst into laughter.

"Oops. I think Kris is mad at us." Farrah's eyes gleamed with amusement and unabashed shamelessness.

"It was worth it."

"A hundred percent," she agreed. Hair tousled, mouth swollen, skin slick with sweat. She was the most beautiful thing he'd ever seen, and he couldn't believe she was his.

Finally.

Completely.

"I love you, Farrah Lin."

Her eyes turned liquid. "I love you too, Blake Ryan."

Their lips met again in a kiss, long and sweet and lingering, and Blake knew, after a lifetime of running, he was finally home.

CHAPTER 41

Six months later

"NO ONE KILLED EACH OTHER, WHICH IS GOOD."
Farrah loaded the plates into the dishwasher while Blake wiped
down the dining table. "It's actually kind of scary how well our
moms get along."

"Which is why they had to leave. I can't have them ganging
up on me." Blake pitched his voice higher to imitate their moms.
"Blake, are you treating Farrah right? Blake, this meatloaf is a
little dry. Blake, why is Farrah the only person who gets a signature drink named after her?"

The Farrah, an orange blossom vodka martini with a splash
of vanilla extract, debuted at Legends New York two months ago
and was a massive hit.

Not to be egotistical or anything, but it was the only drink
Farrah ordered when she visited the bar.

She giggled. "I mean, they're valid questions." She squealed
as Blake swept her up from the ground and tossed her over his
shoulder. "What are you doing? Put me down!"

"This is what you get for taking their side." Blake threw her on the couch and straddled her, his powerful arms and thighs caging her in. His steel-hard erection dug into her stomach, and she was so wet she could feel her drenched panties sticking to her.

"You're the one who invited them for dinner," Farrah pointed out breathlessly.

"True. What was I thinking?" Blake's day-old stubble scraped across her sensitive skin as he licked and sucked on her neck. Her nipples puckered in response, and a strangled moan fell from her throat.

"I don't know," Farrah gasped, lost in a wave of sensation.

Blake had flown both her mom and his family to New York. Joy had earned her master's in educational psychology in May, and she'd begged Blake for a trip to New York as her graduation present. He'd agreed and sprung for their parents to accompany her so they could have a big family celebration.

Farrah met Blake's family a few months ago when she went with him to Austin to consult on a new design for the original Legends bar. After four years, it was time for an update, and she was officially the interior designer for all Legends projects going forward. Though she'd been hesitant about going into business with her boyfriend, they made it work.

Farrah's design business was thriving even without the Legends portfolio, so she wasn't reliant on Blake for income. She'd politely declined the interview offers from the firms that'd reached out after the Kelly scandal. And that magazine editor she'd worked for last fall? Turned out she was the new editor-in-chief of *Mode de Vie*, and she'd loved Farrah's work so much she did an entire profile on her for the magazine. After that, the offers rolled in so fast, Farrah couldn't keep up.

As for Legends, she and Blake agreed she could walk away if it didn't align with her goals anymore, but she didn't have plans to do that anytime soon. As much as Farrah had enjoyed last year's residential projects, hospitality design was her passion, and she loved creating new, innovative concepts for Blake's expanding business and tailoring them to fit with the local culture.

Blake, meanwhile, assisted her with the practical aspects of scaling her now three-person design firm, F&J Creative, which was comprised of Farrah; Jane, her old supervisor from KBI; and their assistant. Jane left KBI soon after New Year's and called Farrah, asking if she'd be interested in partnering together.

Farrah agreed without hesitation. The other woman had the years of experience Farrah lacked, and Farrah had the fresh insight and appeal to a younger demographic. They made the perfect team.

Blake and Farrah took a lot of weekend trips to Austin after their initial visit. His father was a little cold, but she could tell he was trying. Tension remained between Joe and Blake—you couldn't erase years of resentment and bad blood in the blink of an eye—but they were getting there. Meanwhile, his mother and sister welcomed Farrah with open arms. Joy pulled her aside the first night after dinner and thanked her for making Blake smile—for making him truly happy for the first time in a long time—and Farrah burst into tears in the downstairs hallway of the Ryans' house.

The two of them had been great friends since, much to Blake's chagrin. He always grumbled about them conspiring against him, and he wasn't always wrong.

"Do you think your mom likes me?" Blake nibbled on the sensitive skin below her ear, dragging a whimper out of her.

"Probably." Farrah's mom *loved* him. Blake was tall, successful, and had a "wealthy face," according to Chinese face-reading standards. His only flaw was not understanding Chinese customs—he'd bought Cheryl a set of Diptyque candles for her birthday, since Farrah had mentioned how much her mom loved their scents, and Cheryl freaked out because candles were considered unlucky gifts in Chinese culture. Luckily, she forgave him after he followed up with a pair of twenty-four-karat gold and jade earrings. Farrah picked them out herself, just to be safe. If that had failed, Blake flying Cheryl out this weekend so Farrah and Cheryl could spend quality mother-daughter time together sealed the deal. "Let's not talk about my mom right now. It feels wrong."

Blake's chuckle vibrated against her chest. "Why's that?"

"Because I'm about to do very dirty things to you." Farrah reached for Blake's belt buckle, but he grasped her wrist and tugged her hand away.

"Not yet. I have something to show you first."

"I bet you do." She tried to take off his pants again and was rebuffed again.

"Nuh-uh. There'll be time for that later." Blake's eyes sparkled with amusement and veiled lust as he pushed himself off her.

Farrah pouted. *This better be good.*

She followed him onto his balcony, trying to walk properly given the heavy, needy throb between her legs.

"What is it you want to show me?" While Farrah would much rather be having sex, she couldn't tamp down her curiosity.

"I chose a good day for this." Blake smiled, ignoring her question. "Look at this sunset."

It was 7:30 p.m., but since it was summer, the fiery ball of light was just beginning its descent beneath the horizon. Its slow march to slumber streaked the skies with an artist's palette of pale purples, soft oranges, and cotton-candy pinks. In the distance, the lights of Manhattan flicked on, so dense and numerous they looked like a carpet of fallen stars draped across the city's iconic skyline.

It was Farrah's favorite view at her favorite time of the day.

But as much as it took her breath away, she didn't understand why it was so important. They watched the sunset together every day.

She turned. "It's beautiful, but I don't—" Her words died in her throat.

Because Blake was no longer standing behind her. He was bent on one knee, and in his hand, he held a diamond. The most gorgeous, perfect yellow diamond Farrah had ever seen, one that blazed so bright it put the sun to shame.

The world tilted on its axis. Farrah's hand flew to her mouth, her stomach tumbling over itself as her brain struggled to process the sight before her.

Blake's hand shook as he spoke. "Five years ago, I told you I didn't believe in love, and that the crazy, stupid love they showed in movies was a scam. You proved to me, minute by minute, day by day, how wrong I was until one day I woke up and realized I'd fallen so deep, I would never be able to dig myself out. And you know what? I don't want to. But I also realized I wasn't entirely wrong because that crazy, stupid love they showed in movies is nothing compared to what I feel for you. You are the stars in my night, the sun to my earth, and I thank fucking god every day that out of all the cities in all the world, I chose to study abroad in Shanghai. Otherwise, I wouldn't have met you, and you. Are. Everything. But the one thing I want you to be, more than anything else, is my wife." Blake's voice turned hoarse. "Farrah Lin, will you marry me?"

Tears blurred her vision until Blake's face swam before her, beautiful and taut with a mixture of nerves and anticipation.

From the moment she popped out of the womb, Farrah had overthought things. Every decision, from what to eat for breakfast to who she should give her heart to, came with a thousand branches of possibilities, spiraling and curling and tangling until they muddled her true desires.

But for once, Farrah didn't think. She didn't have to. The answer came swiftly, as if it had been a part of her all along.

"Yes," she choked out. "Yes, yes, yes! I'll marry you!"

Blake sagged with relief. He slipped the ring on her finger, and then his lips were on hers. Her arms wrapped around his neck, and Farrah sank into a bliss so complete, she must've died and gone to heaven.

"Future Mrs. Ryan," he murmured. A thrill zipped through her at the moniker. "I love you so fucking much."

"And I, you." So much so her body and soul ached with it. Sensuous heat entered Farrah's voice. "Now, why don't you take me to that beautiful bedroom of yours and show me just how much you love me?"

She'd spent a lot of time designing that bedroom, and she intended to make full use of it.

Blake's eyes lit up with a devilish glint, and he flashed her a smirk so devastating, her knees buckled. "Yes, ma'am."

Farrah squealed again as Blake picked her up and carried her, bridal style, inside the apartment, where he showed her, over and over, how much he loved her, until the darkness of the night melted into the golden warmth of sunrise.

EPILOGUE

"I CAN'T BELIEVE YOU PULLED THIS OFF." FARRAH shook her head in awe. "Unbelievable."

"There's almost nothing money can't buy," Kris drawled. "Consider this my honeymoon present to you, even though you got engaged after me and married before me, you bitch."

"Your fault for prolonging your engagement so you could throw the wedding of the century." Courtney nudged Kris. "Your words, not mine."

Farrah laughed. The "almost" caveat surprised her—what in the world had Kris Carrera ever wanted that she couldn't buy?—but she was too happy to dwell on it.

She was officially Farrah Lin Ryan.

Married to a man who drove her crazy and sent her over the moon with joy at the same time.

A huge grin overtook her face when she looked across Gino's and locked eyes with Blake, who was getting another round of drinks with the guys. He winked at her, and her breath quickened.

They'd been having nonstop sex the past few weeks (because what else are you supposed to do on your honeymoon?) but he still had the ability to turn her inside out with one look.

Farrah and Blake had gotten married a month ago, on a beautiful rooftop garden in New York City. Her mom wanted them to tie the knot in California; his mom wanted to do it in Austin, but they'd stayed in the city that reunited them and that they now called home.

The wedding had been a small intimate affair, planned to perfection by her maid of honor. As expected from an Olivia Tang–coordinated event, the ceremony went off without a hitch. Even the weather cooperated, with clear skies and sunny weather, so they didn't have to draw on one of Olivia's five backup plans.

Everyone they loved had attended: their families, closest friends, colleagues (including Justin, whom Blake had threatened to yank off the guest list after Justin cheated at poker during guys' night), and members of their Shanghai group whom Farrah hadn't seen in years.

She'd invited Leo, Luke, and Nardo on a whim, despite not being close with them anymore, and had been pleasantly surprised when they RSVP'd yes. She was even more surprised they'd agreed to come on this trip.

Blake and Farrah had been getting ready to return home from their honeymoon in the Maldives and Sri Lanka when Kris messaged saying she had a present for them and they "may as well stay in Asia because we're going to Shanghai, bitches." She'd emailed them two first-class tickets to China; when they arrived, a driver whisked them to Kris's penthouse near the Bund, where they found their old group of study abroad friends waiting for them.

Kris. Courtney. Olivia. Sammy. Leo. Nardo. Luke. They were all there.

It was a long-overdue reunion, Kris said, and fitting since Blake and Farrah's story started in FEA. They were a family, and even if you went years without seeing some members, family was family.

Farrah would've teased her friend for her shocking sentimentality had nostalgia not overwhelmed her.

Surrounded by her old friends, in the city that started it all, made everything that happened in Shanghai real and not just a fantasy so beautiful she'd willed it into memory.

The guys returned with beers, fries, and two mojito fishbowl cocktails the size of small aquariums.

Blake slid into the seat next to Farrah and draped an arm over her shoulder; she snuggled into his side and grinned as her friends fought over the fries.

"I bought the fries. I get first dibs." Luke dove into the basket and shoved a handful in his mouth.

"Ugh." Kris crinkled her nose. "They're for *sharing*, you Neanderthal. Now that you've contaminated the basket, we have to get a new order."

"Cry me a river," Luke said through a mouthful of deep-fried potato. "You're rich. You can afford it."

"I love how you work for a university and still have no class."

"I love how you have millions in the bank and still no way to remove that stick from your ass."

"That's it. You're disinvited from my wedding," Kris fumed.

"Fine by me. I'll save money on airfare, hotels, *and* a wedding gift."

"Children." Courtney slammed her hands on the table, her mouth twitching with suppressed laughter. "I swear, it's like we're in college again."

"If we're going to do throwbacks, might as well do it all the way." Sammy grinned. "Never Have I Ever?"

Courtney's face shone with excitement. "Best idea of the night. You always were my favorite."

Beside her, Olivia rolled her eyes.

"I'm offended," Leo drawled, not sounding offended at all.

He and Courtney had ended their fling long before study abroad was over, and the years had placed a comfortable, if somewhat distant, camaraderie between them.

The brunette released a sheepish shrug. "Sorry, Leo. You were a great kisser, though."

"I know."

Everyone laughed.

Blake whispered in Farrah's ear, "Not as good as me." His arm tightened possessively around her shoulder, and she stifled a laugh.

No doubt Blake remembered her fleeting crush on Leo at the beginning of FEA. Even though they were married and it had been years, Blake still eyed the other man with suspicion.

"No one is as good as you." Farrah patted him on the knee.

"Damn right." Blake preened with male satisfaction.

"We should play a different game than Never Have I Ever." Nardo adjusted his glasses. "Something more intellectually stimulating."

Sammy clapped his friend on the back. "Dude. We're in a bar. Chill out."

"Exactly. Besides, *should* and *want* are different things." Courtney's tone brooked no opposition. "I'll start. Never have I ever pierced anything below my neck."

Nardo sighed.

The group stayed at Gino's until last call. It was a long, decadent night, and it made Farrah feel nineteen again—young, wild, and free. Only better, because this time she knew how the story ended, and it was better than she could've hoped for.

Blake ducked into the restroom before they left, and Farrah waited for him outside, trying to piece together what, exactly, was going on between Olivia and Sammy, who stood on opposite ends of the sidewalk. They hadn't exchanged one word all night, but the glances they threw each other could've burned the city down.

Farrah wondered how the sweetest couple in FEA devolved into this weird do-they-hate-each-other-or-love-each-other dynamic.

It was going to be interesting to see how things played out, now that Olivia was moving to California to get her MBA at Stanford.

Farrah was going to miss having her best friend in the same city, but she supposed that was selfish. She had, after all, moved into Blake's apartment after their engagement, leaving Olivia with a subletter in their Chelsea apartment.

"Hey." Leo ambled over with his signature relaxed grin. "Settled into married life yet?"

"It's only been a month, but I have no complaints so far." She smiled at her old friend. "Thanks for coming. You didn't have to."

"Trust me, I wouldn't have missed this for the world." Leo raked a hand through his curly dark hair. "Actually, there's something I want to give you. Another wedding present, though nowhere near as extravagant as a weeklong trip to Shanghai."

"It's ok. I think Kris has the market cornered on extravagant gifts." Curiosity pricked at Farrah. She had not expected a second present from Leo, of all people.

Leo pulled a thick bound stack of papers from his weathered brown messenger bag. "It's the first draft of my next novel. Written under a pen name." He flashed an abashed smile. "The story has been in my head for a while, but I lacked the will to finish it until I received your wedding invite a few months ago. I wanted you to read it first."

Farrah's brow furrowed. "Why me?"

"Read it," Leo said simply.

The next day, Farrah curled up in a seat by the window and

read the manuscript from front to back, until the sun sank beneath the horizon and moonlight streamed through the windows, illuminating the tearstained pages of a story about a girl and a boy who fell in love in a city long ago and far away.

———————

Blake liked his friends. They were great.

But after a week of their nonstop company, he was sick of them. He wanted alone time with his wife. He wanted to kiss her without other people interrupting, and he wanted to make her scream at night without having to deal with seven sets of knowing eyes and shit-eating grins the next morning.

Kris really needed to soundproof her rooms.

So on their last day in China, Blake moved their shit from Kris's penthouse to a suite at Z Hotels Shanghai. He had downright wicked ideas for what he and Farrah could do in that massive hotel bed, but first, they needed to complete their nostalgia walk.

Farrah had insisted on visiting all their old date spots—Moller Villa (that hadn't been an official date, but they'd had their first dinner alone together there), the M50 art district (again, not a real date, but close enough), the ice-skating rink they went to on Valentine's Day—and Blake indulged her. At first, he did it because Farrah wanted to, but as the day wore on, he found himself enjoying the walk down memory lane. It reminded him of how far they'd come.

They ended their night at the Bund. Five years later, and the Shanghai skyline was still a fucking beauty—ageless, timeless, and so dazzling it hurt to look at it.

Blake remembered staring at the spires rising above the city when he was twenty-two and feeling so tiny, so insignificant. Now, when he looked at the sprawl of glittering buildings across the river, he felt like he was on top of the world.

He had a booming business, amazing friends and family, and the woman of his dreams in his arms. He had everything he needed.

"It's like we never left." Farrah sighed, lacing her fingers with his as they continued their leisurely stroll along the waterfront. "god, I missed this place."

"This city has seen some things." Blake's dimples made a sneaky appearance. "Do you remember what I asked you when we came to the Bund for the first time after we kissed?"

Farrah's smile matched his. "You asked me to be your girlfriend. In the clumsiest way possible, I might add."

"It was not clumsy. It was adorable."

"Sure it was." She patted his cheek; he caught her hand in his and brought it to his lips.

"Five years ago, I asked you to be my girlfriend in this very spot. Now, you're my wife." Blake stopped walking and pressed his forehead against hers. "We've come full circle, haven't we?"

Farrah's eyes shimmered brighter than the symphony of lights behind her. "Yes, we have."

"Are you happy?" His lips brushed hers as he spoke. Of all the things in the world, that was what mattered most.

"Yes." Simple, confident, no hesitation or explanation needed.

Blake cupped Farrah's face with his hands and kissed her, a deep, lingering, breathless kiss that had them melting into each other beneath the beaming smile of the city that had changed their lives.

They'd kissed before, many times. But this time was different. This time, it was forever.

Can't get enough of Blake and Farrah?

Type this link into your browser to read a sizzling scene from their honeymoon: Bookhip.com/CBKHFZ

Acknowledgments

Thank you for coming along with me on Blake and Farrah's journey! It's been a wild ride, and while I love all my characters, Blake and Farrah will always have a special place in my heart.

I also want to thank everyone who's made this book possible:

To my beta readers, Carmen, Lola, Jennifer, and Anca, for all your feedback and words of encouragement. I couldn't have done this without you!

To my editor Shelby Perkins and proofreader Krista Burdine for taking care of my book baby and polishing it until it shines.

To early reviewers and bloggers for taking the time to read, share, and love this book. Words cannot express how grateful I am!

Finally, to my readers, both old and new. I am beyond humbled that out of all the books out there, you've decided to give mine a chance. Thank you for your time, support, and patience. It means the world to me.

Sending you all so much love.

xo, Ana

Keep in Touch with
Ana Huang

Reader Group: facebook.com/groups/anastwistedsquad
Website: anahuang.com
BookBub: bookbub.com/profile/ana-huang
Instagram: instagram.com/authoranahuang
TikTok: tiktok.com/@authoranahuang
Goodreads: goodreads.com/authoranahuang

About the Author

Ana Huang is a *New York Times*, *USA Today*, *Publishers Weekly*, *Globe and Mail*, and #1 Amazon bestselling author. She writes new adult and contemporary romance with deliciously alpha heroes, strong heroines, and plenty of steam, angst, and swoon sprinkled in.

A self-professed travel enthusiast, she loves incorporating beautiful destinations into her stories and will never say no to a good chai latte.

When she's not reading or writing, Ana is busy daydreaming, binge-watching Netflix, and scouring Yelp for her next favorite restaurant.

Also by Ana Huang

KINGS OF SIN SERIES
A SERIES OF INTERCONNECTED STANDALONES
King of Wrath
King of Pride
King of Greed
King of Sloth

TWISTED SERIES
A SERIES OF INTERCONNECTED STANDALONES
Twisted Love
Twisted Games
Twisted Hate
Twisted Lies

IF LOVE SERIES
If We Ever Meet Again (DUET BOOK 1)
If The Sun Never Sets (DUET BOOK 2)
If Love Had a Price (STANDALONE)
If We Were Perfect (STANDALONE)